She looked directly into his face. "Please let me go."

His hand slid over the bare skin of her shoulder and beneath the strap of her nightgown. A vibration passed through her, a tremor. She put her robe on and tied the tasseled belt, pulling it taut.

She held out her hand to him. "Come with me," she said, pleased that her voice sounded unafraid.

"I want to help you," she said.

His head tilted at a listening attitude. Abruptly he twisted toward the door.

The boy gave a weird cry as Jean Pierre rushed in and seized him. They struggled and fell heavily to the floor.

"Don't!" she cried. "Don't hurt him!"

THE ADAM PROJECT

William Woolfolk

FAWCETT GOLD MEDAL • NEW YORK

A Fawcett Gold Medal Book
Published by Ballantine Books

Library of Congress Catalog Card Number: 83-91143

ISBN 0-449-12658-7

Manufactured in the United States of America

First Ballantine Books Edition: February 1984

FOR JOANNA
With all my love

Margaret Denning knew they were watching her. After all these months they were still hoping she would lead them to Adam.

She crossed Second Avenue with her long coltish stride while a red light held ravenous traffic at bay. At the corner newsstand she saw the headlines screaming and her taut nerves screamed back.

Obeying compulsion, she turned into the doorway of her favorite bookstore halfway down the block. Two books featured in the window gave different explanations for why the world was in crisis. Their titles menaced each other.

On the shelves marked Travel, set off by a small projecting wooden sign from the weltering storm of books on current affairs, she found two copies of *Letters from New Guinea*.

"May I help you?"

The owner of the store, a gentle, wizened man, had come up behind her. She turned; he smiled a bird's-beak smile.

"Oh, it's you, Miss Denning."

Embarrassed, she realized that she was holding a copy of her book in her hand.

"I promised to send a friend of mine an autographed copy."

"We sold quite a few when it first came out. Every now and then someone still asks for it."

At the cashier's desk she paid for the book and left the store. Across the street a man in a topcoat was standing with his back to her, looking into a store window. The window provided a clear view of the bookstore across the street.

Don't they ever give up?

She walked briskly to the corner. The man in the

1

topcoat left his store window and began strolling casually down the other side of the street.

She reached the huge brown-red building on the East River where she had a small studio apartment. An escalator led up from street level to an open plaza where the building entrance and various shops were located. Near the escalator an elderly woman was seated on a folding chair before a table. A placard was raised on the table: *Sign Here for Peace.* A register was open. The few people who passed seemed to hurry up and avert their faces, as though ashamed that they were not going to stop.

Frightened people, Margaret thought. Frightened that the worst will happen, frightened of what might happen if they put their names in writing to confess their fear.

She stopped at the table and signed her name in the register, appending her address with a flourish.

"God bless you," the woman at the table said.

"God bless us all."

"Amen." The old woman had clear gray eyes. The kind of eyes that could see into the future.

Adam's eyes.

Margaret entered the apartment building. In her mailbox were two advertisements which she promptly threw away, a bill from the pharmacy, and a letter from Jim Halas at the Boston Museum, Division of Anthropology and Archeology.

The watchers were getting careless. Only half the flap of the Halas envelope had restuck and the rest had the repasted look she had come to recognize. Perhaps they wanted her to know her letters were being opened. Perhaps they hoped that if she felt harassed enough, or alarmed enough, she would try to make contact with Adam.

The elevator brought her to the fourth floor. She took out her keys and opened the double lock on her apartment door and went in. The window of the small living room was floor-to-ceiling, giving the illusion of more space.

They had been here.

On the small desk in the corner her papers seemed to be in the same order. But she had made a tiny pencil dot beside the margin of one pile of papers, and the dot was covered now. She had to move the pile back a fraction of an inch in order to reveal it. There was no way that the pile, held down by a brass gavel paperweight, could have moved itself.

She was amazed that they would continue to go to so much trouble for such little reward. The papers were a colleague's manuscript she was reading as a favor, a report on a small band of shepherds on a remote Scottish island. Masses of data were trapped in labyrinthine scholastic prose. Doubtless they had made a photographic copy with one of those ingenious little German or Japanese cameras.

She opened the letter from Jim Halas.

Halas regretted. There simply were no funds to finance another expedition to the upper Sepik River in New Guinea. In these troubled times very few people were interested in funding a scientific study of a culture so primitive it almost did not exist. She had already established that the Mondugami tribe had no history of how they came to be, no real idea of who they were, no knowledge of geography or their place in the world.

That was true. There was very little reason for her to go back.

Why, then, did she feel this strange compulsion to return?

She sat in a chair near the picture window that looked out on the East River. The day was clear with a frosty sun, and all outdoors looked inviting and...sane. It was the kind of day that should be set to music. She spent a moment simply staring out the window.

Something drew her gaze to a mist gathering on the mirror on the opposite wall.

She felt an odd premonitory prickling at the base of her neck.

The mist on the mirror began to shape itself into a

cloudy likeness. The likeness continued to develop slowly, like a strip of film from an instant camera.

She told herself: This is not real, it is not happening. There are reflections in the mind as well as in mirrors.

Then her breath caught. Adam was there, a face glimpsed as though in a car windshield, shadowed and pale.

"Come to me at once. You will be safe here."

He did not speak; she heard him with her mind's ear.

Or did she? There are auditory hallucinations too.

"Adam," she said. "Is it really you?"

"It will begin."

She answered, "What will begin? I don't understand."

A small corner of her mind wondered: Has his ability progressed to where he can project an image of himself to be seen and heard? The ordinary human brain has less power than a twenty-watt light bulb, but Adam's incredible brain blazed with an ability to transcend reality, to surpass experience. Who could say where its development would stop? She could not foresee its evolution any more than the human beings who lived under a Pleistocene sky could foresee the future of their kind.

"Come at once," the voice inside her head repeated.

"Come where?" she cried, knowing that she deceived herself with the question. She knew now that he was the source of her strange compulsion to return.

Adam would guide her each step of the way.

How can I? she asked herself. How can I act on a vision that exists only in my mind, a voice I hear only inside my head?

There was no answer.

Adam's image in the mirror paled, became once more a mist on glass.

Then the mist was gone.

His image, his voice had been as real to her as the empty mirror on the wall. She wanted to believe that Adam had made his presence known to her in order to

4

send an urgent prophetic message. But she knew the terrible nostalgic power of memory. Time was no longer measured for her by the calendar but by the gravitational power of the recent past. Her desires might have summoned up what she saw and heard.

There was no way to be sure.

It will begin.

What did he mean—that the crisis would escalate to its inevitable end in apocalypse? She could not accept that.

For millions of years primitive man had struggled to separate himself from the animal, to subdue it within his skull, to suppress all that was nonhuman, to emerge from the long psychic darkness. She had faith in man's future. It was not possible that human civilization would cease to exist or that other forms of life would dominate the earth. Man must endure. He must prevail. She would continue to believe that. In the silences of things, when she could remember her prayers, she would pray for that.

I cannot come to you, Adam.

The Wild Boy

"Man still bears in his bodily frame the indelible stamp of his lowly origin."

—Charles Darwin

chapter 1

Upper Sepik River
New Guinea

On the day of the man-killing, the women and old men, the sick and the lame were inside the thatch-roofed houses preparing for the feast. The village street was deserted except for an occasional wandering pig or one of the native dogs, so small and thin as hardly to warrant a canine identity—more like rabbits with furless tan skins.

To the west of the village the dense spiky undergrowth divided into two separate paths that ended at a gray-green greasy-looking tributary that meandered its oily way between high banks with a few frondy palms.

Near the shore the water turned dirty yellow and muddy. In dry season there were small patches of squashy quagmire, half-submerged fen lands in which floating islands appeared. Turtles and fish were trapped in shallow puddles between the floating islands. As they plunged about, seeking deeper water, the pygmy men of the village of Mondugami speared them.

A short distance away from this ceremonial gathering of meat, Margaret Denning was seated on a tufted rise of ground. She wore a short-sleeved wrinkled cotton dress with a red bandana tucked inside the open neckline. Her mass of chestnut hair was parted in the middle and her bright blue eyes, intent on her sketching, seemed to disappear into shadowed depths of dark brows and lashes.

As Margaret looked up to confirm an impression for another quick sketch, she became aware that she, in turn, was being observed by the shaman of the tribe. He was a small old ugly man with a shaved head and rubbery features and a dark skeletal body covered with ringworm.

On an impulse she got up, notebook in hand, and crossed the uneven soft ground to where the shaman sat cross-legged. She squatted beside him and opened her notebook. She showed him her sketch of him observing the quick deft little men impaling turtles. A glitter appeared in his small lashless black eyes. She flipped to another page: a full-length portrait of the shaman standing with the skimpy cloth covering his loins and the fiber band that held his penis pressed flat against his belly.

The shaman began to mutter rapidly, his voice making a clacking sound like dice colliding. It was clear that he was angry. His bald scrofulous head twisted back and forth on its scrawny neck. Suddenly he rose to his full four-foot-five-inch height, seized the notebook from her, and flung it down into the mud. He raised a mud-caked foot and planted it firmly on the likeness of himself.

"Don't do that!" Margaret said.

The shaman snapped his head sideways in a gesture of contempt and defiance. He stooped to pick up the notebook, and began methodically tearing pages from it and flinging them away.

He was interrupted by a terrible cry that came from a short distance away. A pygmy hunter appeared to be drawing a log that had a powerful tail and cruel jaws. The little man was screaming and performing a one-legged dance to free himself. Finally in a twisting movement he forced his body into a half turn and thrust his spear's hard obsidian point into the crocodile's eye.

A great tail thrashed. Cruel jaws gaped. The man pulled free and crawled away, the ground under him turning a dark wine color.

A keening chant began, was taken up and amplified in cries and moans and wailing. Ignoring the injured man, the pygmies converged to where the stricken crocodile was in its death paroxysm.

The crocodile was the river god of the Mondugamis,

and the pygmies gathered to mourn their totem god of the river, incongruously dying on land.

The crocodile lay on its back with its stubby forelegs waving feebly. Its great powerful tail stopped thrashing; then all motion stopped. The shaman approached and timidly poked the reptile's white belly. There was no response. He gestured to the pygmies, who wrapped the sixteen-foot length of their totem god in a bark sheath, then drew back into a wide circle with the shaman at its center.

The shaman dropped to his knees and a pygmy brought him two small pots. From one pot the shaman took a handful of red clay and smeared it on his lean-ribbed body and bony arms. When he was daubed to the waist he gathered a chalklike substance from the other pot and painted his face white.

As he rose, the necklace of human teeth around his neck jounced against his red chest. Nearby the injured man was lying on his back, his nearly amputated leg bleeding steadily into the ground. With a terrible effort the injured man forced himself to his knees with his head bowed in penitence.

The shaman positioned himself directly behind him while one of the pygmies handed him a spear. The shaman lifted the spear high, then thrust it down between the man's shoulder blades so that the point emerged through his chest.

Margaret's cry of outrage was lost in the general shout of approval from the pygmies.

By lantern light in the mosquito room of her thatched house, Margaret wrote and sketched a report on the brutal ceremony she had witnessed. Her fingers were still trembling. During the eight months she had spent in the pygmy village she had put everything down in words and sketches, the smells and sounds and visions of village life. Her notebooks were descriptions of how the tribe lived and worked, communicated with each other, and celebrated their various ceremonies and rituals.

11

She had lived among these fierce little people only recently weaned from cannibalism, but had learned very little about the meaning of the tribal rituals she had come to study. Why, for example, did a pygmy woman who allowed another man's infant to feed at her breast never get another husband if she was widowed? Why, if a man became ill, were his women forced to leave his home until he either recovered or died? Did pygmy men feel that their women were "takers of strength" who diminished their chances of survival? Why did the old men drink "brain soup" from hollow human skulls during each male initiation ceremony? Was it a way of making welcome the new adult member of the tribe?

The mosquito room was in the middle of a wide verandah, a boxlike area nine by nine feet made of copper wire and uprights bolted together. Inside there was a worktable, two straight chairs, a small bookcase, and a large basket.

The floor beneath her feet shook a little. She looked up to see that Nambuli had come onto the verandah. Nambuli was her "talk boy," a pygmy girl who had lived for a short time in Alitoa and learned Middle Sepik dialect. Margaret drew down the pulley weighted with a box of cartridges that pulled open the door to the mosquito room.

Nambuli seated herself on the other straight-backed chair and crossed her hands on her lap. At the four corners of the room hung native net bags containing reading matter, clothes to be mended, and items to exchange for talk-talk with informants.

"Talk-talk?" Margaret asked.

Nambuli nodded.

Margaret indicated that the girl should proceed. In the dialect of the Mondugamis, assisted with many gestures, Nambuli said the villagers were fearful of terrible things that would happen because a river god had been slain. Not even the shaman's powerful magic could guarantee their safety.

"Many years ago," Nambuli assured her solemnly, "when a river god was killed, it rained boiling water

12

and all who were not inside their houses perished. After the boiling rain, there was a spirit who came and stole food. Its father was a crocodile and its mother was a water drum. The shaman says the spirit will return if an evil presence is not removed from the village."

Margaret perceived that Nambuli had arrived at the reason for her visit, and guessed what was coming next.

"Do you think I am an evil presence, Nambuli?"

"You are not evil but you are ignorant."

"In what way?"

"You draw pictures that are like-like."

"What is evil about that?"

"A like-like picture captures a person's spirit by drawing it through the windows of his nose."

"Do you believe that, Nambuli?"

The girl nodded vigorously. "That is why the shaman is angry. You tried to capture his spirit so he would not be able to work magic."

Margaret asked, "Will it do any good to meet with the shaman and assure him I have no desire to draw his spirit out through his nose?"

Nambuli shook her head sadly. "You must leave. Otherwise very bad things will happen."

She thanked Nambuli for coming to see her and gave her a can of tinned meat to show there were no hard feelings. Just before retiring for the night she fought her way from the mosquito room to the toilet with a Flit spray. No one else in the village had a toilet but she had cut an old oil tin in half with a machete and converted it into a water tank with a chain. The plumbing was certainly not fancy, but she preferred it to the pygmies' habit of dislodging a piece of bark floor in their houses to urinate through it and using the street or the woods for defecation.

Before she could pull the chain on her improvised tank, the house shuddered and a glass clattered to the floor. Her pet pig, tethered outside the house, must have rubbed against a post again. In the absence of other companionship she had so spoiled and coddled this young animal that it actually hung its head when scolded. She would have to scold it again in the morning.

A few minutes after she got into bed behind thick mosquito netting, she heard a tumult in the village street. She sat up, reluctant to leave the shelter of her netting and confront a ravenous mosquito swarm. Then she heard Nambuli calling, and quickly dressed and armed herself with her Flit spray to venture forth.

Breathless, excited, and frightened, Nambuli arrived to tell her the shaman's prediction of trouble had come true. The evil spirit had returned to rob the village, but he had been caught trying to steal Margaret's young pig.

Margaret followed the girl to the side of her thatched house. The broken tether lay on the ground near the dead pig. Its throat had been cut. This must have happened as she felt the house shaking earlier. It was not the work of a spirit but of a very corporeal killer.

"Where is the one who did this?"

"With the shaman. In the House of Tambaran."

At the far end of the village was the grand house where the shaman received his followers. No women were allowed to enter. Another sign of the unrelenting sexual hostility within the tribe, Margaret thought. She went to the storeroom in back and got a sack of salt and a necklace of ornamental beads.

The House of Tambaran was a long, high-roofed building. She hesitated at the entrance. Go on, she urged herself. Nambuli was watching on the other side of the street, convinced that Margaret would not dare to defy the taboo.

That settled it. She entered the House of Tambaran.

The interior was disappointingly bare, mostly an open shed with a floor of hard-packed dirt. Along the walls were several carvings of the crocodile god. A dead pig was strung up on its hind legs to a pole. Black clusters of insects covered its carcass. The shaman sat smoking a pipe on a chair raised on a bamboo platform.

On the dirt floor beyond a barrier of nettles, a young boy lay facedown, completely naked, with thick hair

14

matted on his head that fell to his shoulders. What was startling was the paleness of his skin. Margaret knew of no white-skinned tribe in this area of New Guinea.

He was fighting for breath with a wrenching effort. A poisoned dart was sticking to his thigh, another clinging lightly to the surface of his arm. His hands were bound at the wrists and his legs at the ankles. His breathing became more labored as the poison continued to paralyze his lungs. From time to time he gave a "Wwwoo!" sound as he expelled a gust of trapped air.

They are going to let him die, she thought angrily. No one has the courage to kill him outright because an evil spirit might identify its murderer and return at some later time to exact a terrible vengeance. She knew how their superstitious minds worked.

The first pygmy to see Margaret simply stared with mouth agape, his eyes shining with surprise. Another saw her and grunted disapproval. Then all were watching every step of her progress toward the shaman. She stopped before him, dry-mouthed with fear, her heart thumping strongly.

The shaman laid his pipe aside. It was a long clay pipe that contained a curved bark leaf filled with bits of excrement, skin, nail filings, and sputum contributed by members of his council. By smoking the pipe, the shaman imbibed their collective wisdom.

In his masklike face his squinting black eyes vibrated with anger. Without speaking, he extended one rigid arm with a finger pointing to the way out of the House of Tambaran.

Margaret placed her gifts of salt and an ornamental necklace at the shaman's feet. She said quietly, "The shaman has said that I must leave the village by the next moon. I do not wish to leave. If I have offended, I am sorry. I will be careful in the future. I have lived here long-long time and have not offended before."

The shaman's arm remained rigidly extended. She was aware of the stench of his pipe and his powerful body odor. She felt herself under scrutiny from everyone in the House of Tambaran.

She said, "If I must go as the shaman orders, I beg one favor." She heard the stertorous breathing of the dying boy. "If you grant this favor, all the possessions in my house, the tinned meat and salt, the matches and sharp knives and other ornaments, I will leave with you."

This prospect clearly intrigued the ringwormed sorcerer. His gaze did not seem quite as angry. His rigidly extended arm slowly lowered.

She said, "Let me take the evil spirit with me."

She did not fully understand why she was making this bold proposal. She had not intended it when she first entered the House of Tambaran. But no human being should be allowed to die as the boy was dying, sick and untended, among people who both feared and scorned him.

To be honest there was another motive involved, the need to salvage something out of her imminent exile. If she could provide a dignified, less painful death for the poor boy, give him food and water and medicine, that would be some consolation to her.

The shaman scratched himself, looking from the boy to Margaret. He picked up his long-stemmed pipe and puffed, surrounding himself in malodor, then with a peremptory gesture he ordered the members of the council to draw back.

Margaret did not know how to interpret this action. She waited as patiently as she could, listening to the hoarse gasping of the dying boy.

Finally the shaman put down his pipe. He motioned to Margaret to come closer. He searched for a while in his scanty clothing until he found a louse, a search that did not take long. He bit the louse in half with his teeth. Holding one of the halves in each of his closed hands, he held out his hands for Margaret to choose.

Behold the oracle, she thought. He had not explained the rules of this curious decision-making process, but she put her faith in a fundamental truth. There are ordinary decisions, logical decisions, and magical decisions. Magical decisions are the kind you can depend on—if the price is right.

Unhesitatingly she chose.

In the morning Nambuli entered Margaret's bedroom with an air of suppressed excitement. A man wearing a headdress of hornbill beaks was walking down the center of the village street carrying a spear with a piece of bark attached to its point. That was a sign, Nambuli said, that he had an important message for everyone to hear. It meant the shaman had decided what to do with the evil spirit.

Margaret dressed quickly and accompanied Nambuli into the street. By then, most of the village was following the man carrying the spear. The man stopped and waited for the villagers to gather around him. By exhortation, scolding, and threats, Nambuli managed to get very close.

Holding his spear above his head, the messenger shook it once as a call for quiet. He was a self-important little man, as swollen with his message as a tuberous root. The chattering of villagers stopped, and he was satisfied enough to proceed. Margaret was not fluent enough in the dialect, so Nambuli gave her a running account. The speaker began with a fulsome tribute to the valor of the men who had run the evil spirit to ground and captured him. No tribe possessed such heroes, willing to do battle against the supernatural. Then he pronounced the shaman's verdict. That very night the evil spirit would be fed to the river god. So said the shaman.

Shortly after Margaret returned to her house, it became apparent that she could expect no useful work from either Nambuli or the cook boy. They were seething with impatience for the sacrificial ceremony, and either whispering and giggling between themselves or mysteriously disappearing to discuss the forthcoming event with their friends in other houses. She told them to take the rest of the day off.

Their excitement proved that the shaman's judg-

17

ment was correct. The pygmies feared him as a powerful magician and obeyed him as leader of the tribe, but they would not allow him to abandon his role as preserver and enforcer of their rituals.

With no servants in the house she had time and privacy to complete the plan she had worked out with the shaman. When she had finished packing, the sun was sliding down the sky on its way, the pygmies believed, to drown in a hot still black lake about thirty miles distant. She wrapped the things she was taking with her in a thin cotton blanket: two bags of rice, some bottles of drinking water, her camera, field glasses, a cookie tin filled with used film cassettes, and her money. She was leaving all her other supplies. The village would have a week-long orgy after she was gone. From the many artifacts she had painstakingly collected, she chose only a life-sized crocodile head on a pole, realistic and ferocious-looking.

During her stay in the pygmy village nothing had ever been stolen from her. The tribe believed that a person's belongings were a part of the person's "spirit," and if something was stolen the spirit would return, even after death, to reclaim its own in a particularly horrible way. Margaret had seen a young girl severely beaten because she had retrieved bits of food floating on the river. Her parents believed that the food had belonged to someone who would inevitably make trouble for her.

She rested for an hour until dusk. The villagers were all in their houses by then preparing their evening meal. Nambuli and the cook boy were undoubtedly dining with friends and discussing the evening's entertainment. Margaret left the house for the last time, carrying her blanket-wrapped supplies, and followed the path used only by taboo (menstruating) women to the riverbank. Pygmy men would not set foot on this path for fear of losing their sexual potency. She came to the large vat where by day the menstruating women prepared dye for grass skirts, the only work they were allowed to do. The women would not return to the vat

18

until morning, and the men would not come because they believed even the sound of their voices would spoil the dye.

In the brown-gray light, the river looked almost black. Occasional circles of white revealed where a crocodile was moving near the surface. She moved a small raft from the shore to the water. Plover birds rose, fluttered, and descended again onto the backs of crocodiles lying dormant amid the floating islands.

She was not sorry to be leaving Mondugami. She had lived among the pygmies for eight months, notebook in hand, asking questions and trying to learn, but in a fundamental sense she did not know any more about them than when she arrived. She had learned to eat smoked fish and taro, to weave a mat and to prepare an offering for a charm, even to converse in their impossible language with its haphazard structure of nine genders, sixteen third-person pronouns, and irregular unguessable verbs. But she had never got to understand them nor had she absorbed the meaning of their culture.

At dusk the mosquitoes were especially ferocious. She had to fight her way through the shivery swarms to the tall grass beside the men's path, where she settled down to wait. She did not dare to use her Flit spray. The odor would be noticed.

Her face and hands were dotted with tiny red bleeding pimples when a shouting informed her that the shaman and his council members had left the House of Tambaran. Soon a procession came in view. The shaman was in the lead, followed by four men who carried the boy lashed to a hammock. Another man carried a torch to light the way. Behind them the entire village seemed to have turned out for the spectacle.

As the procession drew near, she could hear the shaman chanting repetitive phrases meant to nullify the power of the evil spirit. The boy's head lolled idly; he looked unconscious. She hoped he was not dead. Nothing would be more foolish than to go to this much trouble for a corpse.

19

The torchbearer began capering about, and the procession came to a halt while the shaman lectured him for failing to light the way properly. Chastened, he returned to his place in the procession. The oily smoking torch cast a flickering orange light ahead. A vaporous mist rose from the ground. The light of a quartermoon filtered down wanly.

They stopped again at the beginning of the broad men's path that led down to the river. Margaret cursed because mosquitoes were making her feel like a dartboard. She could no longer make herself indifferent to them by an act of will.

The shaman began to address the villagers. This was a ticklish moment. He was telling them they could not come any farther for fear of angering the river god.

There was angry jeering. Apparently, the villagers had counted on being there for the final gulp and swallow.

The shaman became furious. He shouted that the river god had given him very clear instructions. If those instructions were disobeyed, the river god would consume not only the evil spirit but everyone who displeased him. This should have put the matter in a different light, but the villagers still refused to back off.

The flaring torch held motionless—she could smell its rancid sour smokiness—while the shaman harangued the villagers. She grasped her pole tightly in her hands, making sure of her grip. She saw the torchbearer plainly, and just behind him the shaman and the council members carrying the hammock on their shoulders.

Now.

From the high grass a terrible apparition rose. In the flickering uncertain light a ghastly crococile head appeared with teeth and jaws dripping blood. It reared swiftly skyward.

The torch shook in the torchbearer's palsied arms.

The ghastly croc head circled high over the heads of the villagers as if choosing a victim. Then the head swooped down. The victim uttered a strangled cry as the croc head struck him and knocked him to his knees. That was all the others waited to see. They fled. The man who had been knocked down crawled after them on hands and knees. He looked back once at the crocodile with its teeth dripping blood. He had the awed expression of a man seeing the true nature and ferocity of death. As the crocodile head swooped toward him again, he leapt to his feet and bolted.

The shaman flung up his arms and shouted to the council members: "No more, no more. Not good!" They needed no further persuasion from their all-powerful sorcerer. The council members dropped the hammock and fled, with the torchbearer leading the way.

Margaret emerged from the high grass holding the carved crocodile head she had dipped into the vat of red dye. She tossed it away and went to the hammock that had been dumped so precipitously. The boy had been jolted awake, and he watched dazedly as Margaret cut his bindings. A bubbling noise was coming from his clenched lips.

He was too weak to stand alone. She put her arm around his back and under his shoulder, and with the shaman's help guided him the short distance to the riverbank. They got him on board the raft, where he promptly collapsed. The shaman bared his betel-stained teeth and delivered himself of a singsong chant, which she understood to be a message amounting to goodbye and good riddance.

She went back to untie the raft, and climbed on board. Taking the paddle from the raft, she beat furiously at something incredibly long and black at the shore edge. It glided away. She pushed at the ground with the paddle until the raft moved out into the sluggish current of the tributary.

Then she used the paddle to row. At midstream there was a stronger current that moved the raft briskly toward an eventual junction with the Sepik River seventy miles away.

* * *

During the night the raft moved smoothly along the meandering tributary, which sometimes widened into a flatness like a shallow pond and at other times narrowed to where enclosing arches of leaves were so close they brushed against her. At times the air smelled full of rotting vegetation, at other times there was the strong sodden smell of mud. The water teemed with unidentifiable life. Once she heard a sharp series of cracking sounds which might have come from a school of fish attacking the raft. She shuddered and moved closer to the center of the raft.

The boy lay quietly except when his mouth worked as if kneading his gums or he gave a choking whimper. From time to time his open mouth became covered with insects and she had to clear them away. He was afire with fever. Around the edges of the wounds in his thigh and arm the skin was like a fleshy tropical plant, so lush it was almost at the point of decay.

You're going to die no matter what I do, she thought. Then with a sudden rush of anger: Whoever you are up there, who keeps your eye on all the sparrows, how about looking this way?

Morning brought a subdued clarity in which she saw a bare landscape denuded of trees, a long stretch of barren brown earth that resembled a scene of natural devastation. Fire? A flood? Leafless twisted sticks were all that broke the featureless monotony.

By midmorning her eyes were dry and hot and staring, and there was a dull low pain in the back of her neck. The sun's heat was like a blow. Lying on his back, the boy looked split open like a haunch of meat in a slaughterhouse. She spilled out the blanket's contents, centering them on the raft, and used the blanket to cover him. He did not stir.

If he died, there would be so many unresolved questions.

She studied the boy with the detachment of a scientist. The genes that cause hereditary differences between human beings are few compared to the number of genes that human beings share in common. Only by limiting the traits to be considered could she make any useful distinctions.

Skin pigmentation: pale white with a reddish tone caused by sunburn.

Stature: medium to tall for his age, which she guessed was mid-adolescence.

Head form: long.

Hair: light brown in color, and apparently straight and of a fine texture although now so matted and tangled it was hard to be sure.

Nose bridge: high with thin nostrils.

Color of eyes: light green, no epicanthic fold.

Not one characteristic linked the boy to the pygmy group or any other native inhabitants of New Guinea. His physical traits identified him as Caucasoid, not Negroid. There was not even a subgroup in New Guinea that could account for so many variations from the dominant Negroid race of the area.

Where had the boy come from? How could he have survived alone in a harsh and inhospitable jungle? Had he belonged to a tribe that cast him out because of the color of his skin? Who were his parents? Even if he were a feral child raised from infancy by animals, he would have had human parents. Besides, animal nurses were the stuff of fairy tales—there was no proof an animal had ever reared a human child. That myth was kept alive by those who wanted to affirm a connection with our animal ancestors or who believed that such a connection would demonstrate the oneness of God's divine creation.

In a world increasingly known, explored, mapped, its inhabitants classified, categorized, and ranked, the possibility that this was a wild boy who had grown to adolescence without contact with other humans was intriguing. All her months of not very rewarding work in Mondugami would be abundantly rewarded if she could study this boy and discover the truth of his origin. It would be an invaluable contribution to anthropology.

The raft quivered.

In a confused instant she looked to the right. A hideous head appeared out of the water, fully as terrible as the one she had used to frighten the pygmies. A long armored body passed swiftly under the raft, lifting it and letting it plunge back with a splash. Geysers of water shot up between loose logs.

She seized the paddle and on the crocodile's next pass she struck at it. The edge of the paddle came down on a face that was like scaled blue stone with big lightless eyes. With a powerful flip of its tail the crocodile sped away, causing a wave that sent the raft rolling.

A moment later the crocodile attacked from the other side. She struck at it again and heard a grinding awful crunch. Then she was holding a short length of wood that ended in jagged protruding thin straws.

The crocodile whirled, its extended jaws open to show bits of mashed wood clinging to its teeth. It swiftly submerged and did not return. Margaret stared stupidly at the splintered remnant of wood she was holding, then at the widening ripple where the crocodile had gone under. I hope it hates the taste, she thought, and began to giggle. She was not far from hysteria.

What snapped her out of it was a hoarse choking rattle, a sound that brought a new coiling of terror. The boy was lying on his back, gasping for air like a landed fish. Water had poured into his open mouth during the brief violent struggle with the crocodile. Now he seemed to be foaming at the mouth and his youthful face beneath its light beard stubble was a ghastly blue.

She crawled to him on her hands and knees, and tilted his head back so the chin was pointing upward. With his jaw pulled out in a jutting position, his tongue couldn't fall into the back of his throat and block the passage of air. She reached into his mouth and pulled out a clog of mucus. The rattling noise stopped but he still struggled desperately to breathe. She bent over him and fixed her mouth completely over his. She began blowing air into his mouth. His chest rose with

24

each exhalation of her breath, as if she were pumping up a balloon.

She continued mouth-to-mouth resuscitation until she heard a rumbling inside his chest as the air passages unkinked. His breathing became more regular, although it still rumbled with chest noises and sighing sounds came from the back of his throat. She stopped the mouth resuscitation and began giving him a chest pressure arm lift to encourage his respiratory center to keep working. She laid him down gently on the raft.

She said, "No harm will come to you. I'll look after you."

His eyes opened, looked at her, closed. His body shook with another ague-like convulsion. He turned his head to one side and vomited green slime.

Before nightfall the raft passed the body of a newborn infant floating in the river. The natives in this region of the Sepik River had no sense of parental responsibility and quietly disposed of unwanted infants by setting them adrift on bark leaves in the river current. A short life's voyage.

At dawn the raft was gliding past a baret, a canal that flowed from an inland lake to join the tributary. The baret glowed with dull luster and on its surface floated thousands of pink and white lotuses. Ospreys and blue herons rested among them as motionless as birds in a Japanese print. The scene was familiar to her. With a sinking sensation she realized that she was scarcely twenty miles from the village of Mondugami. At this rate the journey would take three more days, and her supply of food and water would be used up. Only one bag of rice remained and one bottle of drinking water. During the battle with the crocodile some items she had placed for safety in the middle of the raft had vanished into the river. She had lost the camera, the field glasses, and the cookie tin filled with film cassettes. But she still had her notebooks. They had been wetted but she had spent an hour lovingly exposing each page to the heat of the sun and they seemed

25

legible. Without the notebooks she would have no record of her eight-months sojourn in the village of Mondugami.

By afternoon she was desperately thirsty. If the boy was to have any chance of survival he would need most of the water, so she resisted the compulsion to drink. During the night she became disoriented from thirst and had a succession of nightmares. In one she was doing battle with the crocodile and felt herself being crushed in its gaping jaws. In another she was aboard the raft accompanied by the bloated body of an infant. Then the shaman was standing on the shore shaking his spear and shouting.

The shaman's angry face became that of her father. What bad thing had she done?

It had to do with the soap.

The Indian girl Ysabel worked hard in the kitchen, scrubbing and scouring. There was no hot water in the dungeon-like kitchen with its wood-burning stove and very low concrete sink with a single faucet. The soap Ysabel scrubbed with was a dark waxy block that made almost no suds.

She had brought Ysabel a bar of soap from a crate given by friends to her father. He would not use the soap because he believed a missionary had no right to separate himself from the lives of the people he served. His friends meant well but did not understand that luxuries widened the gap between a missionary and those being saved for Christ.

Ysabel, who had to scrub furiously just to work up a small lather, considered the new soap a powerful revelation. Did being a Christian mean she would have such soap all her life? The next day she brought Margaret a present, a plastic bracelet that had the power to ward off injuries and illness. To refuse it would be un-Christian and ungenerous, so Margaret wore the bracelet without belief in its magical powers. When her father found out he became very sad—he had a face meant for sadness, an El Greco face. He prayed for her.

It was very dark, she remembered, and the kitchen
26

had a cold floor. He was on his knees apologizing to God for his daughter. Pots and pans were clean and shining on hooks on the wall. When her father finished praying he told her to return the bracelet to Ysabel and explain that magic was the instrument of the devil. Ysabel accepted the bracelet although not the message. Was it not magic that enabled Jesus to walk on the water or feed the multitude with a few loaves and fishes or raise a dead man from the grave? She was surprised by the illogic of Christian faith.

Margaret awoke to a new day of simmering heat. The boy was in poor physical condition. Where he was not covered with the blanket, his skin had burned a frightening crimson. He had shaken off the effects of the poison but he had no strength and spent all day sleeping in a fetal position. As for herself, she was exhausted and had developed a physical trembling so pronounced she could not take her precious sip of water without spilling a few drops. She also suffered badly from sunburn. Her lips were cracked and sore, and wherever her skin was exposed it had blistered.

At noon she felt a small stir of breeze. The raft began to move more quickly. The hope that had sprung up in her mind turned to anxiety as the pace kept increasing.

They were being swept along on a pouring rushing cataract. Logs creaked, lashings strained, water cascaded over the side of the raft. A promontory of reeds and sago palms loomed ahead of them, thrusting halfway out into the river. The raft headed directly for it. A great black spot in a blaze of sun magnified before her terrified gaze.

She felt the blow as the raft struck. In the final terrible moment, prolonged into intolerable suspense, the blaze of sunlight turned into a heavy inundation of water. Her nose, ears, eyes were swamped with it. She had not breath in her lungs to blow out a match.

Then water was streaming from her like enormous tears. She coughed and choked. Through the palms of her hands on the rough logs, she felt the raft begin to move forward again. She looked up with bleary uncomprehension. The promontory was falling quickly behind. The raft had struck the very edge of the islet, spun and twisted along its curving shore, and the powerful current had propelled it on.

The blanket had been swept away from the boy's nude body, but at least he was still on the raft and still breathing. He was not going to drown.

Her notebooks had disappeared into the growling cataract. Gone forever. But that did not matter anymore. Her senses were so dulled that all she could feel was indifference...

In quiet water the raft bobbed slightly, beyond the streaming power of the current. They were not moving in any direction. The tributary rushing into the Sepik River had formed the powerful cataract, but now they were on the river itself.

Less than half a mile away, a government pinnace was heading in her direction.

chapter 2

She was in a bed with clean white sheets and pillows, and she wore a pair of pajamas equally clean and white. The pajamas had been given to her during her stay in the infirmary at Alitoa. Now she was on board the *Malmö Explorer*, of Swedish registry, sailing from Sydney to Boston. She had been on board for three days.

A knock on the door.

"Come in," she said.

The ship's medical officer opened the door and stood in the doorway to assure himself of welcome. He had curly blond hair graying at the temples.

"I hope you weren't asleep."

"I seem to do a lot of that."

He scrutinized her with a professional air. "You've been through quite an ordeal." He came to the bedside, picked up her wrist, and stared fixedly at the wall as he counted her pulsebeats. "Doing remarkably well," he said as he released her wrist.

"When can I do a little work?"

"Nothing strenuous?"

"Just some writing."

He smiled. "A book about your adventures?"

"I lost my notebooks during that raft trip. I'd like to reconstruct as much as I can from memory."

"I'll have writing materials delivered along with your breakfast tray in the morning."

"Thank you." She watched him with a steadiness full of expectation.

With an almost apologetic tone he muttered, "I'll drop in again tomorrow."

"How is he?"

"As well as can be expected."

"You've told me the same thing every day in the same words. I want to see him."

He seemed momentarily perplexed, then he shrugged. "We've been trying not to worry you."

"He's ill?"

"He's refusing nourishment."

"Where is he?"

"We had to move him from the infirmary. He made several attempts to escape."

She flung back the bedcovers and got out of bed. "I'm going to him wherever he is."

In the corner of a large wooden cage in the hold, the boy sat cross-legged. The cage was six feet high, boxlike in dimensions, and the floor was covered with a layer of sawdust. Sawdust was on the boy's arms and body, and flakes of it were scattered in his matted hair. He was naked; his pale body was almost hairless, patchy-colored and peeling from sunburn. The ribs showed plainly in his emaciated torso.

"Why is he in a cage?" she asked the medical officer.

"What could we do? We couldn't keep him in the infirmary, and we can hardly give him the run of the ship. We're carrying fare-paying passengers."

"Why is he refusing food?"

"Pure mulishness. He drinks when he's thirsty, so there's no reason he shouldn't eat."

"There's a difference. Drinking involves much less dexterity and concentration than eating. Therefore less risk."

The medical officer looked puzzled. "Risk?"

"You may have noticed that people are less tense at a drinking place than at a feeding place—more relaxed in a bar than at a restaurant. Our tribal memories go back a long way. When our ancestors fed, they were in danger of being caught off guard by a rival or a predator. Much more danger than when they were just having a quick one."

"He's in no danger here."

"He doesn't know that." She studied the boy, the slack apathy of his whole bearing. "What kind of food are you offering him?"

"The same as our crew gets."

30

"Cooked?"

"Of course." The medical officer sounded shocked. "You can't expect us to feed him raw meat."

The medical officer suffered from the food prejudice common to most people who consider their habits of feeding to be reasonable and sensible and other people's disgusting.

"The boy is used to hunting his dinner," Margaret explained patiently. "He probably caught small game, birds, or fish—and ate them on the spot."

"That's almost like cannibalism."

"Men have dined for thousands of years on human flesh—with not a single reported case of indigestion."

The medical officer looked slightly ill. "I think you'd better discuss this with the captain."

The ship's captain was a rotund red-faced moustached man who wore a rumpled white uniform. He said, "The doctor informs me that the boy is being offered a healthful balanced diet. What's wrong with that?"

"In the boy's opinion the food isn't fit to eat."

"The doctor says that when the boy gets hungry he will eat."

"Not necessarily. In Bengal a few years ago the rice crop failed. Over three million people starved to death because they couldn't bring themselves to accept wheat as a substitute."

"What do you suggest?"

"The boy will not begin eating until he gets what he considers his normal food."

"I am not a medical person and neither are you. I have to follow the doctor's advice. He says raw meat is not a balanced diet."

"Any high-protein food is good food. The only food that provides a completely balanced diet is blood—and only vampire bats live on that alone."

The captain worriedly rolled the end of his drooping moustache between his fingers. "I can't take the responsibility."

"Captain, this boy is a very valuable property. If

31

anything happens to him it will require a great deal of investigation and explanation. And I can assure you that he will starve himself to death unless you do as I say."

"Suppose you're wrong?"

"You can always go back to the doctor's diet. For all I care, you can even give him a menu."

The captain sighed unhappily. "I'm not going to argue. Do it your way."

"Thank you. I'll report how cooperative you've been in the daily cable I send to the museum."

Margaret returned to find the boy sitting as before. Beneath his tan beard stubble, his lean cheeks were hollowed with hunger. In the cross-legged posture his penis hung loosely, flaccidly at rest on his scrotum. She stood beside the cage until he looked at her dully.

"I don't know what they were thinking of," she said cheerfully, "feeding you cooked food from the ship's galley. Things will be better now, I promise."

His ears pricked forward slightly but nothing else in his attitude changed.

"Your feeding habits aren't so strange. At the polar ice cap there's a whole community of species, including men, who are strictly carnivorous. They live on what's available—the meat they provide for each other."

The boy continued to stare expressionlessly. But he was listening. They regarded each other through the bars of the cage.

She said, "You are what primitive man was before he became a farmer. Agriculture was man's ticket to the top but the old carnivorous ways didn't die. They were just superseded by a more efficient feeding method. Humans are still hunting animals."

Question: What makes a human? Is it walking upright? Using tools? Speaking a language?

The boy got up, moving in a shambling crouch and making guttural sounds. He did not approach her, but moved from right to left or backward and forward in a semicircle.

She said, "I understand how it is to be taken out of

32

your natural environment, forced to live a whole new existence. No wonder you tried to escape. But there's no place for you to go. The place you used to live in is far away."

She moved closer to the bars of the cage.

"I am not your enemy. You may not know the meaning of friendship but after what we've been through you must know I will never harm you."

A fly buzzed inside the cage and landed on the boy's shoulder. He looked at it without interest and did not try to brush it away.

She leaned slightly forward and, on an impulse, put her arm inside the cage.

She smiled at him. "I'm on your side. Let's shake on it."

The boy made chattering noises and fanned his face with his hand.

She was guilty of a reflexive caution: her hand was folded over so that none of her fingers were available to him. If she was going to trust him, she had to trust him all the way. She extended her fingers also.

The boy looked at her hand and then at his own. He lifted his hand and extended his fingers in mimicry of her gesture. She reached in farther until their fingers touched.

"It's a deal," she told him.

When she left she went up to the telegraph office. The operator was tapping out messages that were on yellow sheets piled on a spindle near him. She filled out two message forms and waited until he was finished before handing one to him. The first was a cable to James Halas at the Boston Museum informing him she expected the *Malmö Explorer* to arrive in Boston harbor in about two weeks.

The operator tapped it out. Then Margaret told him, "There's another message. To a Dr. Donald Swenson."

The cable asked Don to meet her when the ship docked in Boston.

* * *

In mid-semester of her third year at Barnard College she had received a letter from the Swensons, an older couple living with her father at the mission in Guatemala. They wrote that her father was ill, and their son, a doctor who was visiting them, said he needed the very best medical care to survive.

There was no question in her mind of what to do; she dropped out of school and took the first plane. She traveled by car and burro to the lonely mountainous region near Los Altos where her father had built his mission. She met the Swensons, Amund and Manuela; Amund was a Norwegian missionary who had come to Quezaltenango many years before and married a mestizo woman. Their doctor-son, Don, was an exceedingly slender young man with blond hair combed straight back, high cheekbones, and a coppery complexion he had inherited from his mother. She classified him in the quick shorthand that young women at Barnard were using that year, comparing their dates to old movie stars: he was a Jimmy Stewart.

Don Swenson discussed her father's condition. "I noticed his waxy skin color, and he complained of an accelerated heartbeat with a feeling of thumping in the chest, shortness of breath on exertion, dizziness and headaches, and a general feeling of fatigue. Of course those symptoms might be caused by a number of diseases other than pernicious anemia. But a blood count revealed a severe lack of hemoglobin—what you call red cells."

"Is it serious?"

"Quite serious. Anemia is never a disease in itself but is always caused by other factors. Liver and B-12 injections have had only a temporary effect. The next step in treatment is blood transfusions. But for that he should be in a hospital."

She was shocked by her father's pallor and weight loss—his thin bearded face looked more El Greco than ever.

He said, "Amund and Manuela are lovely people and their son is a brilliant doctor, but they're making too

34

much of this. I feel a little weak, that's all. I'll be quite well soon."

"Dr. Swenson thinks you should go to a hospital."

"I can't leave here. There's far too much work to do. I prayed to the Lord to guide me to the ones who needed Him, and my prayers have been answered. We have a weekly meeting and I read them a portion of the Bible in Quiche, usually one of the Gospels, and we pray together. It's really quite moving. You must stay for the meeting tomorrow."

The next evening more than twenty people crowded into the mission for the service. Dinner was prepared by Manuela Swenson and served by her and Don's father. On this evening Margaret and Don helped in the kitchen and with the serving.

After dinner Don said, "Now there'll be a lot of exhorting. Do you think we can sneak out for a walk? There's a full moon. Somehow in the moonlight you don't notice all the poverty."

"I promised my father I'd stay."

The people, Indians and a few mestizos, listened to her father with bowed heads and repeated the Lord's Prayer after him. He recited the Prayer in Quiche, in Spanish, and in English. Once again she had the familiar lump in her throat when she said, "And forgive us our debts." She knew then that she would stay with her father for as long as he needed her.

"That's very self-sacrificing," Don said. "I probably wouldn't act the same way in your place."

"Not if it was your father?"

"I never got along that well with either of my parents. We don't understand each other."

"I never felt I understood my father either."

"Then how come?"

"When you're adopted you carry around an extra burden of guilt."

"Are you?"

"Yes. My mother—my adoptive mother—lost her first baby in infancy. A girl. She was inconsolable be-

35

cause the doctor told her she could never have another. My father found her a replacement—me."

"That's nice."

"She was never able to accept me as a replacement for the daughter she lost. I was only nine when she died. I remember my father giving the eulogy in church. His face was illuminated. It was as if he had transcended her illness and death."

"Religious people always seem to take any tragedy as a test of their faith. When did you come here?"

"Less than a year after she died. My father had decided to dedicate the rest of his years to the poor and afflicted. He came here to the mission where he spent his days witnessing, translating the Bible, treating the illnesses of the people, and making inroads for Christ."

"It sounds like an unhappy time for you. Did you have any friends?"

"One. An Indian girl named Ysabel who left after a couple of years to get married. Most of the time I was quite lonely. I got rather used to it. Loneliness became my companion."

"You must have hated it."

"Not really. I became interested in learning about the Indians. I wanted to know more about their culture, not convert them. That's still how I feel."

"Your father couldn't have been pleased."

"We had one of those old-fashioned confrontations. I told him I wanted to live in the world and I had absolutely no interest in being saintly. At eighteen I left to attend college in New York."

"No regrets?"

"No. There's a legacy though. I still say the Lord's Prayer every night before going to bed."

"Really?"

"Whenever I come to the words 'forgive us our debts,' I get a lump in my throat. I can easily say 'as we forgive our debtors.' So I guess the link is not broken."

"A shrink would tell you it never is. Sometimes peo-

36

ple feel closer to each other after they put some distance between themselves."

"I don't know. I wrote him regularly. But he never answered me with much affection. How long do you think he has?"

"Not long, I'm afraid. Weeks, not months."

"Can you do anything to help him?"

"Nothing I haven't already told you. I could risk a blood transfusion without removing him to a hospital. But I wouldn't advise it under these conditions."

"If he's down to weeks, what does it matter? What are the problems?"

"Sanitation. I'd also need to find a donor with the same blood type. And I'd have to know that the donor is healthy, has not had an infectious liver disease or syphilis or God knows what. Frankly, even then I'd only be alleviating his symptoms. I can't change the fact that his body won't produce the amount of red blood cells it needs."

"If you alleviate his symptoms he'll be able to work. That's all that matters to him. We have the same blood type."

Despite her father's protests and Don Swenson's doubts, she went ahead. The transfusion was done the day after the tests were completed. She and her father lay on adjoining cots, in a kind of embrace, her blood flowing freely in his veins.

Don told her after the third transfusion: "Your father needs a lot more blood than you can provide. I won't do another transfusion."

"Can you order blood from a hospital?"

"There isn't any refrigeration in this area. I can probably get dry powdered plasma and redissolve it in water."

"All right. Let's try that."

He looked at her seriously for a moment. "How long do you intend to stick it out?"

"As long as it takes."

For nearly five weeks she was her father's devoted nurse. The failure of the blood-making system located

37

in his bone marrow was fully as serious as Don suspected. Her father had cancer. She thought of his life as reducing itself to a pure and narrow simplicity, as clean and bare as a fossilized bone.

His end was agonizing. On a rainy day, watching a plain wooden box being lowered into the ground, she found herself repeating the Lord's Prayer. For the first time her throat did not choke up when she came to the words "forgive us our debts..." She had repaid her debt.

chapter 3

Margaret saw Don Swenson coming up the gangplank between a two-man police escort. He wore an overcoat and his hatless blond hair flamed. He was smiling and waving. She waved back. When he arrived on deck he hugged her, and she offered him her cheek to kiss, a message he understood so well that he partly released her.

"The captain's waiting to talk to us," she said.

As they were walking along the deck Don said, "That other business is all over, you know. Even before you left."

That cost her a little of her balance, her psychological safety net.

She said, "We have more important things to discuss."

In the captain's cabin, over small glasses of sherry, Margaret explained the problem in getting the boy ashore.

"We've managed to keep any word of this from the press. And we'd like to keep it that way."

"I can have the boy and his cage put into an empty crate. When we remove it from the hold it'll go on top of other cargo crates on a flatbed truck. No one will know it isn't part of our regular cargo."

"Will there be any danger to the boy?" Margaret asked.

"We carry live cargo that way," the captain replied. "Last trip we delivered a whole lot of monkeys to a zoo. They all got there without a scratch."

"The boy isn't a monkey."

"Don't see a lot of difference myself." The captain chuckled. As he realized he was chuckling alone, his red face grew a shade redder. "You know what I mean. He's kind of a missing link—or so you might say."

39

"The missing link between monkeys and a higher form of civilization," Margaret said, "is us."

The captain muttered, "By damn, you're right," then excused himself to make the arrangements for the boy's ship-to-shore delivery.

"I saw that look in your eyes," Don said. "I could have warned him. Have you decided where you're taking the boy from here?"

"To the farmhouse in Vermont."

"Is he really a feral child?"

"I'm convinced he is."

"Raised in the bush without any human contact. Fascinating. Modern science confronted with a creature of legend—a wild child. Why did you want me to be here?"

"This is right down your alley. You've done work on the brain and the physiology of intelligence."

"Is he mentally retarded?"

"By our standards, yes. What I need to know is whether his condition is the result of inherited defect, disease, some unknown organic deficiency, or merely his unique upbringing."

"Interesting question. Has he shown any aptitude for learning?"

"I haven't been able to hold his attention long enough to find out."

"A bad sign. How about communication? Does he have any language?"

"Not words. No."

"Gestures?"

"Generalized. He can show fear. Or hunger."

"Doesn't sound promising. Exactly what do you want me to do?"

"Examine him. Give me a complete evaluation of his present condition and his future prospects."

"It would take a while. How many are working with you on this project?"

"Just me."

"Alone with him at the farm?"

"There's a caretaker who worked for my father. Jean

Pierre. He was my best friend when I lived on the farm as a child. A Quebecois."

"Where will you keep the boy?"

"I sent Jean Pierre detailed instructions on how to fix the place for the boy's arrival. There's a huge cellar being remodeled to resemble the boy's original habitat. Even the temperature and humidity."

"A good idea. Custody?"

"I'm his temporary guardian until final disposition by the courts. Jim Halas at the Boston Museum arranged all that. The authorities have been very helpful with problems of visas and the like. They realize what a unique opportunity the boy represents for scientific study."

"Well, you can trust me to keep your secret. But this doesn't sound like the kind of job you can handle alone."

"If I need an assistant, I'll get one."

"How about me? At the moment I'm at loose ends."

"This would be a long-term project. Months, maybe." She gave him the cool appraising look of a woman checking the price tag on merchandise for sale. "You might pack up and leave the minute you get a better offer."

"Not a chance. I'll stick around because this is a great opportunity. The chance of a lifetime."

She was drawn, ambivalently, to the proposal. "There would be nothing personal. Strictly a working arrangement."

"Afraid, Meg?"

She was annoyed by his discerning eye. "No, but that has to be understood."

"Understood," he replied while the familiar quirky smile gathered at a corner of his mouth.

The captain reappeared in the cabin's doorway. "Crate's ashore," he said. "Passengers are starting down the gangplank now."

They met the flatbed truck outside the city limits. Fortunately the ship's medical officer had given the boy a sedative before he began the trip and he was still

41

semicomatose when they opened the crate and removed him from the cage to Don's Volvo. They put him into the rear of the two-door sedan, where he sat with his legs drawn up, his arms crossed over his chest, and his head drooping.

The Volvo headed northward toward Vermont and the isolated countryside between St. Albans and Enosburg Landing. Securely contained in the rear seat, the boy slowly came awake during the car journey. He stared listlessly out the window at symmetrical dark green cones of tall spruce trees weighted down with snow.

The farmhouse was a three-story spacious wooden building with a wide porch in front and a barn and toolshed in the rear. The buildings were painted a durable maroon color that resisted the harsh winter weather.

Seeing the house again after so many years, Margaret felt a kind of umbilical numbness where the cord had snapped that connected her to this place. She was reminded of a way of life completely different from any she had known since. Everything that happened since she left here seemed a dizzying stream of done-and-lost compared to the life on the farm, building a barn, giving inoculation shots to sheep, repairing a broken water pump. Other memories clamored to be let in. Her grandfather had kept a large flock of sheep, but most of the sheep were gone by the time she was a child. Her favorite of those remaining was an old ram. Jean Pierre would set her on his back and she held a dish of sweet corn in front of the ram to guide him where she wanted him to go, giving him a little taste from time to time so he wouldn't get impatient.

Enough. If she continued to look back she would turn into a pillar of salt.

"That's Jean Pierre," she told Don.

The familiar figure approached the Volvo. Jean Pierre was now a sturdy man of fifty-two who wore a plaid shirt, brown corduroy trousers, and high-laced brown boots. His hair, black when she first knew him, was iron-gray.

"Welcome home, Miss Margaret."

She got out of the car to hug him.

"Jean Pierre, this is Don Swenson." Jean Pierre knew that she had married but she doubted he knew about the divorce.

"Pleased." Jean Pierre wiped his hand to shake hands as Don got out of the car. His eyes shifted to the rear seat. "And who is he?"

Jean Pierre moved forward the front seat to help the boy out, and in a flash the boy, who had appeared in a state of dormancy, bolted past. He flung off his blanket and ran naked with giant steps through the snow. Don went after him.

Margaret cried to Jean Pierre: "Catch him!"

Jean Pierre started after the boy. So did Margaret.

Ten paces ahead of Don the boy's pace slowed. Then he was standing still, his legs planted in the dark holes they made in the snowdrift. Before Don reached him the boy spun in a half circle, partly raising his leg to force it through the fluffy surface. He began heaping flaky snow in both hands to throw it against his face and chest.

Margaret caught up with Don and Jean Pierre. "It's a new sensation. He's enjoying it!"

The boy plunged his head up to the neck in a snowdrift. As he withdrew his head his hair was streaked with white. Melting flakes trickled down his skin. He stuck out his tongue to catch the drops. Then with a loud cry of delight he began running again with giant steps.

Margaret and Don and Jean Pierre followed.

The boy stopped, looked at them, then squatted down.

"What the hell!" Jean Pierre said, startled.

The boy had shit in the snow.

From Margaret Denning's journal:
Enosburg Landing, Vermont
February 4:

The boy is about five feet ten inches tall, but seems shorter because he moves in a sloping crouch. I judge him to be sixteen or seventeen years old. His skin is pale except for the faintly visible marks where his recent sunburn turned to tan. His body is marked with many healed nicks and scratches—stigmata of life in the bush. A scar above the right elbow looks as though it might have been made by the sharp teeth of an animal. His teeth are strong and comprise a full set, for which he can probably thank his carnivorous eating habits.

All his five senses are in working order, although their importance has a different priority than if he had been raised in a civilized community. His sense of smell is extraordinary, and he relies on it as much as his eyesight. He can smell from a considerable distance. We tested him, taking him outdoors on a harness that Jean Pierre made for him. The boy smelled the raw meat we had left on the far side of the barn—at least a hundred yards away—and led us directly to it.

His hearing I would describe as acute but selective; he hears what is important for him to hear. I can talk to him without arousing any interest or response, but if someone knocks at the door, or if any of the mice in permanent residence behind the cellar walls begins to scratch, he is instantly alert.

His health is good. He has made a good adaptation to the artificial climate in his cellar, which we keep as sultry and hot as his former environment. He has suffered no illness, not even a case of sniffles, and has gained weight, from approximately 105 pounds when I first saw him to his present 132 pounds. He is still slender but has lost the starved look.

His reaction to us varies from tolerance to hostility. I am the one he tolerates, Don is the one to whom he is hostile. He and Jean Pierre simply ignore each other. Jean Pierre thinks the boy is no better than an animal and wants nothing to do with him.

I doubt that he is capable of a friendly emotion. I see more of him because in addition to his lessons I share

44

with Jean Pierre the chores connected with feeding him. This provides him with a limited form of companionship, but I have no doubt he is lonely. Loneliness, though, is something he has been accustomed to all his life. I have no reason to say even that much, however. I know the number and location of his body scars, the condition of his teeth, his gait, but nothing about what goes on inside his skull.

Don is frustrated because he cannot conduct a preliminary neurological examination, such as testing the boy's reflexes, his hand-and-eye coordination, and the like. Whenever he attempts to, the boy runs away. If cornered, he bares his teeth and tries to bite. The boy apparently fears Don and reacts to him with real hostility.

Don says the only way I will teach the boy to do anything else is to make him obey me first. My problem is how to discipline and control him without breaking his spirit. Yesterday, for example, we fought a small war at his feeding time. He will not eat food off a plate. He throws the meat to the floor and eats it there. This time I was determined to teach him to eat from a plate. Each time he threw the food off, I would not let him eat but instead returned the food to the plate. It became a test of wills—the food thrown off the plate, and just as firmly put back again. He has a quick temper and is stubborn—we are alike in that. The struggle went on for an hour. At one point he fell to the floor kicking and screaming. The contest began to strike me as silly, but I knew that if I did not win this small point I would never be able to teach him the simplest thing. It was an ordeal for both of us.

Finally I had to take his food and the plate out of the room. That bewildered him. When I returned a few minutes later with the food on a plate, he was sitting on the floor, a picture of despair. I felt so sorry for him that I would have given in. But this time he fell right to eating with both hands—from the plate. When he finished I smiled at him and patted his head. He was indifferent to that, having eaten his fill. As for me, I went up to my room, fell exhausted into bed, and had a good cry. I felt better.

February 18:
Very gradually the boy's behavior is becoming less animal-like. He no longer relieves himself whenever and wherever he chooses, squatting to defecate, standing to urinate, but uses the toilet in the small partitioned area built for him. Clearly he can be trained to a degree—a feat I might have considered impossible a short time ago. He also seems pleased when I show signs of approval.

I don't mean that he has suddenly become semi-civilized. He still sniffs food before eating it, and won't use utensils to eat with. He will eat no food that has been salted or spiced, and will rub it on his plate, the floor, or even against his body to get rid of seasoning. I have tried mixing fruit and vegetables with blood and meat in a kind of stew. He will pick out the meat, drink the blood, and leave the rest untouched. During his occasional forays, harnessed, into the backyard, he still digs up a root to gnaw on it.

He does not stand upright—that vertical station which Aristotle set as a criterion for dividing man and beast. He stands and moves in a perpetual semicrouch. He does not make an articulate sound, although his tongue can move freely and he has no deformity of the larynx. Nor will he sleep in the bed we provided for him in the cellar habitat. He prefers to sleep on the floor.

February 22:
The boy's training calls for the utmost in painstaking patience. There are literally hundreds of steps involved in learning to do the simplest thing. I have finally made him understand that when he is thirsty he can drink from the gallon container of well water that is left for him. We had to go over the whole laborious process each time as if he had not learned before. When I consider how much effort is involved to train him in the
46

workings and responsibilities of home—about closets, cabinets, shelves, how to put things away, how to use faucets, lock doors, use a kitchen, even turn the knobs of a television set—the job ahead seems defeating. How can he ever live alone if he does not know such things? He will never learn to use a can opener or even tie his shoes unless there is some dramatic improvement in his basic ability to understand. For him to master a simple mechanical skill, something he might use to earn his living, such as light assembly and repair work, seems about as likely to me at this stage as his writing a doctoral dissertation.

There may be a fundamental problem with the boy's genetic endowment. After all, the botch-up that causes mongolism is merely one extra chromosome on the twenty-first set. The result is a human with little potential for developing human intelligence. The boy does not suffer from mongolism. But who knows what other problems he may have? We won't know until Don can make a complete neurological examination.

February 26:
Don decided that the only way he can give the boy a neurological examination is to tranquilize him. The first attempt failed today. The boy's keen sense of smell warned him not to eat the food that had been tampered with. Reverting to his old custom, he threw the raw meat off the plate to the floor, then circled it suspiciously, making chattering noises. The pupils of his eyes darted from side to side and he moved his jaw, thrusting it out, then closing it with a sharp clattering of teeth. Hunger was clearly at war with the instinct of danger. He dropped to all fours and approached the meat, sniffing it, then touched it and sniffed at his fingers. He rocked his body back and forth, anxious to eat but held in by his great uneasiness. At last he turned and sat with his back to the food and would not go near it.

Don says he has observed enough to form an idea of the boy's physiological condition, which is not encouraging. Among the reasons: the boy's spasmodic movements, frequent grimacing, inability to pay attention for more than a minute at a time to anything. The boy does not respond to loud noises and cannot discriminate between human voices—mine and Don's and Jean Pierre's seem to sound alike to him. He only appears to understand alterations in tone. If I rebuke him, for example, for throwing off clothing that I put on him, he will exhibit a kind of frantic perturbation—gnashing his teeth or pressing his closed fists to his eyes.

He can be sitting quietly, staring off into space with a sad expression, and the next moment he will give a piercing cry and fall and roll over, biting at the grass carpet. Such extreme reactions and the boy's failure to respond in any consistent or predictable way to stimuli lead Don to suspect that his faculties are seriously impaired and he is incapable of being trained much beyond his present state.

I hope he's wrong, of course. I continue to hope that the boy's failure to learn more quickly is not due to any mental incapacity but to the fact that I haven't learned how to reach him. If there is a failure here, let it be in the teacher, not the student.

February 28:

Last evening I brought the boy up for a brief visit from his cellar habitat. He was attracted by the heat of the fireplace and immediately took up a place on the worn rug in front of it and allowed me to cover him with a blanket.

Don and I had been planning to roast marshmallows, and the box and a long pair of tongs were on the mantel. I was interested in observing the boy's reaction as I roasted a marshmallow in the fire and ate it. His eyes followed every step of the operation. After I had repeated it several times, he suddenly lunged forward to snatch a marshmallow from the tong. It was extremely hot but he showed nothing but a tiny grimace. The grimace soon gave way to an unmistakable expression of pleasure as he swallowed the delicacy without chew-

ing it. From then on he continued to snatch the marshmallows before I could cool them off. Once when a
marshmallow dropped, he even scrabbled in the hot
ashes for it.

Knowing his predilection, I have suggested to Don
that we try to conceal the tranquilizer inside the marshmallows. I think this should work. Don thinks so too.
He proposes to skip preliminary tests and proceed directly with an extensive and significant evaluation. He
even intends to give him a brain scan. He has made
arrangements, with help from Jim Halas at the museum, to borrow an EEG from Massachusetts General
Hospital.

And because Don knows how important this is to me
he's arranged for Dr. Miles Kanter, one of the leading
figures in neurobiology, to be on hand during the examination. Don says, "You're entitled to a second opinion—though I'm sure Miles will agree with me."

Margaret liked Miles Kanter at first sight. He was
a genial, white-haired, plump man who had lived and
worked at the large government hospital at Haifa and
the Medical Center of Hadassah University in Jerusalem for more than thirty years.

Over dinner, Miles and Don discussed the tests that
had been given to the boy. Margaret was baffled by
their technical jargon. It had seemed simple when Don
explained the procedure to her, but he had been re-
stricting himself to layman's terms. Now the conversation was full of arcane words such as glial cells,
dendrites, and axons.

Margaret asked, "If he's incapable of learning, how
did he survive for so many years in the bush? He had
to secure food, prepare shelter, evade predators. Doesn't
that prove he learned something?"

"Limbic brain activity," Don replied laconically.

Miles noted her puzzled look. "The limbic brain is
embedded in the cortex and controls such behavior," he
explained. "We make a distinction between the kind of

49

brain activity we share with animals and the kind that makes language, thought, and culture."

Don added, "There isn't enough activity in the boy's cerebral cortex. That's why he's incapable of learning."

Margaret said reprovingly, "I thought that's what Miles came here to help us decide."

Miles Kanter made a preliminary examination of the boy the next morning.

"I find no indication of a brain tumor, injury, or other abnormality." Miles' mild gaze managed to be full of compassion. "My guess is that the boy's problem is inherent and biological. A brain needs references, particularly in the very early years. His brain never got a chance. Atrophy set in, and right there in the cerebral cortex where he needs them he doesn't have the neural passageways to process information. It's an irreversible condition."

Margaret thought: *The education of this child will be the distinguishing event of my life.* Annie Sullivan had said that. Annie Sullivan who taught blind, deaf, mute Helen Keller to be one of the world's great women. If that miracle could be accomplished, why couldn't a similar miracle happen now?

"Can't atrophied passageways be opened up?" she asked.

"No way that I know of."

"Aren't there other tests you can make?"

"Well, yes. A CAT-scan will give a cross-sectional view which would probably show his brain size is a little small. But brain size isn't that important. Lord Byron had one of the biggest brains on record, Anatole France had one of the smallest. Einstein's was only average."

Don grinned. "A woman's brain is about one hundred and fifty centimeters smaller than a man's. But I wouldn't dare try to tell you that a woman is dumber than a man."

"This isn't a joking matter. I want to know why something can't be done for him. You're supposed to be such great doctors. Don't you have any ideas?"

Don turned to Miles. "Would it be worth testing him with the new brain scan they have at Boston Memorial? It has a computer attachment that can sort out important information from the midst of all the electrical activity going on in the brain. I've heard it even detects the actual firing of electrochemical discharges from individual nerve cells."

"That might give us a clearer picture of what's going on inside the boy's brain," Miles said. "If we can see the microenvironment of his brain and study the structure and interrelationships of neural elements, it would help us to locate the electrical switches in his cortex."

"What kind of electrical switches?" Margaret asked.

"Each one is less than a ten thousandth of a centimeter," Don explained. "Operating on less than one percent of the voltage needed to stimulate an ordinary neuron. But those tiny electrical circuits process the trillions of bits of information that go into the brain. Without them the brain is shut off from the possibility of acquiring information and making the necessary connections."

"We can't move the boy. That would be too upsetting."

Don said, "I don't know if Boston Memorial can be persuaded to part with their brain scan for a while. But Dr. Kanter might have a few friends over there willing to do him a favor."

Miles opened his hands palms outward. "It won't hurt to ask."

Five days later a delivery van parked in front of the farmhouse. Three men working with extreme care unloaded several large crates that contained the disassembled parts of the brain scan machine. It had been forwarded directly from Boston Memorial Hospital.

Miles and Don assembled the machine in a corner room on the second floor. There was a waist-high tilt-table, a computer, an oscilloscope, an amplifier, a screen, a large cone projector, and a profusion of wires connected to an electrical console. The glistening metal apparatus took up almost half of the room.

"A little ungainly," Don said. "But beauty is as beauty does. In a few years they'll probably have small hand-held models selling for under twenty dollars. Step right up and find out if you've got a brain worth bothering about."

Miles looked fondly at the brain scan. He said, "New terms must be invented since our tongue is poor and the material is new."

"A nice saying," Margaret observed. "Whose?"

"Lucretius. A couple of thousand years ago." He patted the gray metal of the cone projector approvingly. "This should enable us to have quite a talk with the boy's brain."

"I didn't know brains could talk."

"They do. Brain waves go right on talking even when you're unconscious—they talk about every breath you take, every time you blink your eyes. They tell all kinds of things. Even what kinds of dreams you're having."

Don nodded. "By checking a chimpanzee's brain waves we can predict—quite accurately—what he'll do next."

"Let's leave out monkeys," Margaret suggested.

"Okay. We can tell whether a child in a training program is learning its lessons efficiently or not at all. Pretty soon we'll be able to interpret the actual process of thinking while it's going on. We'll pinpoint exactly where a thought originates."

Miles sighed. "Right now, I'm thinking about sleep. And I know exactly where the thought originated. I'm tired."

"Will you begin the test first thing in the morning?" Margaret asked.

"Not too early." Miles' smile was a semicircle revolving around irregular white teeth. "I don't trust those old proverbs. What really happens is that the early worm always gets the bird."

Miles left, limping slightly, and after the door closed there was a heartbeat of silence.

52

Margaret said, "Don, I know you don't have any faith in this test, but I thank you for suggesting it. Whatever it proves."

He took both her hands in his. She said, "We have a deal, remember?"

"I remember. I just want you to know."

He bent forward to kiss her, but she turned her head slightly so his lips found only the corner of her mouth.

Through the living room window the next morning Margaret watched soft glistening snowflakes falling. A snowflake landed on the windowpane and turned slowly liquid as it trickled to oblivion. She thought: Vermont gets more than its fair share of precipitation and we need it in a state that is more than eighty percent forested. She tried to hold to that thought in order not to wonder what was going on in the large corner room on the second floor of the farmhouse. It was no use.

At eleven-fifteen Don and Miles came down the stairs. She had not intended to be direct, but she could not waste time on preliminaries.

"How is he?"

"Sleeping off the tranquilizer," Don said.

"You know what I mean."

Miles crossed, limping, to the worn brocade sofa and sat down. He stretched his left leg muscles with both hands.

"I'd rather Miles told you the rest," Don said.

"What did you find out about the boy?" she asked impatiently.

"It's just as we thought," Miles said. "Nothing can be done for him."

"I won't accept that."

"Look at it this way. His brain was starved too long. Now it can't digest food."

Don said unexpectedly, "I don't agree that it's entirely hopeless."

"No?"

"What about the experiment you've been working on? NGF?"

53

Margaret said, "What's that?"

"Nerve growth factor," Don said. "Miles succeeded in isolating the hormone which stimulates the growth of nerve cells. By applying it to human tissue, he caused actual regeneration of nerve tissue."

Miles said dryly, "There's all the difference in the world between regenerating ordinary nerve tissue and brain tissue. Ordinary tissue is not in the business of transforming matter into states of consciousness."

Don persisted: "A little while ago tests were conducted with laboratory rats that showed that their cerebral cortex can be thickened by altering their environment and providing them with a more lively, varied amount of experience. Even more recently a piece of brain was transplanted from one laboratory rat to another, where the rat not only survived but functioned normally. The brain cells grew and sent out nerve fibers that hooked up with the rest of the brain. Somehow the transplant knew just where to grow and make the right connections."

"We're talking about the human brain. The most complex biological entity that has evolved in more than three billion years of life on earth."

"There might be a surgical means of improving human intelligence."

Margaret understood that Don was proposing a way of helping the boy. She listened intently.

"What's your theory?" Miles asked.

"Those laboratory rats were all in their infancy. That's when the brain, even a rat's brain, is beginning to form synapses. We know that the ability to learn corresponds exactly with the ability to form new synapses. I could implant a strip of brain tissue containing the part of DNA believed to control intelligence. With the aid of your hormone therapy plus electrical stimulation, the strip would bind itself to the boy's cortex. The DNA would make new connections. The tissue would become an integral part of the brain's function."

Margaret asked, "Wouldn't there be a problem with rejection?"

54

"No. The brain is a privileged area for transplants. Unlike other parts of the body, it doesn't reject transplants."

"What makes you think that would cause a real change?" Miles asked.

"In a more civilized brain an implant might not have a profound effect. The preexisting circuitry—the conduits—would already have made connections that resist change. But a brain like this boy's—it would be like exploring virgin territory."

"A thousand things could go wrong," Miles said.

"For instance?" Don challenged.

"The hormone that stimulates nerve growth might cross the blood brain barrier. Ordinarily, those blood vessel walls don't permit certain substances known to be harmful to pass into the brain. But who knows whether it would let the hormone through? If it does, who knows what neuroanatomical novelties might result. It might kill him."

Don said, "There's nothing else that can prevent him from spending the rest of his life in an institution."

"It's highly innovative surgery."

"The operation itself isn't dangerous. It's quite similar to surgery I performed on a young man with dyslexia except in that case I inserted a mechanical contrivance. Computer implants in the brain have been used for years for altering personality and inducing certain kinds of behavior. There's a chimpanzee in a laboratory at Yale that's had one hundred electrodes implanted in his brain for years."

"You're talking about monkeys again," Margaret said.

"It's been done with humans too. In Stockholm, surgeons implanted cells from a patient's adrenal glands into his brain to cure Parkinson's disease. The technique is being used to treat other brain disorders—such as strokes and Huntington's chorea."

"You can't predict what would happen," Miles said. "Experimental surgery is only justified when all other alternatives have failed."

"Then you're against the operation?" Margaret asked.

"Personally, I wouldn't mind being a martyr for science. But the boy isn't given a choice." Miles went through the peculiar ritual of stretching the muscles of his left leg. "On the other hand, you could look at it Don's way. Gene transfer, gene grafting, is a recognized therapeutic technique. As the boy stands, he has no future, no hope, no prospect of a life worth living. He hasn't a lot to lose."

"I want to know what *you* think."

"Will you feel guilty if the operation doesn't work? Or if he dies?" Miles asked.

"Of course I will."

Don gave her a long searching glance. "Meg, I want to give the boy a chance at life. You know what I can do. There's no one better qualified to perform this operation."

"I can't authorize it. Not now." A forlorn expression came over Don's face and she added quickly, "But I'd like you to go a little further with the idea. Just to see if it can be done."

The look of gratitude in his eyes caused a pleasant warmth to steal through her body.

"I won't forget this, Meg."

The flow of warm feeling carried her thoughts back to the final weeks at the missionary outpost in Quezaltenango when she first realized that Don Swenson was going to play a meaningful role in her life.

chapter 4

Waiting for the inevitable to happen to her father, existing in a void, she found that Don's company made everything bearable. During long hot evenings they strolled together and listened to any records he could find that were not, as he put it, "devotional." In matters of religion he was a "devout doubter."

She loved the shy smile that seemed to come out of nowhere to light his face, his habit of responding affirmatively with a kind of indrawn breath that he released in a friendly *uhhh-Hahhh!*

One evening shortly after her father's funeral, they sat talking over a bottle of red wine. Amund and Manuela had retired for the evening.

"What are your plans now?" he asked.

"I'm going to try to pick up where I left off."

"I think we ought to get married."

The humid night crept in through the window like a hot mist. She had not seriously considered marriage. She was too young and had no particular reason to settle down. Besides, their careers led in different directions. Don was interested in surgery, especially brain surgery, as part of his overall specialty in the physiology of intelligence. She wanted to be a working anthropologist, to travel and observe strange exotic cultures she had only read about.

But at the thought of not seeing him a hard painful knot formed around her heart.

"Do you really think we could make it work?" she asked.

His hazel eyes brightened and he released an indrawn breath in the familiar *uhhh-Hahhh!*

Later that night they made love. Don was not her first lover; that distinction belonged to an attractively callow Columbia graduate student with whom she had spent three physically active days on Cape Cod. Don was so tentative she was afraid he was going to apologize for undressing her. But then his lovemaking took on a fierce urgency, and she was bruised and excited by his passion. When he climaxed she quivered with satisfied yearning.

Three years later, driving along La Cienega in hazy Southern California sunshine, she was making plans to celebrate their anniversary. Don had suggested their favorite hideaway restaurant in the hills above Bel Air, but gladly yielded when she preferred a quiet dinner at home and unquiet lovemaking afterward. Thinking about the evening ahead, she felt a thrill chill her body. Marriage had uncovered unsuspected depths of sensuality in her. She was not sure that good sex was enough for a good marriage but it helped.

In other areas differences between them had surfaced when Don achieved a measure of fleeting fame. While he was on emergency duty at the hospital, Diane Fleming, a well-known rock 'n' roll star, was brought in with a serious brain injury suffered in a bizarre accident. Speeding along the freeway on a morning of heavy fog, she had raced up on a truck carrying protruding steel rods. She did not see the warning flag in time. The two vehicles collided, and one rod penetrated the windshield and her brain. At the hospital no one thought she could live. The rod had penetrated above her left eyebrow and pierced the right hemisphere of her brain to stop near her ear. Don operated and removed the rod. Using microsurgical techniques, he managed to stop the bleeding from a punctured artery in the brain in time to preserve vital brain tissue. Otherwise his famous patient might have survived only as a nonfunctioning human being. Her recovery was extraordinary, and the chief surgeon at the hospital said there was nothing he could have done to improve on Don's performance.

Diane Fleming's first television special after her recovery was a media event, and she invited Don to appear as her guest. Before an audience of nearly fifty million viewers Diane credited him with saving her life and dedicated her new hit recording to him.

That episode encouraged a certain reckless tendency that was part of Don's nature. "You know how much I'll be making after I pass my boards? It's obscene!" He bought a new sports car, they moved to an expensive apartment on Kings Road between Melrose and La Cienega, and he acquired an interest in dressing up and dining out. He told her, "Nobody works harder than I do. After a month of twenty-hour days I'm entitled to a splurge. We're *both* entitled. The time to live it up is when we're young enough to enjoy it."

His extravagance was a way of pacifying his ferocious restlessness. Even when he appeared to be calm, he was full of inward motion. During a quiet conversation he would leap up to pace around the room, gesticulate, act out what he was saying.

When she accused him of being money-oriented, more interested in doing well than doing good, he flared angrily. "I've only got one aim, and that's to be the very top in my field. Hell, that's why I got interested in brain surgery in the first place. I want to find out why I'm smarter than anybody."

His ambition was a torturing affliction, almost like physical pain. It left no room for any kind of contentment. For relief he turned to drugs; marijuana and cocaine because they were less addictive. He kept trying to persuade Margaret to "turn on" with him. She refused, but couldn't make him stop. The level of tension in their marriage kept rising like steam in a faulty boiler. How long would it be before something burst?

As she turned into Kings Road she willed such thoughts out of her mind. She stopped the car in front of the garage gate. She rolled down the car window and inserted her key into the post lock. As the gate swung open, she drove through to her assigned parking space beside a concrete pillar. The rear service elevator let her off nearest their corner third-floor apartment. A dog was barking loudly as she went down the green-carpeted corridor of the building.

As she opened the apartment door she picked up, at the lowest level of hearing, a sound she was not quite sure she had even heard. A very short foyer opened into the living room. On the bar counter that divided the kitchen from the living room area—all so California style, open and free and unwalled—two highball glasses contained several cubes of melting ice. One was empty, the other a third full.

The door to the bedroom was closed. That was where the sound had come from, and when it came again she knew exactly what it was. Anyone who went to the movies would have recognized it. All acting schools should give compulsory courses in how to vocalize the orgasm.

Standing at the counter and reaching over, she emptied the highball glasses into the sink. The ice cubes made tiny rattling noises. Happy anniversary. She turned on the small radio on the bar counter. She turned the volume on full.

The bedroom door opened.

Don wore only his undershorts; his tall skinny body was standing on stilts of bone. His blond hair was tousled, not combed straight back neatly as usual.

He ran his fingers through his hair. "Jesus, Meg. I didn't expect you."

"I thought I'd get an early start. Our anniversary, you know. I see you had the same idea about getting an early start."

He put on a questioning look. Without being aware, she had acquired an entire rogue's gallery of Don's expressions. Next would come the oh-I've-got-the-answer-to-what-she-means-now look.

"Oh," he said. "You mean the drink?"

"In two glasses."

"Were there two glasses?" He was trying hard to find a way through a hopeless tangle of ridiculous explanation. "I guess I was more squiffed than I thought."

"Where is she?"

"She?"

The big walk-in closet in the bedroom or the bathroom. Wherever she was hiding, she'd have to come out. "This is silly, Don. Tell her to get her things, get dressed, and get out."

"Now, Meg, I hope you're not going to make a scene."

"Get her, whatever her name is, out of here."

He seemed to hesitate, as if he wanted to say more by way of explanation. Then he went back into the bedroom.

She was looking out the window in the living room when the visitor left. In the glass she saw the blurred reflection of a statuesque figure in a dark dress cut in a deep U to show cleavage, an ebullience of overflowing shoulder-length hair. Diane Fleming.

The door opened and closed.

Outside the traffic rumbled along Melrose Avenue, past the antique stores and Ma Maison restaurant with its canopy and outdoor dining patio.

Don came up behind her and tried to put his arms around her. She turned out of his grasp, feeling a physical revulsion at his touch.

He had put on trousers and a shirt.

"I'm a bastard," he said. "I know."

"Is that all you're going to say?"

"We were a little high. It was a rough day. An operation that took all morning and I lost the patient. Diane stopped at the hospital for a checkup. And then, well, we just got started drinking and . . . it happened."

Funny how you can be married to a man and not know him, she was thinking. She felt a gasping in her chest and her heart was beating too fast to make up for the scarcity of oxygen. She wished he had not admitted it, had lied. Lies can be comforting.

"Was this the first time?"

That was not the question she meant to ask, or was it? Her thoughts were not coming in sequential coherent fashion.

"Of course," he said. "And it will never happen again. I swear to you."

He was lying now. It had happened more than once. She had not realized how important that detail was.

61

She might have forced a single event out of her mind and pretended it didn't matter. But repetition proved it was no accident, that it was something *willed* to happen; Don wanted it to happen.

"Why did you bring her here?"

Unspoken was the question: Why did you make love in our bed?

"Don't make a big thing out of it. It didn't mean anything to me."

"You're more sophisticated than I am. It means something to me."

How quickly everything had changed, her view of herself, her marriage, Don; her world had turned topsy-turvy in the past few minutes. There was nothing to rely on any more. There was no one she could trust.

"I suppose you're going to call her," she said, "and apologize."

"Don't start that."

"You owe her an apology, don't you? For putting her into an embarrassing position. You didn't mean for her to be caught, did you?"

"Meg, stop it!"

She did not feel anger, at least not yet. Just fear because her life could be turned around so easily. Suddenly a chasm had opened before her and she saw how close to the edge she was. If she did not stop now, she would go tumbling in and everything would come tumbling after.

"You know I love you," he said.

"I'm not sure what I know."

She saw the plank that would lead across the chasm, not to where he was but to a place where there was at least a temporary refuge. A place beyond recriminations and accusations and lies.

"You've helped me to make up my mind about something." Her voice was shaking a little. "I had an offer last month I didn't tell you about. The Boston Museum is sponsoring a field trip, a rather long one, and they want me to go."

"You can't run away at a time like this. That's the worst possible thing to do."

"I was going to tell them I wasn't interested. But it's something I want very much."

"Meg, I promise you that—"

"I might have felt I made a mistake if I had turned it down. Now I don't have to. Perhaps I should thank you for that. Thank you, Don."

He said angrily, "I hate you when you're like this. So damn superior."

Not superior at all, she thought, surprised that he understood her so little. Just trying to pull something together that fell into pieces a little while ago.

"I'll write," she told him.

She wrote often. She wanted him to share everything that happened so that when she returned they would not be strangers. The expedition consisted of four anthropologists who had settled near Arapesh in New Guinea to study an aboriginal tribe. Each had a different task, to study the tribe's language, culture, history, and sexual habits. Margaret was assigned to study the sexual habits of the tribe, not only its ceremonies and rituals surrounding marriage and birth, but the attitudes toward incest, the relationship between men and women, and how they reared their children. She found it all fascinating, and her letters to Don were crammed with the freshness and wonder of her encounters. Because she wanted him to understand what her work was about, she wrote letters in great detail— about the difficulties and rewards of being in the field, amusing stories about learning the aboriginal language and describing the intricacies of their sexual customs. She included data her colleagues were also collecting, some rich material on religious ceremonies which had been observed by others but never fully understood. She intended to write a scientific paper about this, but Don showed her letters to a doctor at the hospital who had published a book about his experiences while an intern. The doctor was charmed by the frank and personal revealing style of the letters and sent them to his publisher, who immediately agreed to publish them in a book. *Letters from New Guinea* was an instant success and Margaret returned to discover that she was famous.

Don, however, was in the midst of a scandal that threatened to put a premature end to his career. During an international conference of scientists, he had incautiously revealed the results of a daring surgical experiment in which he operated on a man with a dyslexia that had made it impossible for him to read or deal in numbers. He inserted into the young man's brain a tiny silicon chip microcomputer, about the size of a fingernail, that was powered by an outside battery, and the young man's dyslexia was corrected. But the silicon chip microcomputer was used in the military and space program, and the scientist to whom Don revealed its existence was the Russian delegate to the convention.

On the very day Margaret returned, Don was called for questioning by a government investigating committee.

"I'm going to tell the truth," he assured her. "I don't have anything to apologize for. What I did has the potential to benefit other patients suffering from learning problems."

"I don't think they object to what you did in a medical way. They're only concerned that by telling the wrong person about it you might have endangered the security of the country."

"These stupid flagwavers can't seem to understand that scientific knowledge is meant to be shared. It belongs to everyone, not just one country."

"If you talk like that to the committee, you'll put your neck on the block. You're a smart man in many ways, Don, but not when it comes to politics."

"What do you think I should do?"

"Be contrite. Convince them you didn't act with any wrongful intent."

"I'm damned if I will. I didn't commit a crime. If the

whole world has gone mad, that's no reason for me to join them."

During the hearing the chairman of the committee threatened four times to have Don jailed for contempt. In the end the committee decided not to press charges, but the National Institute of Health revoked his federal grants for research. Their spokesman said he had violated federal regulations concerning the protection of human subjects of medical research, and that his attempt to "redesign human heredity" might be disastrous in ways that could not be predicted.

Don scoffed: "Redesign heredity? That's a fine way to describe curing dyslexia. They could say the same thing about Pasteur or Semmelweis or even the doctors doing heart transplants. Any therapy that reduces suffering or death changes the so-called natural order of things."

Don was asked to resign from the staff of his hospital because his continued employment might risk their own federal grants. That was the hardest blow. After that, he began using drugs more heavily and resumed an affair with Diane Fleming. Margaret's marriage became one in which few promises were kept, all hopes were unfulfilled. She began to realize that their love was destined to have a beginning and an end, but no middle. Nonetheless she stayed with him until he told her he wanted a divorce in order to marry Diane.

Free at last to pursue her own work, she went to see James Halas, head of the Division of Anthropology and Archeology of the Boston Museum. He was about sixty years old, a pleasant smiling man whose bald pink head was fringed with gray hair.

Margaret gave him her proposal for an expedition up the Sepik River and its tributary to the village of Mondugami, inhabited by an almost unknown pygmy tribe.

Halas told her, "I suppose at this point we could raise the money for almost anything you wanted to do. But why are you interested in pygmies?"

"We know so little about them. I only heard of them

during my previous trip to New Guinea. Apparently they're a closed society—not native to the region. They probably emigrated from the New Hebrides about a thousand years ago."

"It would be safer and more productive if there were a team going with you."

"The pygmies might accept one stranger but never a whole party." She did not mention that she was feeling too depressed to be a cooperative member of a team. "I don't except any trouble."

Within two weeks a foundation agreed to support the proposed expedition for a period of up to one year. There were still the problems of visas, permissions, inoculations, arranging for supplies and transportation. But two weeks later she journeyed from Boston to Sydney by steamer, then from Madang to Arapesh, from Arapesh to Alitoa, and by government pinnace up the Sepik to a tributary where supplies and equipment were transferred to rafts poled by native bearers that took her to the pygmy village of Mondugami.

She was in Mondugami when her divorce decree became final, but she did not know it until she received the official notification during her stay in the infirmary at Alitoa eight months later.

chapter 5

Shortly after Don left to catch the six forty-five morning train to New York City, a delivery truck stopped at the side door of the farmhouse with a swishing of snow tires. Jean Pierre and Margaret helped Rory to unload the week's delivery of groceries. Rory was eighteen years old and wore tight jeans, cowboy boots, and a belt with a giant square buckle engraved with silver letters, R-O-R-Y. He had a pronounced Adam's apple.

"Story about you in the paper today," he said to Margaret in an almost comically deep voice as Jean Pierre carried the last box of canned goods into the kitchen.

"What paper?"

"New York *Times*. I brought it along in case you'd like to see it."

"I certainly would."

Rory climbed up into the driver's seat. He tossed a rolled-up paper bound with twine to her through the window.

"It'll be on your bill."

She went into the kitchen and cut the twine and unrolled the late-night edition of the newspaper. Jean Pierre was putting away canned goods in the pantry. Halfway down the front page, on the left side, she saw the heading: NEW GUINEA WILD BOY UNDERGOING TESTS. In the first few lines she read that the wild boy was the subject of an experimental project taking place in an otherwise unidentified town in New England. The goal of the experiment, the *Times* said, was to discover whether the boy could be brought up to a level in which he could function as a normal human being in a modern industrial society. At the end of the second paragraph she was named as the person in charge of the project, working under the aegis of the Boston Museum. Before

67

she could turn the page to where the story was continued, the telephone rang.

"Margaret? Jim Halas. Have you seen the *Times*?"

"I was just reading it."

"I guess we couldn't expect to keep the lid on forever."

The thought suddenly occurred to her that James Halas was not averse to garnering publicity for the Museum, of which he was a director. Halas was also in a position to reveal exactly where the experiment was taking place.

Halas said, "That idea of training him to reenter society apparently made him newsworthy. He isn't just Tarzan or Mowgli."

"Jim, I can't have reporters swarming around. You should have known—"

He broke in. "I got an unexpected call this morning after the story appeared. Have you heard of Cornelia De Wein?"

"Damn it, I'm trying to tell you—"

"The De Wein family owns eighty-five percent of all the diamonds produced in the world. She was calling to get more information about the wild boy."

Despite herself, she was intrigued. "What's her interest?"

"She'd like to see him."

"Did she give a reason?"

"Cornelia De Wein doesn't have to."

"Oh, yes, she does."

"It would be nice if you'd go along. I'd consider it a personal favor."

"I don't owe you a personal favor."

"This is important, Margaret. Someone like Cornelia De Wein can finance a dozen anthropological expeditions. You owe it to others working in your profession."

"If you put it that way, I can't say no. Good Lord!" Through the front window of the living room a caravan of vehicles was approaching along the narrow snow-covered road. "They're here!" she said as she hung up the telephone.

Miles Kanter appeared sleepily at the head of the corridor that led to his room. He was wearing pajamas and robe.

"We're about to be invaded," she told him. "Newspapermen. There's a story in the *Times*. Jean Pierre!"

Jean Pierre appeared from the pantry, where he had been unloading more provisions.

"People are coming. I don't want them getting in or even looking in. Make sure all doors and windows are locked. Draw the shutters and curtains."

The telephone rang again. She picked it up.

"Miss Denning, I'm from the Boston Globe. I—"

She slammed the phone back on the receiver. "Hurry!" she told Jean Pierre.

"I'll help," Miles said. He locked and bolted the front door just as the telephone rang again.

A voice said, "This is the Washington *Post*," and Margaret pushed the disconnect button. Then she left the telephone receiver off the hook. Anyone who called now would get a busy signal.

The caravan had arrived at the front door. She heard engines shutting off one by one.

A voice said clearly, "Doesn't look like they want visitors, Sheriff."

The metal knocker on the front door rapped loudly.

"Miss Denning, this is Sheriff Hamilton. I'd like to speak to you for a minute."

"What do you want?"

"I'd rather talk to you inside if you don't mind."

"This is my property, Sheriff. Those people you've brought with you are trespassing."

"They're representatives of the press and television. If you'll give them a little of your time, I'm sure they'll leave quietly."

"They won't get any cooperation from me."

"Miss Denning, they didn't come to make trouble. This can be handled in a nice dignified manner."

"I want them off my property. I know my legal rights. It's your duty as sheriff to get trespassers off my property."

The sheriff's voice lowered: "If I can have a word with you privately."

Perhaps the sheriff was right, and if she granted an interview everyone would leave peaceably. But she doubted it. They'd want to know all about the boy. They'd want to see him and photograph him. She would not permit him to be exploited.

"Impossible today, Sheriff. Perhaps some other time."

The sheriff called her name again, but she did not answer nor did she reply to the loud rapping of the knocker. After a minute she heard swearing and footsteps moving away from the door.

She ran upstairs. Looking through the shutters in the large front room, she glimpsed the sheriff, a tall large slouching figure, surrounded by a number of gesticulating men and women. A short distance away two men were lounging against a television sound truck. They seemed amused.

Half an hour later the sheriff's car departed. Some cars followed him, but others remained; so did the television sound truck. Moments later the side door to the house rattled loudly. Someone shouted an obscenity.

Jean Pierre said, "I can load a shotgun with birdshot."

"That won't be necessary."

At lunchtime four cars and the sound truck were still waiting outside.

"Why don't they go away and leave us alone?" she asked Miles and Jean Pierre in the kitchen.

Miles said, "The house is locked up tight and they can't get in without breaking in. Of course, we can't go out either."

Jean Pierre said, "In the blizzard seventeen years ago I couldn't go out of the house for two months."

"That's what we need," Margaret said. "A blizzard."

Miles said, "They're just doing their job."

"I may feel that way later. Not now." She had a sinking feeling that the house was under seige and she couldn't hold out. Another problem worried her. They could not arrange for surgery if their every move was being watched by the media.

70

She wished Don were there to consult with. She didn't even know where to get in touch with him, and he couldn't telephone her because she had the telephone off the hook.

It had begun to snow and drifts were starting to cover the road. At four o'clock the cars and the sound truck were gone. Their line of retreat might have been cut off if they stayed.

She put the telephone receiver back in place, but the phone rang instantly. A voice said, "This is the Associated Press—" Margaret broke the connection and left the telephone off the hook.

On the long train ride to New York City, Don's exhilaration began to fade. He had been given a big opportunity, a challenge equal to his ambition and talent. What he needed was a medical miracle. But suppose he failed? This would be the first leg of another journey back to nowhere. Nowhere was an office he shared in Plattsburg in upper New York State with an oculist who handled nose and throat diseases and an internist who was a GP. No one could afford to specialize in a small town. After Don lost his hospital accreditation and the federal funds needed to continue with his research, there had been no place for him to go but to an obscure practice in general surgery.

Restless, he got up and went to the bar car. It was crowded and there was nowhere to sit down. A young woman moved to clear a space at the bar so Don could stand beside her. He asked her what she was drinking. She said she was having a Charles Dickens—a martini with olive 'r twist. She was attractive, superficially bright. Just what he needed at the moment.

After two Charles Dickens cocktails, the liquid solvent began to penetrate the series of filters that protected his brain, crossing the blood barrier with ease and seeping into his thoughts. He began to wonder if he should ask her to have dinner with him in New York.

Outside the train window, the landscape was rushing by like time.

"Another drink before we get in?" he asked his companion, touching her elbow, letting his hand remain there. "Charles Dickens, thou should'st be living at this hour."

The young woman laughed immoderately.

Don looked at his reflection in the mirror behind the bar. So far, he had proved unequal to his talent. He should ask more of himself than he believed it was possible to do—and then do it.

If he did not perform the surgery, a unique creature whose education might contribute invaluable knowledge to science would be lost forever because he could not accept systematic training. If the surgery were successful on the other hand, Margaret could begin a sensible program for the boy's long-term education. Train his senses, expand his physical and social adaptability, teach him to respond and communicate in some form of speech. Above all, teach him to think.

Determination turned fierce in him.

This time I will not fail my talent.

I will not.

When the train arrived at Grand Central Station he and the young woman exchanged telephone numbers. He went up the escalator and through the Pan Am Building. A short walk took him to a modern skyscraper not far from St. Bartholomew's Church. He rode up in a glare-free soundless elevator. On the eighth floor he paused before a plain wood-grained door with dignified lettering: CCS.

He opened the door and went in.

A stocky, amiable woman seated at a severely modern functional desk smiled at him.

"My name is Dr. Swenson. I have an appointment with Dr. Bristol."

"You're right on time. He's expecting you."

Ted Bristol looked more like a former athlete than a renowned scientist. His grip was like a grappling iron. His voice had a sonic boom.

"A pleasure to see you again."

As soon as they were seated, Bristol made a swift

segue to the business at hand: "What's the reason for this unexpected visit? Have you changed your mind about joining us?"

At their last meeting Don had refused an invitation to join the Committee of Concerned Scientists. He was concerned, but not enough to join an organization. In his opinion, the only sure guide in a situation was self-interest. It was in the pursuit of self-interest that he had come.

He said, "I have a proposition that may interest you and your Committee."

Ted Bristol sat in a swivel chair behind his desk, thoughtfully twirling a pencil between two fingers while Don explained the nature of the vital substance he needed.

"Why come to me?" Bristol asked.

"There isn't time to acquire this through normal channels even if I could obtain the necessary permissions and find a donor. And this is the kind of project that will certainly contribute to the cause of science around the world."

"Where do you plan for this operation to take place?"

"A small private hospital in Plattsburg. That's in New York State. Across the state line from where the boy is now. No one in the hospital will know who the patient is. Officially, this will be an emergency operation for intercranial bleeding."

"How about the people in the operating room?"

"I'll be the surgeon. Miles Kanter will assist me. No one else will know much about what's going on. The implant can be accomplished with no one suspecting a thing."

"Tell me again exactly what you need."

"A strip of human brain tissue that contains the DNA supposed to control intelligence."

"What makes you think I can get it?"

"You have contacts with scientists all over the world, some of whom work in this field."

"What quid pro quo are you offering?"

"If you can deliver what I need, I'll turn over all the

73

research and post-op notes to your Committee. You'll be kept fully informed as to the results of the operation."

"No restrictions on sharing the information?"

"None."

"We're interested in anything that promotes cooperation within the world scientific community. But this isn't something that can be accomplished through normal channels. If it can be done, at least four or five laws will be broken. I don't want anyone to end up in jail, so I must insist that you tell no one where you got it. That's an absolute condition."

"Understood."

Bristol said after a moment, "I'll see what I can do."

On the way down in the elevator, Don wondered why he was not more excited by the prospect of success. Perhaps, he decided, he was too aware of the difficulties still ahead and the very good chance of failure.

As he emerged on the street the setting sun cast its last rays of light on the topmost floors of a glass-sheathed tower. A taxi to La Guardia and a flight to Burlington might bring him to the farmhouse by midnight. But he did not feel like going back. He would call Margaret and explain that he had to stay in the city overnight.

His fingers touched the scrap of paper the attractive young woman had given him. It might be possible for them to have dinner. She might be exactly what he needed.

At four-thirty that afternoon a white Silver Cloud Rolls-Royce stopped outside the farmhouse. A uniformed chauffeur opened the rear door, and a tall woman emerged. She wore a white fur hood and an immense white fur coat that made her look like a sheepdog.

Margaret opened the front door. "Mrs. De Wein?"

"Miss. You're Margaret Denning." She stamped her boots on the rubber mat and shook snow from her fur hood which she had untied. When she removed the coat she emerged as a slender woman of about forty. She wore black hip-hugging slacks, a white cowl-necked blouse, and a red cashmere sweater-vest. She extended a freckled hand. "I recognize you from your photograph."

"My photograph?"

"On the back cover of your book. I looked through it this morning before I came. I like to become acquainted with a person before I meet them."

She was striking-looking, a bit too long and thin in the nose and too bony in the cheek to be really attractive.

"I'm curious about your request," Margaret said.

"The news did not reach me in Johannesburg when you first found the boy. I became interested when I read about him in the newspaper. I called the man at the Museum, I forget his name..."

"James Halas."

"...and asked him for an interview." She sat gracefully on the brocade sofa, crossing trousered legs. "Twelve years ago my brother Philippe, his wife, and their four-year-old son were lost in a plane crash in the New Guinea jungle."

"I see."

"It was during a flight to Port Moresby. No expense was spared to find them, but not a trace of the missing plane was found."

"And you think your missing four-year-old nephew may be the boy we found in the jungle?"

"He would be sixteen years old now. I'm told that is the boy's approximate age. It is possible that the child survived the crash."

"At four years of age your nephew would have learned how to speak—and to understand what was said to him. The wild boy can't do either. It's true that even older children regress to a primitive state when cut off from all human contact. But the doctors who have examined the wild boy think his condition is caused by a total lack of any brain stimulation even in infancy."

"I took the trouble to make certain medical inquiries before deciding to come here. I've been assured that a traumatic event—such as a plane crash—could also lead to such a condition."

"If he is your nephew, how do you expect to identify him? There's no possibility of communication. He won't understand anything you say."

"If he is my nephew I will know him. We are wasting time, Miss Denning. I would like to see the boy."

Margaret shrugged. "It's probably best if I let you observe him during his lesson. There's a special viewing area where you can watch without his being aware. If you'll come this way."

That afternoon's lesson was part of a continuing series in which Margaret was trying to foster the boy's familiarity with objects in his environment. She wanted to make him grasp that objects have names which can be spoken and that information about them can be communicated through sense experiences and language. The subject of today's lesson was paper. She began with writing paper from a lined school notebook, showed him the look of it, letting him hear the crackling noise it made when she crumpled it, telling him over and over what it was. He showed no particular interest. When she offered him an uncrumpled page he would not even sniff at it—his sense of smell was still his chief means of acquainting himself with anything new.

She repeated the procedure with a copy of yesterday's newspaper and again elicited no reaction. The boy watched impassively. She tossed the newspaper away, and picked up a photography magazine. She ran her hand over its glossy pages and tried to induce him to do the same. His gaze wandered idly away. When she finally crushed, squeezed, and ripped out the pages of the magazine, it was a useful way to vent her frustration.

Finally the lesson was over and it was feeding time. She brought a plate of raw meat to the boy, who squatted and began to feed, using both hands to thrust raw hunks into his mouth.

When Margaret went upstairs Cornelia was not

looking at the viewing glass set into the floor above the cellar. She was a shade paler.

"I've seen enough," she said. "Revolting. He even eats like an animal."

"He hasn't had much chance to learn table manners."

"He's a subhuman. How long are you going to continue trying with him?"

"As long as there's a chance of improvement."

"In my opinion he should have been left in the jungle where you found him. I feel sorry for the little beast."

"You're convinced he isn't your brother's son?"

Cornelia appeared to recoil at the suggestion. "There is no question of that. My curiosity is completely satisfied."

A few minutes after Cornelia left, the telephone rang and it was Don calling from New York.

"Good news. We can start making arrangements for the surgery."

"There's been a complication here. Have you seen the New York *Times*?"

"Today? No."

She related the events of that morning. "The reporters are gone now, but they'll be back. Now they know where the boy is they'll keep coming around."

"I can't get transportation back tonight. But I'll be there tomorrow and we'll figure it out. The first step is the step that counts and that's already been taken. We're on our way."

Margaret returned to the viewing area in the floor of the room above the cellar. The boy was sleeping. She thought: What we know is always changing into something else. One form of life is destroyed to evolve into another form. The babe is destroyed by the child, the child by the adolescent, the adolescent by the adult. Looked at in a certain way, the process of becoming is a series of linked disasters.

The boy's brain was a blank tape waiting for the first thoughts to appear. The problem was how to start the recorder going. Watching the boy sleeping, she wondered: Do you have any emotions other than hunger or
77

fear, the survival emotions controlled by the so-called limbic brain? Does anything amuse you? Are you happy, are you sad? Do you like anyone? Are you aware of anyone else's existence except as a person who satisfies or frustrates your wants? If the answer to these questions is no, then you are not in danger of losing very much with your life, are you?

She had gone along with Don's proposal for an operation impetuously, failing to reckon with his need to prove something to himself. Now she decided she had been right. She was trying to save a life, not endanger it. There was no alternative.

The boy heard a very faint scratching sound. He kept his eyes shut tightly, simulating sleep while breathing lightly. His fingers moved quickly across the tufted grasslike floor seeking a good purchase. His ears pricked forward, listening for danger. His muscles tensed. He sat up quickly on his haunches, ready to run or fight.

He waited without moving again for a long time until he heard another scratching sound. In his home place he knew the meaning of every rustling in the bush, every smell on the hot moist air. He even dreamt of the splash of fish jumping in the stream and himself leaping like a wallaby through bush and tall grass. He slept and hunted and ate and slept and hunted again. But in this strange place there was no hunting. Food was brought to him.

The taste of fear was in his mouth. He clicked his strong teeth.

And heard scratching again.

He sniffed, trying to pick up a scent. The air was strange, like home place but not. He smelled nothing dangerous. With his tongue he tasted warm wet air. His eyes darted but saw nothing.

More scratching.

Slowly he came down from a squatting position to all fours, and with rear elevated, bare buttocks showing, he moved toward the scratching sound.

Smell came. Something alive. Good for eat.

78

In a far corner of the large cellar room a mouse was burrowing through part of the wall weakened by damp and erosion. The scratching was its tiny raking claws pulling down the fragments of plaster. A sharp micronate nose peered through the wall. Shoulders and powerful little forelegs followed. Then a small dark brown-gray body. The mouse peered about, nose twitching, whiskers probing.

The mouse made a great leap, barely in time to avoid the predator's clutch. Squealing, it fled, closely pursued. Twisting, turning, wheeling, doubling on its tracks. The predator was quick too. In panic the mouse scurried for its hole, for safety. It leapt into the hole with a last flick of a hairless tail. A clutching hand barely missed it. Inside the wall the mouse scrambled upward, tiny heart racing with its burden of enormous fear.

The boy lowered himself back to floor level and peered into the hole. Dark. Food gone. He reached out to probe with his hand. Wet crumbling plaster fell on his hand. He pulled his hand back, then put it in the wall again. When he pulled it back against the side of the hole, the hole became larger. He pulled at the sides of the hole with his fingers and the plaster came away easily. He sniffed his fingers. No-food. He threw the fragment of plaster away. Then he began pulling at both sides of the hole with his hands.

The hole grew steadily bigger.

And bigger.

chapter 6

An hour's drive from Fort Meade in Maryland is a spacious Victorian home set on a knoll. The knoll was formerly covered with a stand of trees that provided shelter and privacy. Now the trees have been cut down to provide a clear expanse of view. At the bottom of the knoll, surrounding the house on all sides, is a ten-foot-high stone fence surmounted by three feet of electrified barbed wire.

This Victorian residence is the headquarters of a small but efficient government agency whose existence is known only to a few in the highest echelons of government. The Security Bureau, as it is called, is funded within the budget of the National Security Agency, and operates as an unchartered arm of COINTELPRO, the counterintelligence program.

On this morning Commander Wilson Richards walked from the parking lot, where he had left his car, across the long path that led to the portico of the house. As he entered, a guard standing just inside, dressed in a semiuniform of black turtleneck and dark tight-fitting trousers, nodded to him.

"Good morning, sir."

Commander Richards walked down a narrow corridor past two closed doors and into a wide high-ceilinged pleasantly spacious room in which a dozen men and women were working at desks. Everyone looked up and smiled as he passed. The commander liked to have smiling people around him. He liked to create an environment in which people were happy to work.

As he passed from the large room, all smiles vanished behind him.

He entered the anteroom of his private office, an inviting atmosphere in which a well groomed woman

80

secretary sat at a large curved desk. The anteroom had thick carpets and artfully recessed lighting.

The secretary said, "Good morning, Commander," and smiled. "Mr. Holcomb is waiting in your office."

"Hold all phone calls."

The commander had no idea what Martin was about to tell him, but the number-two man in the Security Bureau would not have asked for an early morning meeting unless the matter was urgent. The commander sat in the leather armchair at his desk. Behind his metal-framed glasses his eyes were large, cool, and appraising.

"We have exactly twenty minutes," he said.

"The problem concerns Dr. Donald Swenson. You may remember that Dr. Swenson is the man who delivered valuable scientific material to a representative of the U.S.S.R."

"Whether he did so advertently has not been determined. But we assume the worst."

"Swenson has been under surveillance since that incident," Martin went on. "His career is in decline. Federal funding was withdrawn from his research projects, he lost his hospital accreditation—"

"I believe we can take some credit for that."

"Indeed, sir. In addition to our usual methods we undertook special measures. When an independent laboratory was interested in hiring Swenson, we created evidence that he had faked research in his previous employment and conveyed this secretly to the laboratory. After the laboratory decided not to employ him, Swenson moved to upper New York State where he shares an office with two other doctors. A nonsensitive occupation. We were about to withdraw low-level surveillance when a new development occurred. He took a leave of absence in order to join his former wife, Miss Margaret Denning, and Dr. Miles Kanter in the training and evaluation of the wild boy discovered in New Guinea. In view of the abrupt change in occupation, we decided to continue low-level surveillance."

"Sensible."

81

"While under surveillance Swenson paid a visit to the Committee of Concerned Scientists."

The commander's expression did not change. He was prepared for surprising information at all times and invariably responded with patronizing patience, affecting the kind of boredom that comes only from having endured countless such episodes before. It was as if he were saying, "You think you are revealing something of the first importance, but when you have been around as long as I have..." But it was difficult for him to pretend indifference about anything concerning Ted Bristol and his insufferable Committee.

Martin said, "I asked Gert for a complete rundown on Miles Kanter."

Gert was the vast, complex thirty-two-bit computer that occupied most of the basement of the building.

"Summarize," the commander said, "anything of interest."

"Dr. Kanter is a very distinguished medical scientist, the winner of last year's Lasker Award for his discoveries about regenerating nerve tissue. Ordinarily, nerves of the central nervous system do not regenerate, but when Dr. Kanter's method was used nerve fibers from the spinal cord grew and sent fibers into neighboring tissue. He healed a man who'd been paralyzed for almost a year."

"I'd like to know more of his personal history."

"Kanter is an Israeli citizen who emigrated here a few years ago. Miles Kanter is not his real name. He was christened Miles Wenedge and born in Brooklyn to middle-class parents. He is not Jewish. He adopted the Jewish religion and took another man's name. A man who died at Buchenwald."

Commander Richards believed there was always a clue that, if recognized, would reveal the secret of a man's character and greatly increase the probability of being able to predict what he would do under certain circumstances. The trick was to recognize the clue when it appeared.

"There must be a reason for that."

"If so, Kanter has not confided it to anyone. He lived for thirty years in Israel, first in Haifa and then in Jerusalem. Apparently he now considers himself a Jew. He became acquainted with Swenson soon after his arrival in the United States, and they conducted an infrequent correspondence. He was enlisted by Swenson to work on the project involving the wild boy. I believe the situation bears watching, and I recommend upgrading surveillance to Class One on Swenson, Kanter, and the Denning woman."

The commander's magnified eyes blinked behind his glasses. Miles Kanter was certainly a factor to be weighed, but Martin was overlooking the vital clue. The commander reflected with pleasure that there were valid reasons why Martin was his second-in-command.

"*L'shana ha-ba-nah b'Yerushailayim.*"

Martin stared. "What did you say, sir?"

"It means 'next year in Jerusalem.'" The commander was proud of his mastery of languages, a skill he had gone to trouble to acquire. "The traditional Jewish parting at the end of Passover service. Jerusalem is every religious Jew's heaven."

"Yes, sir," Martin said dubiously. "But my question—"

"I know your question," the commander said indulgently. "There will be no need for close surveillance of Dr. Kanter." His secretary appeared in the doorway. "Our time is up, Martin."

The hole was almost big enough. He could put his head inside it and one shoulder. Dark. Across a little space was another wall.

Someone coming.

He withdrew his head and quickly scrambled away from the wall. The door made a funny click-click noise. It would open soon. His eyes darted to the hole mostly concealed by the fronds of a jungle plant.

The door opened. Man appeared and put down food and drink on a tray. Man left. He waited for door to close and then waited more, looking at hole, looking at

83

food. He loped over to the food and ate quickly, stuffing his mouth.

Back to hole. With hard bare feet he kicked at it. Hole became wider. He put head and upper body inside. He could reach another wall. Pushed hard at the other wall. Kept pushing until it yielded, like throat of animal that gives up fight.

Part of wall gave way. He looked through. Not outside. Other place. He tore at the crumbling plaster. It came away in his hands.

Finally the opening was large enough to crawl through. The other place smelled of heat that came from a black round metal tree with silver branches spreading upward. The trunk hummed faintly, and when he touched it his hand stung. Hot. He rubbed his singed palm against his naked thigh.

This other place was dimly lit from a small window high on the wall. He climbed the rough stone wall. The window had bars outside. Like cage. Through the bars he saw the pale moon in a dark sky. The glass was cool to his touch. He pushed and there was a cracking sound. Something sharp cut his fingers.

He dropped down from the wall and put his bleeding fingers into his mouth. He sucked at the liquid oozing. As he turned away, holding his hurt fingers in his mouth, he saw a door set into the far wall. In his experience doors were always locked.

This one was not. At a push it swung partly open.

Escape!

Leaving the oil burner room, the boy loped up the stairs.

Margaret was in bed reading a textbook on ethnology, a ponderous volume in which the footnotes overwhelmed the text. The author had mastered everything about his subject except its essence, and he expressed what he knew in a style that had mastered everything but clarity.

Sleepily, her mind wandered. She put the book down, aware of being in her parents' bedroom. Everything had a soft nostalgic glow. White-painted walls had the enclosing power of memory. The room was redolent with long-forgotten intimacies.

Life repeats patterns from one generation to the next. Her father had consummated his religious passion in a form of sacrifice for the glory of the Lord. Idealists are the most selfish of God's creatures. The progress of the world may depend on those willing to sacrifice for a cause, but don't invite them to lunch.

She turned out the light.

She awoke to the clock faintly ticking on her bedside table. Its luminous green hands pointed to quarter to two.

What had wakened her? The wind was rattling lightly against the side of the house, but she was used to that— and to the clock ticking. Familiar sounds are absorbed into the deep soft cushion of sleep.

She decided it was the creaking door that had wakened her and she turned on her side, her cheek pressed tight against the pillow. Then her heartbeat picked up a quicker rhythm as with cold awareness she heard a floorboard complaining beneath the pressure of a foot.

The wind rose in a gust and the frame exterior of the house rattled. Then the gust of wind died and she heard a footfall. Close to her bed.

Cautiously she reached for the lamp, found it. She moved her finger up to the light switch.

Sudden orange-white radiance revealed the boy standing beside her bed and looking down at her.

Anger overcame her fear. "What are you doing here?"

His eyes were open and empty of expression. He was naked. Something about the way he was standing, staring blankly, one shoulder drooping lower than the other, made him appear dangerous.

His hand moved along the edge of the sheet and left a thin trail of blood.

She said quietly, "I'll get my robe and take you back where you belong."

Slowly she pushed back the sheet that covered her and swung her feet off the bed. As she tried to stand

85

up, the boy's hand shot forward to grab her bare shoulder.

She looked directly into his face. "Please let me go."

His hand slid over the bare skin of her shoulder and beneath the strap of her nightgown. He pushed the strap down so that part of her bare breast was revealed. A vibration passed through her, a tremor. His stiff hairless penis was protruding, gleaming in the subdued light. Then his hand fell away. She drew up her nightgown strap. Her robe was draped over a nearby chair. She put it on and tied the tasseled belt, pulling it taut.

She held out her hand to him. "Come with me."

The hand she was holding out to him began to tremble.

"Come with me," she repeated, and was pleased that her voice sounded unafraid.

In the stillness she was aware of the wind humming at the windowpanes.

"I want to help you," she said.

His head tilted at a listening attitude. Abruptly he twisted toward the door. His body blurred with swift movement.

Jean Pierre rushed into the room.

The boy gave a weird cry as Jean Pierre seized him. They struggled and fell heavily to the floor.

"Don't!" she said loudly. "Don't hurt him!"

The boy was continuing to struggle and Jean Pierre concentrated on subduing him. Finally he straddled him, got hold of the boy's arms, and forced them back to the floor.

The boy screamed, the piercing plea of a trapped animal.

Margaret said, "He didn't mean any harm. He doesn't understand what's happening."

"Give me something to tie him with."

She gave Jean Pierre the tasseled cord of her robe and he used it to tie the boy's hands. The boy's slender naked legs kept thrashing.

"Something for the legs," Jean Pierre said.

"There isn't anything."

He loosened his own trouser belt and tied the boy's feet together at the ankles. Naked and bony, the boy now looked like a plucked chicken. He no longer had an erection.

Jean Pierre stood up.

"I went down to get his food plate. When I looked in he was gone.

"How?"

"Through a hole in the wall he made. I'll get that hole fixed right away."

"Where can we keep him meanwhile?"

"Someplace he can't get out."

"The pantry has a dead bolt. It has no windows."

Jean Pierre hoisted the boy over his shoulder. The boy's face had a crumpled look and his eyes were tight shut. She followed them down to the pantry, where Jean Pierre lowered the boy from his shoulder. She had seen dead animals carried the same way by hunters— trussed, defeated, savage creatures.

They went out and locked the pantry.

"We'll talk about it in the morning," she told Jean Pierre. "Thank you for everything."

When she returned to her bedroom she carefully closed and locked the door. She went into the bathroom and turned on the light, throwing back her robe from her shoulder. In the mirror she could detect no sign of the spot where his hand had gripped her. She touched it and felt tenderness, but there was no bruise.

The next morning Jean Pierre sealed the hole in the cellar wall, fortifying the inside space with heavy cross-bars and filling it with insulating foam as an extra precaution. Then he covered it with quick-drying cement.

Margaret visited the boy in the pantry, bringing him his meal of raw meat. He sat against the wall, his ankles still loosely bound with the belt. He had made no move to free himself. She loosened, then removed the belt. He did not look at her or acknowledge her presence.

She stayed with him until she heard the choppy whining sound of a motor outside the house. On her way to the living room she saw through a window a snowmobile driving away from the farmhouse. In the living room Don Swenson was sprawled in the large upholstered chair.

He lifted one hand limply. "Don't scold me. I feel rotten. I really tied one on."

She said, "The boy nearly escaped last night. He cut a hole in the wall and got through. I woke up to find him in my room."

He sat up straighter.

She continued, "Jean Pierre came in and between us we tied him up and brought him down to the pantry."

"Did he try to attack you?"

"No. Actually, I don't know what was in his mind. But everything's going to be more difficult now. Jean Pierre was a little too rough with him. And locking him up in the pantry didn't help. I've probably lost what little rapport with him I had."

"I wish I'd been here."

"I wish that too."

"We can't have a repeat performance. I'll proceed with surgery as soon as possible."

"In order to get the boy out, we'll have to sneak him past the collective noses of the media and Sheriff Hamilton."

"I've got a plan that may work." He wavered to his feet. He was making a real effort to gather the remnants of his dignity. "Right now I've got to get some sleep. I'm worn down to the bone."

She watched him go unsteadily toward the stairs. She felt sympathy for him. His problems were rooted in a past they had shared, and she was not as bored with his failings as he was.

chapter 7

At six-thirty in the morning Margaret telephoned
Rory at McNamen's Food Market. She asked him to
show up with the van at seven o'clock, an hour before
he would ordinarily begin his regular deliveries. She
told Rory she would hire him to move some valuable
medical equipment, explaining that the regular truck-
ing service would charge too much to take a direct
pickup at the farmhouse. She would pay him twenty-
five dollars. Rory told her he'd be there.

Margaret went down to the cellar. The boy became
eager as soon as he saw the harness and knew that he
was going upstairs. He put on the harness willingly
and practically pulled her after him up the stairs. The
moment he saw the fire and the box of marshmallows
he became impatient. He made guttural noises, pointing at the fireplace and at Margaret. When she held a
marshmallow in the fire a little too long and some of
the confection oozed off and fell, he uttered an angry
growl and yanked at her hand to make her withdraw
the tongs. He pulled the remainder of the delicacy free
and swallowed it.

After a few minutes the tranquilizer in the roasted
marshmallows began to take effect. The drug worked
by changing the body's normal controls that linked the
nerve cells together. It caused a temporary impair-
ment, a short circuit in the boy's ability to stay awake
and to perceive his surroundings. It was simple, natural, and very effective.

He stretched and yawned. Moments later he was
asleep.

Jean Pierre and Don were putting the boy into an
empty crate. The boy's legs were drawn up and his
shoulders hunched so that he looked like a fetus in a

womb. Jean Pierre began to nail down the lid of the crate.

"Will he be able to breathe in there?" Margaret asked worriedly.

"Plenty air. Between boards. Under lid."

"Sedated," Don said, "he won't need as much air anyway. And Miles and I will be going along with him."

Rory would drive them only a few miles to a diner at Sheldon Junction, where the crate would be transferred to a leased truck to make the last part of the journey to the hospital in Plattsburg. Ostensibly, Don and Miles were going along to guard the valuable medical equipment.

As Jean Pierre finished nailing the lid of the crate, Margaret looked out the window and saw a caravan of cars led by the sheriff's car and followed by a television sound truck.

"Oh, damn!" she said. "They're back!"

The caravan of cars and the sound truck stopped a short distance from the house, on the road. The sheriff's car came on to the front door.

"Get that crate out of sight into the kitchen. I'll try to keep the sheriff occupied until Rory gets here."

A few moments later she opened the door to the sheriff.

"I'm sorry to bother you, Miss Denning. But I have a search warrant for this domicile. I intend to look for the boy you have here."

The van from McNamen's Food Market moved down the road past the parked cars and the sound truck, and turned into the driveway. Rory had arrived.

Margaret said, "May I see the search warrant, Sheriff?"

She pretended to study it. From behind the closed doors of the kitchen she heard the subdued scraping of the crate being moved outdoors.

She said quickly, "There's no mention of anyone but yourself, Sheriff, being permitted to search."

"That's right."

"The others will have to wait outside the house."

"Fair enough," Sheriff Hamilton said.

Listening intently, Margaret heard the sound of the crate being loaded onto the van.

"And, of course, this warrant says nothing about reporters or photographers or television people being allowed to trespass on my property."

"They're not trespassing, Miss Denning. They're on a public road."

Outside the kitchen she heard van doors close. It was done so quietly that only someone listening for the sound would hear it. Nevertheless, Sheriff Hamilton looked up, puzzled.

Margaret said, "Please wipe your boots on the rubber mat before coming into the house."

"Oh, I'm sorry."

The sheriff bent down and carefully removed his zippered overshoes. Through the window Margaret saw the van slowly back out of the driveway.

Sheriff Hamilton straightened up. "Where is the boy?"

"You're going to be disappointed. He isn't here."

"We'll see about that."

On the road McNamen's van was now driving past the line of waiting cars and the television sound truck. Sheriff Hamilton headed straight for the stairs leading down to the cellar. Margaret sat on the brocade sofa to wait until his large presence returned to the living room.

"I told you you'd be disappointed," Margaret said.

"I'll have to go through the rest of the house."

"Go ahead."

Ten minutes later the sheriff returned.

"I want to know where he is."

"I'll answer that in court."

"I'm sorry you're taking this attitude. I'm trying to uphold the law."

"I believe you. It isn't people like you I'm worried about. But as long as the boy is in my custody he's a lot better off than in an institution."

Sheriff Hamilton tilted his head down. "I'm not saying you're wrong. But they can take custody away from you."

"They'll have to do it in court. And I'll fight every step of the way."

He appeared to be distinctly uncomfortable. "I don't think you'll win, Miss Denning, but I admire your spirit."

"You're a nice man."

The sheriff's car departed a few minutes later, and the caravan of other cars and the sound truck followed it.

She went into the kitchen. Jean Pierre was seated at the wooden table, peeling an apple with a paring knife held between thumb and forefinger.

He asked, "What you going to do now?"

"As soon as I can I'll join Don and Miles at the hospital."

"If the operation kill him, maybe he be better off."

She felt pressure tightening behind her eyes. "Don't say that, Pierre. Please."

He finished peeling the apple, removing the skin in a single long connected strip. "This thing bothering you, hey?"

"Yes. It's bothering me a great deal."

Her head ached. What right did she have to make a decision involving the life and death of another human being? She might be set on a path that led nowhere but to disaster. She went down the stairs to the cellar habitat and opened the door to a room inhabited now only by memories. The imitation jungle ambiance looked futile and silly; it was like a deserted sound stage for a movie of Tarzan of the Apes.

She had tried hard and she had failed. Now she was abandoning her inching progress (or lack of it) for a wild leap into the unknown. The chances of failure were great. It was all right to fail at something oneself, for then the punishment would be exact and merited. The punishment for this failure would fall elsewhere, on a boy who was a nonparticipant in his fate.

Somberly she reviewed the choice she might have

made, the road not taken. She might have authorized Don to proceed with a less extreme surgery. He had once performed an operation that cured a man of dyslexia by implanting a computer microchip in the brain. But she knew the arguments against it. A computer microchip required an outside source of power. That meant wires and a battery that the boy would pull off at the first opportunity. And an operation of that kind would improve only one specific area: his primitive mind might learn to do calculus or to speak several languages. But the boy would become, in effect, an idiot savant. His brain's basic ability to perform, to integrate and interpret experience, would not be affected.

On the other hand, if the genetic implant worked, a fundamental change might occur in his ability to learn. He might achieve true normalcy.

There was no way to assay the risk without confronting the malignant shadow that lurked, waiting to become real.

If the operation kill him, maybe he be better off.

She felt suddenly very cold.

A messenger delivered a package wrapped in brown paper to Don at the hospital. There was an unsigned card attached. *Good Luck.* Inside, packed in dry ice, was a thermal container with a small frozen section of grayish-white tissue. Don invited Miles to help him make a careful examination with a scanning electron microscope. The tissue sample was magnified more than three thousand times to reveal its underlying structural detail. A thin slice of cell was fixed chemically, dehydrated and freeze-dried, then coated with a thin layer of gold-palladium mixture to enhance surface detail.

"It's human brain tissue, all right," Miles said.

"We can't prove that it contains DNA," Don said. "Not without further testing. We have to trust the people who sent it. Has Margaret called?"

"Not yet."

"I hope she gets here in time. How's our patient?"

"I told the nurse he has to be kept deeply sedated to avoid unnecessary movement."

"I'm beginning to realize what a risky thing we're about to do."

"You realized that a long time ago. You're beginning to get worried. A good sign."

"I'd better get dressed."

Forty-five minutes before the operation was scheduled, Don, attired in surgical greens, joined Miles in the doctors' lounge. Miles, also wearing surgical greens, was having a snack of tea and cookies.

The wall telephone rang and because Miles was nearest he answered it.

"Margaret's arrived. She's coming up."

They walked to the elevator to meet her. Margaret stepped off the elevator, breathless and looking particularly lovely.

"I didn't think I'd make it," she said. "How is the patient?"

Don glanced at the wall clock. "He's had his pre-op medication. He'll be leaving his room about now, headed for the sterile area."

Miles said, "Time to go."

Don and Miles finished their scrub and entered the operating room. A nurse helped them to put on rubber gloves and reported the boy resting quietly. He was not on an operating table but seated in a cushioned chair that resembled a dentist's chair. His arms and legs were strapped, and a sterile towel was wrapped around his shaved head. His head looked smaller and wrinkled without hair.

The anesthetist started the IV, insinuating a long thin plastic tube in the right and left forearms of the patient. Bubbles began rising into a bottle positioned overhead. The nurse catheterized, taping the catheter in place inside the left thigh. Meanwhile, Don took a last look at the series of X-rays on the back wall of the operating room. When he returned, the nurse had taken the sterilized instruments from the steamer and arranged them on the tray. The anesthetist put a blood-pressure cuff on the boy's arm, and another nurse attached EKG leads to his bare chest. The cardiac monitor began a regular beeping. Other monitor leads were fixed to the body with electrolytic paste and connected to a tangle of wires that led to the equipment.

All physical responses were normal.

"Is the equipment shielded?" Miles asked a nurse.

"Yes, Doctor."

Unless the equipment was shielded, minor radiation was emitted—not enough to be dangerous to humans, but it might cause trouble with the delicate machinery in the operating room.

Don nodded to the anesthetist, who placed his needle precisely between the second and third lumbar spaces of the boy's spine.

"X-ray, please," Don said. The television screen began showing black and white images of the skull.

As a boxlike frame was placed over the boy's head, Don looked at Miles. Since Miles was wearing his surgical mask, only his eyes were visible. Very slowly one eye closed in a wink.

Don positioned the boy's head and drew a line with a marking pen from ear to ear and another line from the middle of the forehead straight back to the occipital area of the skull.

He recognized the second stage of his anxiety ritual. There was nothing to do but endure it. The operation was highly experimental and sure to fail. He was about to enter a wilderness full of unseen danger, to test and feel his way along a trackless trail where a surprise could mean death. He had no weapon but his skill. His arms felt so heavy he knew he would not be able to move them. The fingers inside the rubber gloves were too stiff and inflexible.

He watched the computer screen, which showed a schematic drawing of the brain. The computer's encyclopedic knowledge of cranial anatomy and its faultless memory would indicate when even the most minute change of direction should be made after entry. It's like a video game, Don told himself. Space Invaders or Battlezone. The attack can come at any minute from any quarter. He had to be ready to meet it. His anxiety level kept rising. I am not a surgeon about to open a human skull but a hairdresser doing a transplant for a bald eagle. Now he began to feel better. The anesthetist fixed the burr hold locations where Miles indicated, then injected anesthetic into these points. Don and Miles put on their loupes.

"Scalpel, please," Don said.

Success preexists in the mind. Everything was going to be fine. It was going to be perfect. On the elapsed-time clock the numerals no longer registered for him. Time had become discontinuous. He was one with his purpose.

With a quick sure movement he cut through the skin and peeled back the scalp to expose the bony surface.

"Drill, please."

He expected the operation to take five hours. When he finished, the elapsed-time clock read four hours and thirty-two minutes.

Miles said, "Take it from one who's watched thousands. That was a gorgeous piece of work."

"Thank you."

"You must be tired."

"A little. But I'm staying in the recovery room until he's out of danger."

In the recovery room they watched the boy transferred from the rolling stretcher to the bed.

"How does he look to you?" he asked Miles.

"Fine."

The boy was hooked up to monitor his brain-wave activity. The first patterns were normal.

"Check his vital signs every five minutes the first hour," Don told the nurse. "Every ten minutes the second hour. Then every half hour for the rest of the day. If he's stable, we'll move him back to his room tonight."

He dialed an extension and began to dictate his notes about the operation to the transcribing machine. Ordinarily the cassette would be typed up by a secretary and inserted into the patient's record. When Don finished dictating, however, he ordered that the cassette and one duplicate be turned over to him without being typed.

"Will you notify Margaret that everything's okay?" he asked Miles.

"Of course."

Above the boy's bed a monitor showed the tracing of the EEG. The alpha rhythms were slow because of the sedation but were within the statistically normal range. Nearby, a computer was checking related brain electrical activities, the evoked potentials which are responses to external stimuli.

Don pulled up a folding chair near the foot of the bed. The boy's head was completely bandaged and he was strapped to the bed to prevent movement. The situation inside his skull was totally unpredictable. The DNA strip inserted into the boy's brain might not spark increased activity. How many electrical neurons would have to be generated before there was measurable improvement?

This was the time when, everything he could do having been done, doubt caught him in its net. He was very tired. His head dropped. He dozed briefly. When he looked up the boy's eyes were wide open and staring directly at him.

Don gave a slight start. "Nurse," he said quietly. "Two grams of Pentothal."

He administered the two grams of Pentothal through the IV attached to the boy's arm. All the while the boy's eyes kept staring at him. Finally the sedative took effect and the boy's eyes closed.

"Keep him well under until morning," Don told the nurse a bit shakily.

Margaret was waiting in the small downstairs cafeteria, which had only six tables and was serviced by the hospital's kitchen. An untouched club sandwich was on the Formica table before her. She had been waiting since the operation had begun.

97

At last Miles was coming toward her.

"He's in the recovery room. Don is with him."

Alarm released its cold grip on her heart. "Did everything go well?"

"Better than I expected."

"You look all wrung out."

"I feel like I just had a sixteen-pound baby. I never want to go through *that* again." He eyed the club sandwich. "Are you going to eat that?"

"Would you like it?"

He moved her plate over to him. "I'm ravenous. I'd like hot tea also."

"I'll get it for you."

"A living doll."

By the time she returned he had devoured the sandwich and was studying the blackboard menu listings above the small serving counter. "They've got lamb. Think it's any good?"

"Somebody was having it at the next table. It comes with a mashed potato. The potato had a pool of gravy in the middle that looked metallic."

He made a face. "I've gotten used to your cooking. I'm spoiled."

"What happens next?"

"With the boy?"

She nodded.

"Well, he isn't ready to go home and start having callers. But I have no doubt he'll be fine." He sipped his tea and then corrected himself: "Almost no doubt. He'll be hospitalized about two weeks. We have to get by a number of possible post-op complications."

She frowned. "And then? When will the results start to show?"

He swirled the tea in his cup. "There is no scenario. This whole operation is unprecedented. If anything goes wrong there will be a lot of explaining to do. On the other hand, if everything goes right, we have no idea if there will be any improvement. Meshuggeneh odds."

Don entered the cafeteria and came to their table. He said wearily, "The patient is asleep. I hope he'll stay

98

that way until morning." He looked at Miles sipping his tea.

"Would you like some?" Margaret asked.

"I prefer coffee."

"I'll get it for you."

She brought him hot coffee. After a few swallows he sat back and said, "I feel as though a large bolus of fresh blood has just been injected by ventricular contraction into my general circulation."

The loudspeaker on the wall announced, "Dr. Swenson. Please call Number Four." Don got up immediately.

"What's that about?" Margaret asked.

"I'll soon know."

He spoke on the wall telephone for about two minutes, looking annoyed but not as though there was an impending crisis.

When he returned to the table he said, "That was the chief of surgery. He's received an inquiry about the identity of our patient. Apparently there's very little information on the hospital admission card for Henry Fairchild."

That was the pseudonym they had chosen for the boy.

"Who was the inquiry from?" Margaret asked.

"I didn't want to seem too curious. My guess is that it's one of the news services—a fishing expedition. Checking hospitals would be a natural line of investigation. 'Was a young man about sixteen admitted to your hospital in the last forty-eight hours?' It turned up Henry Fairchild."

"We should invent a history for the patient in case there are more inquiries," Miles said.

"I intend to. As it is, the question stirred up a bit of a ruckus. The chief surgeon checked the notes I filed after the operation and all they had was my short hand-written note covering pre-op, dx, and post-op procedure. I kept the cassette with the detailed report."

"Are you going to turn that over to them?" Miles asked.

"Not on your life. They'd know just what went on in that operating room. I'll expand my written report a little and say the surgery was exploratory. We were looking for a possible brain tumor as a source of intercranial bleeding. We found no tumor, the intercranial bleeding was minor and has been corrected. The patient is recovering normally."

Miles sighed. "I hope they never find out what we've done. It wouldn't sound very ethical."

Don grinned. "We're obeying the highest standard of medical ethics. A doctor's first duty is to his patient."

Commander Richards looked across a treeless expanse of fairway to the putting green one hundred and thirty yards away. He chose a seven iron from the golf bag that the caddy held toward him, and stepped up to a white golf ball nestled just an inch inside the rough grass.

The day was bright with thin lemony sunshine, the temperature was in the high sixties. It was an excellent day to play golf and the commander was enjoying himself.

The others in the golfing foursome were the chairman of the board of an electrical utility company, a highly respected corporation lawyer, and an investment banker. They had taken their second shots. The commander, being nearest the green, was shooting last.

He stepped up to address his shot, waggled his club to loosen his wrists, and gauged the distance for a last time. At that moment a flash of light came from the woods on his left where thickly clustered trees bordered the rough.

The flash of light appeared once, then after an interval twice more; finally, after a shorter interval, it flashed again. No one else was in a position to see this. The message was meant for the commander alone.

Cursing softly under his breath, he positioned himself over the ball, drew back his arms, uncocked his wrists, and drove the ball in a low whistling drive that hooked sharply. He heard the ball's thunking progress amid the trees. Then silence.

"Too bad," said the investment banker. "You looked up on that one."

"About time you goofed," said the corporation lawyer, hiding his pleasure under gruff complaint. "This give us a chance to catch up."

"Drop another ball," advised the utility company chairman.

"Damned if I will," the commander said. "I'm going to find my ball. I saw where it went. If I can see my way out of there, I'll take my chances."

The others didn't argue. They knew that in trying to rescue himself from his predicament he would probably get into more serious trouble.

He told them, "I'll join you in a few minutes."

He watched them trudging obediently toward the distant green. He ducked quickly into the woods, taking his seven iron. Martin Holcomb stepped from behind a tree, holding the flasher signal in his left hand.

"What's this all about?" Commander Richards demanded.

"We've located the missing boy. Swenson operated on him this morning in a hospital in Plattsburg, New York."

Checking hospitals had been only one line of investigation. *"Has a young man about sixteen been admitted to your hospital in the last forty-eight hours?"* The inquiry, purportedly from local police looking for a runaway boy, had turned up "Henry Fairchild" and the fact that "Henry Fairchild" was operated on by Drs. Donald Swenson and Miles Kanter. A short time after Don Swenson's expanded report on the operation was filed with the hospital administration, a duplicate copy was telexed to the headquarters of the Security Bureau in Fort Meade, Maryland. Commander Richards glanced through the report.

He said, "I don't think this describes the operation that actually took place. They would not go to such lengths to avoid publicity if the surgery were intended
101

to save the boy's life. Clearly some kind of medical experiment was undertaken."

"Do you think they implanted a mechanical device in the boy's brain?"

The commander was pleased with another opportunity to lead Martin along the devious passageways of logic. "No, I do not think that," he said, his voice reprovingly soft. "They could not conceal it from others present in the operating room. There would have to be outside batteries and projecting wires to connect such a device to a power source."

"What do you think they did?"

"It was only a question of time before someone daring enough would attempt to transplant living brain tissue."

He expected Martin to react with surprise or skepticism.

Instead, Martin answered, "That would explain it. We learned that a package was delivered to Swenson at the hospital shortly before the operation. A small brown paper package, contents unknown. As soon as we learned that, we began trying to trace it. Delivery was made via a messenger, and the messenger came from the Committee of Concerned Scientists."

The commander felt as though the skin at his mouth corners was becoming unstretchably tight. His aversion to Ted Bristol derived from a traumatic experience some years earlier. Bristol's pioneering work with plant viruses had led to the discovery of an exceptionally virulent strain. When this became known to NSA, Commander Richards was told to make Bristol a very handsome offer to produce the virus in mass quantities for biological warfare. Bristol promptly reported the offer to the press. The resulting furor forced an embarrassed President to make one thing perfectly clear: the United States Government had no intention of engaging in biological warfare. NSA accepted the blame for the episode, and the head of NSA privately blamed Commander Richards. For a time he had feared that he might be relieved of his duties as head of the Security Bureau. It was a close call and he never forgave Ted Bristol.

Now he regarded Martin Holcomb with the expression of a man who has just opened a letter whose contents displeased him. "It's possible that what was in that package is now inside the boy's brain. Upgrade surveillance to Unrestricted."

"On Dr. Kanter also?"

"No. Call the Israeli embassy. Tell them I want to see Moshe Yarosh."

As soon as Martin left, the commander moved through the woods to where he had a clear line of sight toward the green. Two of the foursome were on the green and one had just made a wedge shot from the sand trap.

Commander Richards took a ball from his pocket and dropped it on the ground. He waited until he saw the wedge shot roll past the green.

"Fore!" he cried.

He used his seven iron to hit a sharp groundcutter out of the woods. The ball rolled to within three feet of the cup.

He woke up knowing he was badly hurt. He had not been so weak since the little men attacked him.

He was in a sleeping place, tied to a bed as the little men had once tied him to a hammock and carried him to the river. He could not move.

When he heard people nearby he closed his eyes and feigned sleep. Like the possum who could pretend to be dead so an enemy would go away. He was so weak that pretending was easy. As soon as he closed his eyes darkness began to come.

A dart was piercing his arm. It was connected to a bottle of poison that brought illness. He would die at the hands of his enemies.

After a long time a woman-in-white came and took the dart from his arm. After bottle was removed, hunger bit him. A long time since his belly felt empty-pain.

103

He pretended to sleep. Soon he would stop pretend and escape. Then run.

Run.

Run!

For two days after the operation the boy was fed intravenously, avoiding a ticklish problem.

As Don put it, "Somehow, I can't see the attendant bringing him a tray of raw meat at mealtime." He added, smiling, "Not unless we put an anchovy on it and call it steak tartare."

Margaret said, "Sooner or later he'll have to be taken off the IV and fed solid food."

"Then we'll prepare and serve his meals ourselves," Don replied.

On the third day the patient's recovery was proceeding according to schedule except for an unexplained tendency to slide off into a long coma-like sleep. On the fourth day the IV feeding was discontinued. Don told the nurse the boy was likely to display hostility to strangers, so special arrangements were being made to serve his meals.

"You can take the first shift," he told Margaret.

As she entered Room 209 daylight was streaming in past the drawn curtains. An arc of light fell across the bed and seemed to divide the boy's face, part in light, part in shadow. His head, wrapped in bandages, lay unmoving on the pillow. His eyes were shut. He was breathing lightly, soundlessly.

She put the tray on the table near the bed, and undid a heavy buckle secured under the left side of the bed. Then she removed the leather strap that held his chest and arms. The restraints were to prevent him from trying to get out of bed, but he couldn't eat with the strap holding him down.

She said, "We have a nice surprise for you today. Real food."

His pale face remained immobile. There was not the slightest response. A drop of spittle had dried in a corner of his mouth. She wiped it off with the corner of a tissue.

"Everything's going to be much nicer from now on," she said. She crossed to the window and parted the curtains. As light poured into the semidarkened room, she heard a curious hissing sound.

She turned and saw a white-headed apparition coming toward her. His open mouth was making the hissing sound. His face was twisted into a grimace.

His hands choked off the scream rising in her throat. He pushed her back against the wall. His sharp nails were digging into her throat and she felt warm blood trickle down her skin. Glaring eyes were close to her face.

They struggled in a kind of bearlike embrace until she broke his hold. "Damn it!" she gasped through a shivering burning in her throat. "Don't you ever—"

Something hurtled through the air toward her. She felt a terrible blow. She was falling. She felt her face strike the floor; then she was rushing outward into illimitable darkness.

"Did you hear anything?" Don asked.

He and Miles were in an alcove at the end of the hospital corridor. They had promised to be nearby if the boy gave her any trouble.

Without waiting for a reply, Don started off at a dead run. Midway down the corridor two nurses emerged suddenly from a door into his path. He careened off them, knocking one nurse to a sitting position. The other yelped angrily:

"Why don't you look..."

He kept his balance and raced on. Miles stopped to help the nurse to her feet.

Before Don reached Room 209 he heard shattering glass. He plunged through the door, slamming it back. The lower part of the window was knocked out. Jagged shards caught the sunlight with an orange-white glinting.

All at once his heart felt as though it were being squeezed into a space too small for it.

Margaret!

She lay sprawled on her side, one arm flung out above her head. There was blood on her throat. He knelt beside her and his fingers fumbled for a pulse in her neck. He felt it, but his fingers came away sticky with blood. She gave a catching gasp and his own breath stopped until she breathed again.

A heavy lamp lay on the floor nearby, its cord attached to a socket in the wall that had almost pulled out.

Miles hurried in.

"Get a stretcher," Don said. "Quickly!"

Only then did he become aware that the boy was gone.

Miles Kanter was confined to his room in a nearby motel with a bad cold for which he blamed the air conditioning. He could not visit Margaret with a cold. Don said she would recover; there was no skull fracture or acute subdural hematoma causing extreme pressure inside the skull. All she had suffered was a moderate concussion. But he couldn't risk giving her his cold.

He was relieved that Margaret was going to be all right and disturbed that the boy had managed to escape. How had he managed? God alone knew. He should have been too weak to do much more than sit up in bed. His recuperative powers were astonishing. But unless they found him soon there might be dangerous consequences. Only a few days ago he had undergone major surgery and he still needed close medical supervision. This was no time to be traipsing around on his own. If anything happened to him, if, God forbid, he suffered any kind of blow to the head... Miles warned himself not to think about that. The boy would be found soon and returned to the hospital. That was the only allowable outcome.

There was no work for him to do in the motel. During the afternoon he tuned in a television rerun of Lillian's favorite movie, *Exodus*. He sat there thinking of her and the first time they saw *Exodus* together. Severed nerve ends of his memory were recalling pain like messages from an amputated limb.

Someone knocked at the door. A welcome interruption. Outside was a man he had never seen.

"Dr. Miles Kanter?"

Miles nodded speculatively, noncommittally. "Are you selling something?"

"I'd like to ask you a few questions. May I come in?"

He was already inside the door when he asked. He was about thirty, slim and well muscled, wearing a dark brown suit, a plumply knotted tie, and a white shirt with a widespread collar. His hair was cut short, and he wore well-shined, elegant-looking shoes.

Miles said, "What do you want?"

The young man extracted a flat thin wallet from his inside breast pocket. He took out a glassine square with his photograph. His name was Moshe Yarosh and he worked for the Israeli embassy in Washington.

"Did I forget to pay tax?" Miles asked.

"Nothing like that." Yarosh smiled; he had perfectly white even teeth. He could have been a dentist, Miles thought. "Actually, that identification does not tell the whole truth. I am with a special agency attached to the Israeli embassy. Part of our secret service."

"What business do you have with me?"

"I came to ask you a few questions concerning your friend Dr. Swenson. Naturally, anything you tell me will remain entirely confidential."

"If you have questions for Dr. Swenson, go ask Dr. Swenson."

"That wouldn't be practical."

"Why are you so interested in him?"

"We work closely with an intelligence agency of the United States Government."

"This agency, has it got a name? FBI? CIA? Army Intelligence? NSA?"

"NSA is close. It's a special bureau. You probably never heard of it."

107

"Well, Mr. Yarosh..."

"My friends here often call me Morris."

"Well, Mr. Yarosh, I'm not going to tell you anything. If you're bothering Dr. Swenson about that business with the Russian scientist, you ought to be ashamed. What's it got to do with Israel anyway?"

"It's in Israel's interest to keep the Russians from acquiring military secrets that the United States shares with us."

"How paranoid is everyone getting?"

"Perhaps you don't understand the situation. Let me give you an example of what I mean. Not long ago a Russian electronic buoy was fished out of the Atlantic near the East Coast of the United States. The buoy was designed to collect vital data for Russian submarines. It contained computer circuits that duplicated American circuits exactly, so exactly that when the U.S. circuits were plugged into the buoy it worked."

"Maybe the Russians learned from the Japanese how to be good copycats."

"Data stamped on the Russian computer circuits showed that the Russians began reproducing the tiny computer chips involved within a few months of finding out about them from Dr. Swenson."

"It was a harmless mistake on Dr. Swenson's part. A slip of the tongue."

"Perhaps, but that microchip is also part of an early warning radar system that the United States just gave to Israel. If we had had such an early warning system in place in 1973, the Egyptians could never have surprised us—even by attacking on the holy day of Yom Kippur. A lot of young men in Israel would be alive today."

They must have a dossier on him. They knew about his lost son.

"Are you suggesting that Dr. Swenson deliberately passed on that information?"

"The evidence points that way. Do you know that he has been in friendly contact with an outfit called the Committee of Concerned Scientists?"

"I was asked to join that Committee myself."

"And you refused."

"Not because I disagreed with their principles. Only because I am not a politician."

"Do you know where Swenson got the DNA brain tissue you inserted in that operation?"

"If you know so much about what's going on, why come to me?"

"That brain tissue Swenson obtained came from a Peking laboratory. A laboratory that has been doing highly secret research on the human brain. It was delivered to Ted Bristol in a Chinese diplomatic pouch."

Miles almost let his composure slip. This was shocking news, and he understood now why Don had not confided it to him.

He said, "Dr. Swenson can't be working for both the Russians and the Chinese. Maybe you haven't heard how those two countries hate each other."

"Both are Communist countries."

"Communists are often wrong. But it doesn't follow that they are wrong simply because they are Communists." He was temporizing, trying to adjust his thoughts to the revelation of what Don Swenson had been up to. "What do you want from me?"

"Swenson is under surveillance and has been for some time. But U.S. intelligence now wants someone right there, working with him. They asked me to recruit you because it's important to know if Swenson has any further contacts with Ted Bristol and his Committee."

"You want me to spy? I can't do it. It's not my kind of work."

"Compared to what you've sacrificed for your country, this isn't much to ask."

"I don't understand such things. I wouldn't know how to go about it. You wouldn't find out anything. Besides, aren't you overlooking something? The boy is missing. He escaped from the hospital."

"It isn't likely he'll be at liberty very long."

"He may die. That would be the end of the experiment, the end of your interest in Dr. Swenson."

"We don't anticipate that."

"Does everything happen the way you anticipate?"

"The real issue, Dr. Kanter, is whether we can count on your cooperation."

"Not by spying on Dr. Swenson. I don't believe he is a traitor. Not for a minute."

"We'll be delighted if our suspicions are wrong. But suppose we're right. That is a possibility too. And it might have very grave consequences."

"It's a hard thing you're asking."

"You can be of real service. And we'll make it easy for you."

"How?"

"Some special equipment that's the latest in electronic eavesdropping. A suitcase and a phonograph. Who is your favorite composer?"

"Chopin."

"Second favorite?"

"Mozart."

"We'll supply you with records. You'll enjoy them. You can even pack the suitcase."

chapter 8

He was hiding beside a road where cars passed. An old truck with chicken coops piled high in the rear labored very slowly up a hill, staying close to the inside lane so other cars could pass. The truck neared the top of the incline, traveling no more than ten miles an hour.

He saw the crates and the white feathered bodies and querulous heads peeking out between the boards. Pain in his belly sharply reminded him of his hunger. As the truck turtled by he ran out of hiding, caught hold of the latticed wooden supports at the rear. Scrambling agilely, he got to the top. He dropped down onto the chicken crates.

The old truck rumbled over the top of the hill and picked up speed on the downside. It was traveling north on Route 87. The truck kept up its laggard pace until nightfall. In the back, replete after a meal, the boy slept. Neither the jolting truck nor the cackling of disturbed chickens wakened him.

At nightfall the truck pulled off at a roadside truck stop. As the truck ambled into the parking lot and came to a wheezing halt, the boy awoke. Quickly, he climbed out. He ran swiftly away through the parking lot, vaulted a brick wall at the far end, and sprinted into concealing darkness.

The trucker, an old man wearing overalls with a red bandana sticking out of the back pocket, stretched his back muscles as he walked toward the diner. A white-faced young man wearing a cap and probing his mouth with a toothpick was in the entranceway.

"Your passenger skipped out."

"My what?"

"The guy in back of your truck. Went running off that way." The toothpick indicated the direction.

"I'll be damned!"

111

"You didn't know?"

"Sure didn't. Maybe I better have a look."

The young man with a cap accompanied him back to the truck.

"Oh, my good Jesus Christ," the trucker said. "What a mess!"

"He must've tore the poor thing apart. *Ugh!* Ate most from the look of it."

"What a nut!"

"What'd he look like?"

"I didn't see him close. Wore a kind of turban on his head. And a kind of outfit looked like pajamas."

"A foreigner. Indian maybe. *India* Indian. They eat anything."

"You gonna report it?"

"Nah. What's the good? What's one chicken?"

"Or one nut for that matter." The young man laughed.

"You said it. I'm gonna have my dinner."

"Just don't have chicken, Pops."

He wore only hospital pajamas and the night air was cool. But he could easily endure extremes of heat and cold. He paused, without shivering, then climbed the iron gate to a waterfront estate. Three cars were parked in a long curved gravel driveway. A window was open on the second floor of the large house and music was coming from it. On the ground floor only a corner window was lit.

He edged his way along a high stone fence that bordered the iron gate. Lanterns were hanging from tree limbs to illuminate the gravel driveway. He stayed at the far edge of the lawn where darkness reigned. There was no moon and the sky reflected its blackness upon the earth. Once he whirled about at a barely audible sound, the passage of a swift tiny creature of the night. His neck stretched, his ears pricked forward.

He sniffed, then moved on, taking what cover he could find. He had the wild creature's ability to travel silently over unfamiliar terrain in pitch darkness.

Another, smaller building was behind the large house, and he saw the dull glintless motion of water. The build-

112

ing was a boathouse on the shore of Lake Champlain. He approached cautiously. There were no lights. A short dock groped blindly into the fog-shrouded lake. On the right side of the dock a cabin cruiser creaked in a gentle swell. On the other side a small canoe rode the swell easily. A paddle was lying athwart the middle seat. He had seen canoes before. The pygmies traveled only on rafts but other tribes used canoes on the Sepik tributary.

He did not wish to travel anymore on water or on land. He was tired and his head was full of thundering pain that would not stop. The door of the boathouse was slightly ajar. He pulled the door open and entered, unaware that as he did so he tripped a motion detector.

Piercing sound shrilled. His hands flew to the sides of his head. He heard distant voices, men's voices, excited. He turned and fled. Other lights flashed on at the great house, and searchlights lit up the backyard. The searchlights reached out into the darkness at the water.

He ran out onto the dock. The water was dark, limitless. He leapt into the canoe. He picked up the paddle and began to use it as he had seen the tribesmen do.

The canoe moved silently into the concealing darkness and fog of Lake Champlain.

He paddled for some time until he came ashore on a pebbled beach. He left the canoe there and moved inland. After a while he saw a road and beyond the road a meadow that ended in a deep woods. His senses were alert for danger. Many houses were near the woods on both sides. Before he crossed the road he hid behind a large rock. An occasional car sped down the road with staring headlights like blank white eyes looking for him.

A dog barked.

He flattened himself against the rock. A man came down the dirt path bordering the road. He was led by a collie on a leash. The collie caught the boy's scent and pulled against the leash, barking loudly.

"Easy!"

The boy pressed his body tight against the rock's surface. The collie was barking excitedly, lunging, trying to get off the path to investigate what he knew was there. The man could not understand why the dog was excited. The man saw nothing, smelled nothing, heard nothing.

"Shut up!" he shouted at the dog. "You'll wake up everyone!"

The man was dragged a little way off the path by the collie's eager lunging. The dog's barking ascended the scale to an excited yapping.

"Heel!"

The collie, ears flattened, tail drooping, abandoned his quest. He returned with the man to the dirt path.

"Midnight is no time to chase squirrels," the man said with annoyance.

When they were out of sight and no cars were moving in either direction along the road, the boy loped across and entered the woods. Everything here was more familiar to him, the dense growth, the leafy feel of ground under his bare feet, the mingling odors of animal spoor. In the darkness the least sound attracted his attention. He gave his head a little jerk now and then to listen more attentively.

A fleeting shape crossed before him. A startled rabbit. The boy took off at once in pursuit, following the rabbit deeper into the forest. Craftily he cut the rabbit off, but the frightened creature was too swift. The boy had to stop. His head was pounding. It hurt. The rabbit leapt through a V-shaped crevice between two trees growing jointly from the same root and vanished into thick shrubbery. The boy was too weak and sick to follow. Dizziness overcame him, and he sat down at the base of a tree to rest. His chin sank onto his chest and his eyes closed.

Light filtering through branches overhead woke him. It was late morning and he had slept a long time. He looked up through entwined branches at the sky. A breeze stirred leaves on the topmost branches.

He stretched stiffness from his neck and shoulders. His pajamas were wet with dew and clinging. He tore them off. Naked, he felt free. He drew in a deep breath of sharp, keen air. He did not feel dizzy anymore, al-

114

though his head still pained dully. His stomach clamored with hunger.

He began to lope through the woods. Once he stopped to grub in the ground for roots but did not find any. He descended ground covered with blackened tree stumps. At the bottom of the descent a stream flowed, soundless, fast, and smooth. He crouched beside it and cupped his hands and drank. His hands smelled good to him from burrowing in the earth. But they were shaking with weakness and his head ached badly.

A fish cleared the water to snatch an insect, and made a dimpling circle on the stream as it sank back. The rushing current sucked at the boy's legs as he waded out. The speckled fish zigzagged. The boy moved quickly but barely touched the fish's scales as it fled downstream.

His reflexes were much slower because of his weakness. He waded out and crouched by the bank and waited for insects to attract other fish. He was very hungry. He was also very patient.

After a while a faint odor came to him from a distance. He sniffed it, drawing in more air through his nostrils until the odor became distinct. Pressing down on his knees, he rose from his cramped position. He left the stream and began to pursue the smell that enticed him.

He came to a steep rise where saplings grew. A gully was in front of the ascent. Higher up, at the top of the hill, he saw wispy puffs of gray-white smoke. He leapt the gully and began to climb. Bent low, his hands touching dirt, he proceeded upward almost on all fours. The slender trees grew at an angle, lying almost parallel to the ground, and he was able to use their trunks to haul himself up farther.

He peered over the edge at a flat area. Expressionless, he took in the scene before him. A plateau of scraggly bush and rock extended about twelve feet deep and perhaps twenty feet wide. Behind it was a natural rock cave with a small low entrance.

On the plateau a young girl was roasting plump frankfurters on a metal grill over a fire. The grill was fixed between two large stones. Heated air shimmered above the fire.

The girl was slender with dark blond hair, and she wore a brown quilted jacket, dark wool slacks, and hiking boots. She sat on a stool of rock, poking at the frankfurters with a long-handled fork.

The boy watched for several minutes as the meat broiled and darkened. His salivary glands filled his mouth with juices. His whole body yearned toward the food. The smell was maddening.

He could wait no longer. Hunger made him advance with defiant boldness. He came up beside her and snatched one of the frankfurters from the grill. It burned his fingers but he swallowed it in two bits. The girl's eyes widened slightly but she said nothing.

He snatched another frankfurter. It scorched his fingers also as he wolfed it down. The girl did not protest. She sat absolutely still before the fire until it began to die. He too stood watching. Pale flame licked at charred wood, vanished, and reappeared at another place, settled, rose, trembled, puffed a whorl of smoke, and expired at last in a long tendril of grayness.

Without turning to him or speaking a word, the girl stood up and carried the empty grill back into the cave. Her body was bony and angular. She came out of the cave and the boy watched her descend the hill between rocks and scraggly bushes until she disappeared. He stared at the charred dead wood where the fire had been.

That night he slept inside the cave. In the morning he went down and drank his fill from the stream. He splashed water on his naked body. Sunlight came through tree branches.

He could not catch any fish because when he moved too quickly a clanging pain in his head began. He climbed slowly back to the cave. The girl had returned and was gathering twigs to add to a pile. He found more twigs to add to the pile on the crumpled paper.

She lit the paper with a match. He thought her finger had burst into flame. She reached into a bag to remove
116

two ears of corn and unwrap them from their husks. Her movements were not smooth and confident, but jerky.

She put the corncobs on the grill and set the grill over the fire, placed between the two large stones.

When the corn was roasted he snatched one from the grill. The smell and taste were wonderful to him. She took the other cob and started to munch it.

They finished their repast without speaking, comfortable with each other's silence. She returned the empty grill to the inside of the cave. As she emerged, she turned to him and put out her right hand, holding the elbow close to her body. He recalled a similar gesture made to him by the woman-who-had-saved-him. He held out his hand in the same way. When their palms touched she drew her hand back quickly.

Then she was gone.

He went back to the fire. A tiny flickering tongue of flame was not yet out. He picked up a rock and beat at it until it was dead.

The next morning he awoke early and went back to the stream. He had better luck. When she arrived an hour later he showed her two fish he had caught.

She had brought a brown wool blanket. A blanket was a thing he had worn before. He wrapped it around his shoulders. She wore a white loose sweater and slacks.

To his surprise she did not proceed at once to eat the fish he had brought. Instead, from a hiding place in the cave, she brought a knife and slit the fish's body from the tail to the tip of the jaw. The insides of the fish came out clean and compact, and she threw the insides away.

When she brought out the grill from the cave, he could not believe she was going to put his fish into the fire. But he helped her to gather the twigs, and soon the fish were cooking on the grill. He had eaten many raw fish but he had never seen a fish treated this way. He waited patiently until the fish were cooked, and ate his with extreme pleasure. The girl watched him eat. She had the faintest suggestion of a smile. When he

117

finished one fish, she gave him hers. He ate that with equal gusto and licked his fingertips.

Later they went down the hill to the stream where he had caught the fish. He waded, still holding the wool blanket about him with one hand. Speckled fish were swimming swiftly over the gravelly stream bottom. She seemed afraid of their swift darting movements.

The sky was a high clear blue with occasional fleecy white clouds. She dipped her fingers in the cold water. She let the water dry on her skin. Her hands were brown.

A breeze picked up, and a shadow began to march across the land, but they did not go back to the cave. They stayed on the soft earthen bank of the stream until he sensed that she was going to leave. Before she left, she made marks in the earth with her finger. She made a girl's head. He could tell it was a girl because she had long hair and long lashes. She pointed to it, then to herself. She stooped again and quickly made more marks. This time the boy could not make out a resemblance to anything. The girl had written her name: *Amelia.*

She waited, indicating he should do the same. Impatiently she showed him her dirty finger, the one she used to make the marks. She took hold of his finger. He let her guide his finger to the earth but it only made a hole. When she let go of his hand he withdrew his finger.

She walked away from him. He started to follow but stopped, and she continued walking until she was out of sight.

He returned to the bank of the stream to stare at the girl's head. He could not make out the queer markings beneath the head portrait. But a dim apprehension was forming. He stooped and put his finger into the hole in the earth he had made previously. He pulled his finger through the ground to make a mark. Then he made other marks that resembled those she had made. They spelled the name: *Amelia.* He looked at the two markings together, his and hers. *Amelia* and *Amelia.* Then he smudged over all the marks with his bare foot. He left the girl's head intact.

* * *

118

At dinner that evening in Amelia's house, her father said the police were looking for a hospital patient who had escaped after nearly killing someone.

"You mean some sort of a lunatic?" her mother asked, reaching for the butter. She had plump shiny pink arms on which the flesh seemed to run down in ripples.

"Sounds like. A young boy according to the description I heard. He'd just had some sort of operation."

Like many long-married couples, they had acquired each other's quirks of speech. "Some sort of" was an example.

"They shouldn't let people like that out."

"They didn't let him out. He escaped."

"They shouldn't let him escape."

Her father was short, thick-shouldered, blue-jowled. He picked up a slice of ham with his fork, put it in his mouth, and slowly masticated it.

"You know what would go good with this?" he said. "Corn on the cob."

"Ask your daughter about that."

"What?"

"I had two ears of corn in the fridge this morning. Tonight they're gone."

"She cooked and ate 'em? *Her?*"

"I don't believe she cooked them in our kitchen."

He banged his fork down on his plate. "Will you stop talking around me? How many times have I got to tell you?"

"How many times have I got to tell you not to use that tone of voice on me? If you want to know something, ask in a nice way."

"I'm asking in a nice way."

Amelia sat silently, looking down at her plate with her fork poised a fractional inch above a piece of broiled ham. The fork did not move up or down.

"What do you think she did with the corn?" her father asked.

"How do I know? She goes out every day on her own. Right after I go to work."

"How do you know?"

"Neighbors tell me. Sometimes in the morning, sometimes later. I think she goes to the wildlife refuge."

"Why would she do that?"

"Why does she do anything? I can't give her around-the-clock care, can I? I work too, don't I? If you want her to have twenty-four hour nursing care, then send her away to a place where they give twenty-four-hour-a-day nursing care."

"I don't want her leaving the house. It's not like she can look after herself."

"Lock her in a closet then. I've had all I can stand. Look at her. Look at her fork."

The fork was suspended, unmoving.

"That's what I'm saying. She's not a normal. We both know that. The doctors told us. That's what it is to be autistic."

"I can't wait for her special class to start again. It's the in-between times that's hard." Shiny arms raised a napkin to dab at one eye. "It's not only food missing."

"What else?"

"An old grill I had, that's gone. Yesterday a blanket. A brown blanket I kept in the linen closet."

Her father turned to Amelia. "Well, girl?"

Amelia stared down at her plate.

Her mother said, "There's no use asking. She won't tell you anything."

Her father reached over and took the motionless fork from Amelia's hand. "What have you got to say for yourself?"

She started to get up from the table. Her father reached over, put his hand on her shoulder, and pushed her firmly down into her chair.

"You're not excused. I intend to get some answers around here, and I'm not going to stop until I hear you say you're sorry."

Her mother said sternly, "If she was really sorry, she'd try to do something about it. She'd try to act better. But she won't so she's got no right to say she's sorry."

The father said, "Look, girl, I know you're mixed up
120

in your head. But you're not so mixed up you don't know right from wrong. At least, I hope not. You know it's wrong to steal, don't you?"

Amelia stood up suddenly.

"You sit right down. This is your father talking."

Amelia hurried away.

"You see what I mean?" her mother said. "It's getting harder to deal with her all the time."

He looked at the almost full plate Amelia had left at the table. "Okay," he agreed. "Maybe the time has come to do something about her."

At ten-thirty that night the door to Amelia's bedroom opened, and she came out wearing a nightgown. She listened at the door to her parents' bedroom. Her father's deep snoring alternated with her mother's, a deep bass cello accompanying a flute. She went downstairs, moving with an arms-akimbo awkwardness. In the kitchen she opened the door to the closet, where along with a mop and broom and cleaning supplies, brown shopping bags from the supermarket were folded. From beneath she pulled out a black plastic trash bag. She began removing food from the refrigerator and the freezer to put into the trash bag. She took only uncanned food; cans weighed too much and were too hard to open. She tied the top of the half-filled trash bag with the closer, twisting it as she had seen her mother do many times. Only then did she take off her nightgown. Underneath she wore the clothes she had worn at dinner. Over these she put a heavy wool cardigan.

She tried carrying the bag, but had to settle for dragging it. She dragged it out the kitchen door, onto the back lawn, across the lawn to the big wide meadow. Just beyond the meadow the woods began which marked the boundary of the wildlife refuge. Alternately carrying and dragging her burden, she headed in that direction.

It was quite dark inside the cave and he was asleep when he heard the noise of someone climbing the hill. Venturing outside, he saw her.

He was pleased to see her. He took the bag, which was ripped in places from its journey, and carried it up the slope. She picked up a few small items that had fallen out. He put the bag into the cave, and she began to empty and store food on the natural rock ledge where she kept the grill and the two-pronged fork.

He went to her and indicated that he wanted her to watch. Then he squatted and began to make marks in the ground. He made a girl's head with long hair and long lashes. Beneath the head he made the other marks that spelled Amelia. She clapped her hands and laughed. As he stood up beside her, their bodies touched. Her aroma drew him without his willing it. A quickening heart beat beneath his ribs. Confronted with her body so close to him, he began to feel an enormous tension. He wanted to move still closer to her, to enclose her in the same warmth that stirred him.

The girl turned and silently raised her eyes to his face. She touched his hand with one finger, then clasped it. Just as suddenly she walked away. She went outside, and he saw her bending in the soft moonlight, gathering more twigs. She held the twigs she had gathered tight to her breast. A pained expression crossed her face.

Abruptly she dropped the bundle and took a step toward him. Her foot slid on a small stone and she became unsteady. In a confusion of feeling he put out a hand to steady her. She slipped into the circle of his arms.

They lay under the blanket inside the cave. Her hand was entwined with his and they were asleep. As daylight entered the cave the boy wakened. Immediately he wished to do something to please her. She moved her sleeping position, pulling up part of the blanket over her. Cold, the thought flashed. She is cold. Into his mind flashed a picture of her making a fire. Fire would be good.

He went outside to where the pile of twigs lay. He carried the twigs to the place where she had cooked meals. He returned and took the plastic bag and crumpled it as she had done with paper. He put the plastic bag under the twigs. He found the fire sticks in a small square box on the ledge.

He returned to the pile of twigs, and holding a fire stick against the box moved it as he had seen the girl do. On the third attempt a flame spurted and he dropped the stick. He tried to retrieve it but the flame was gone. He took another fire stick and moved it against the box. This time, when a flame flared, he did not drop the stick. He held it to the crumpled plastic bag beneath the twigs. The plastic did not flame. He tried again with another fire stick, and this time a corner of the bag smoldered. There was an unpleasant odor. He tried to brush the odor away but it grew worse and a spiraling column of black smoke rose in the air.

He retreated into the cave. She was sitting up, bewildered, having smelled the smoky odor. She ran outside the cave, and when she saw the smoke she gave a harsh blatant cry. She ran back and forth flapping her arms to make the smoke go away. She tried to reach into the fire to seize the smoldering plastic bag. He joined her, and they dragged the smoking seared noxious-smelling plastic out of the flames.

They scooped dirt onto it. As they were doing this, he suddenly raised his head and sniffed. The heavy penetrating bad smell of burning plastic obscured his keenest sense. But his ears pricked foward as he heard a sound.

He made two unfocused flings of his arms in the direction of approaching danger. His agitation communicated a message to her. They had to run. But instead of running she became totally stiff and rigid.

Loose stones, rattling of boots, scratching on hard ground. A voice called, "Someone's up there!"

He turned to go, then hesitated and turned back and crouched beside the girl. He put his arm about her. He felt her body trembling and he began to tremble too. But he did not leave her.

That is how the search party found them, two frightened young people clinging to each other.

chapter 9

The hospital corridor on Sunday afternoon was a mob scene. Friends and relatives of patients were spilling out from the visitors' lounge. The lounge resembled the aftermath of a picnic, with beer and soda cans, pizza boxes spread on the tables, scattered magazines and newspapers. At the nurse's station the crowd was thicker. "Did the X-rays come down yet? Have you seen them? Can my husband go home tomorrow?"

Don Swenson walked past a room where a patient was holding court for a group of friends. There was great hilarity. In the next room a young boy was lying unconscious, scarcely breathing through an oxygen mask. Both his legs were in traction and his body was in a foam rubber cast.

In the next room Margaret was sitting up in bed, working with a pencil stub in a large paperbound book of word games.

She tossed down her book. "If I have to do one more word game, I'll have a relapse. Can I go home today?"

"Tomorrow. The concussion is clearing up nicely but I want to be sure."

"It's ridiculous. I feel fine."

"Doctor's orders. You don't know how lucky you are."

"What is this—your graveside manner?"

He did not wish to elaborate. If the lamp base had not been partially arrested by the cord connected to that socket, she would probably be in intensive care right now.

"No more dizzy spells?"

"None. Any word about him?"

He shook his head. "He shouldn't be hard to find, wearing pajamas and with his head bandaged like that. I'm surprised it's taken this long."

124

"Obviously he was feigning weakness. Isn't that a sign of intelligence?"

"Many animals know how to play doggo."

"No animal would use a chair to break a window and escape."

"I wouldn't put it past a monkey. There have been experiments in which a stick was left in a monkey's cage and he used it to reach food he couldn't reach with his hands. In fact, a monkey has even fit two hollow bamboo poles together to accomplish that."

"How's the patient?" Miles Kanter asked, entering the room. "Does she appreciate the good care we're taking of her?"

"Oh, I do. In fact, I..." She sensed Miles' repressed excitement. "Is it the boy?"

Miles nodded. "They've found him."

"Where? How?"

"No details. The hospital got a telephone call a few minutes ago. From the sheriff's office in Franklin County."

"I'm going with you," Margaret said firmly.

Don did not bother to argue; he knew there was no stopping her.

The sheriff's office was in a one-story brick building that also contained the post office and a realty firm. They entered through glass entrance doors and went down a corridor past the post office on the right and the realty firm on the left. As they opened the door to the office they heard a man's loud voice.

"I should have shot the son of a bitch right then and there. I'd have saved the trouble of hanging him."

Just inside the door was a wooden railing where a stocky blue-jowled man, wearing a wrinkled work shirt with an American flag sewn onto its shoulder, was haranguing Sheriff Hamilton.

Sheriff Hamilton said in a slow heavy voice, "I'd probably feel the same way if it was my daughter. But we've got to go one step at a time. As soon as the people from the hospital arrive..." He saw Margaret and the

125

two men approaching. He seemed as surprised to see her as she was to see him. "What are you doing here?"

Margaret said, "This is Dr. Swenson and Dr. Kanter."

The stocky blue-jowled man turned on them. "Are you from the hospital?"

Sheriff Hamilton said, "This is the father of the young girl who was with him when he was found."

The father said, "A criminal maniac. How the hell could you let a degenerate like that get away?"

Sheriff Hamilton laid a restraining hand on the man's shoulder. The sheriff was a big man with a careless uncoordinated look but he gave the impression that he could pull himself together in a hurry if he had to.

He said to Margaret, "I think you and I had better have a talk. Alone."

He led the way into a small private office with a desk, a chair, a battered gray metal filing cabinet. She sat in a chair opposite his desk. He remained standing.

"It's pretty clear this is the same boy," he said. "The one you had up at your house."

Margaret nodded. "I don't understand why you're in charge. Wasn't he picked up in New York State?"

"He crossed the state line at the wildlife refuge. That put him back in my jurisdiction. Now I'll ask the questions. What was he doing in the hospital?"

She decided the best course was to tell him the truth. "Dr. Swenson and Dr. Kanter thought they could help him by performing an operation. We want him to have a normal life if that's possible."

"And he escaped from the hospital?"

"Yes." She decided against telling him about how he escaped. She didn't want the sheriff to think the boy was dangerous.

"How come nothing got into the newspapers about this?"

"No one knows who he is. The hospital thinks a young man named Henry Fairchild left prematurely following surgery. That isn't exactly headline news."

126

"The newspapers would make a big thing of it if they knew the real story."

"Yes, they would. But there's no reason for them to know. We have the best possible reason to withhold that information, Sheriff. We're trying to save a life. We don't want the boy to spend the rest of his life in an institution."

"What happens to him isn't my affair. My job is to uphold the law."

"No law has been violated that I know of."

"The girl's father wouldn't agree. He's talking about a kidnapping charge."

"That's ridiculous."

"His daughter is underage. If the boy took advantage of her, he would be in pretty serious trouble."

"He can't look after himself, much less take advantage of anyone."

Sheriff Hamilton appeared to think that over. He was the kind of man who took his time arriving at a conclusion.

"What do you expect me to do?"

"I hope you'll let us take the boy back to the hospital and continue his treatment. It certainly won't help to arrest him. It would just put everyone to a lot of trouble and cost a lot of money, and do you think anyone would convict him? At his age and in his condition?"

"No, I don't."

"Even if they decided he'd done something wrong—which he hasn't—they'd send him to the same kind of institution we're trying to keep him out of."

"You're probably right about that."

"Well, then?"

"Well..." the sheriff's slow heavy voice turned unexpectedly soft, "we'll have to see what can be done to help Henry Fairchild."

When they returned to the main room, the father was glaring at Don and Miles. "I want him charged with kidnapping. I want the crazy bastard put away for life."

Sheriff Hamilton nodded sympathetically. Then he

127

said, "It's not all cut and dried. Some of your daughter's things were found in the cave. If she brought those things there, it would indicate she went of her own free will."

"The hell she did!"

Hamilton shrugged. "I guess that will have to come out at the hearing."

"What hearing?"

"The grand jury will be asked to bring an indictment. They're going to need all the information they can get. You'll have to testify and so will your daughter."

"My daughter!"

"There can't be an indictment without her testimony. Who else can swear she didn't go with Mr. Fairchild of her own free will?"

"It's plain as anything what happened."

"Plain to you and me. The law has its own way of looking at things. There's got to be proof. It's even tougher when it comes to a trial. The law insists on hearing from both sides then."

"She's in no condition to testify!"

"My deputy says that when the search party found your daughter and this Henry Fairchild, they were acting pretty friendly. At a trial he'd have to tell the judge and jury just how he found them. It won't sound as if she were kidnapped or anything like that."

"I don't care how it sounds. It's the truth!"

"The defense lawyer will put on doctors to testify about Henry Fairchild having an operation on his head and how he wasn't responsible. I don't know how a jury will feel about that. They're usually pretty impressed with medical testimony. Of course, when your daughter gets up on the stand to tell a different story, they'll be likely to believe her. That is, supposing she's willing to testify against the young man."

"She can't. *Jesus!*"

"I really sympathize. I wouldn't want to put my own daughter through that either."

"I won't let her. She's the *victim*!"

"Did any actual harm come to her?"

"The whole goddamn experience was a harm to her. We look after her like a baby. Then some crazy dangerous moron kidnaps her..."

"I'm saying how it looks to me. If she isn't willing to testify, I don't think the DA will go to a trial."

"You telling me to forget about it?"

"You go home and talk it over with your wife. See how you both feel. If you still want to bring charges, why that's your decision."

"Somebody had better be punished. That's all I can say." Sullenly the father looked at Don and Miles. "I ought to sue the hospital and everybody connected with it."

Sheriff Hamilton put his arm about the man's shoulder. "I don't blame you for feeling that way." He walked with him to the door. "You talk it over with your wife."

"That crazy moron has got to pay!"

"Sure he does."

Hamilton walked slowly back to them. "I don't expect he'll press charges."

Don said, "I gather from what you were telling him that the boy did not commit a hostile act toward the girl. If there are no charges, I'd like to take him back to the hospital."

"I'd have to know where to find him if I want him."

"I'll be responsible for him, Sheriff," Margaret said. "He'll be under close supervision at all times. And before he leaves the hospital we'll let you know."

"Well, that sounds fair. I guess you'd like to visit with him now."

"May I?" Margaret asked.

Another door led off from the large main room to a narrow detention area. The area was four feet by eight feet long, with a short curved wooden bench and two wooden chairs and in opposite corners a water cooler and a standing coatrack.

Seated on the linoleum floor with his back against the bench was the boy. He wore denim trousers, a shirt, and a pair of scuffed unlaced shoes too big for him. His hands were palms up on the floor beside him. There were red chafe marks on his wrists where he had been handcuffed.

He did not react when she came in. He appeared to be in a completely withdrawn state.

"Aren't you thirsty?" she asked.

She filled a paper cup at the water cooler and brought it to him. There was no response and she expected none. His stillness and silence were impassable. If only there were a physical cause for this mental isolation—the lack of a necessary hormone or the loss of too much salt from the body. Those conditions could be dealt with; there was a chance of improvement.

What chance was there for him?

Suddenly she felt an overwhelming discouragement. It might have been better for him to have died in the muddy Sepik River rather than to undergo the long-drawn-out living death that probably awaited him. She drank the water in the paper cup and crushed it in her fingers. It was foolish of her to think she could change what God or fate or destiny, or simple genetics, had ordained.

The boy stared straight ahead, as rigid and blank-eyed as a statue.

I'm so sorry, she thought.

"What sort of relationship did you establish with the girl?" she asked aloud. "Did you communicate with her?"

His eyes did not even blink.

It's like in Poe's *The Raven*, she thought. I'm asking questions that will never get a meaningful reply.

Nevermore.

"Oh, it doesn't matter," she said, impatient with herself, adding harshly, "The girl has gone away. You'll never see her again."

To her astonishment tears formed in the boy's eyes.

chapter 10

The delivery truck pulled to a stop at the side door of the farmhouse. Rory cut the motor, hopped out, and let down the back panel. Jean Pierre and Margaret helped to remove the boxes of groceries.

"Your star boarder isn't around anymore," Rory said.

"How can you tell?" Margaret asked.

"No fresh-killed meat. Just your regular order."

Jean Pierre carried a small wooden crate filled with canned goods into the kitchen.

"No sense buying what we don't need," Margaret said.

"Whatever became of the guy?"

"If you hear, be sure to let me know," Margaret replied, hoisting a small crate off the truck.

"For a while people used to ask about him. But they don't ask anymore."

"That's how people are."

She watched as Rory backed the delivery van out of the driveway.

Jear Pierre was piling a crate on top of another near the kitchen cabinet. "That kid has a long nose."

"I put a message onto the local telegraph. We can depend on Rory to deliver it."

Actually her star boarder was again in residence, and had been for almost a month. They had returned him to the farmhouse, driving back at three o'clock in the morning and traveling deserted roads in order to escape detection.

Rory was deceived because the boy was eating cooked food. At some time during the episode with the girl he had learned to prefer cooked food. Miles and Don discounted this sort of progress as they discounted his newly learned ability to control his body functions ("A cat is toilet-trained from infancy," Don said deridingly)

131

and the fact that he was wearing clothing and walking with an erect posture.

"None of that indicates an advance in intelligence," Don said, and Miles agreed.

They had been equally unimpressed when Margaret told them about the boy's strange reaction when she had mentioned he would not see the girl anymore.

"It was as though he understood what I was saying," she had insisted.

Don scoffed: "He hasn't progressed to even the simplest form of speech. When you show him an object and tell him what the name is, can he repeat it? At the age of seven, blind, deaf, and mute Helen Keller had learned over four hundred words, not including proper nouns."

Miles added gently, "It's possible that just hearing a friendly voice might have evoked the response you mention. I think Don is right when he says that so far the operation has had no real effect. That's just as disappointing to us as to you. What we are hoping for is some sign of progress in his daily lessons."

The regime of daily lessons was disheartening, for the boy showed no interest. She felt like a blind woman groping for the key that would unlock the world to him. He sat in attentionless silence, a ghostlike presence. She could not rid herself of a feeling that there was an imprecise area, a darkness like a smudged fingerprint, that she could not see into. At times she even imagined that there were depths in his blank gaze, a softness, a look almost of dreaming.

She had furnished the cellar habitat with a table and chairs. At noon she set the table for lunch with cloth and napkins. The boy ate with utensils, but he was clumsy and lacked coordination. During a meal she always talked to him, hoping in vain she might strike some response that would persist like the vibrations of a tuning fork.

After lunch, she cleared the table and began another effort to interest the boy in a game. Game-playing was tremendously important in rating intelligence, and if a small sign of skill could be developed it would represent progress. Today she tried a simple variation of the shell game. With a marble and the used cups from the lunch table, she tried to persuade him to follow her moves and pick the cup that had the marble under it.

She could not capture his attention, and after a while she gave up the shell game. She placed a large square flat box on the table. Inside the box was a maze with cunningly constructed narrow passageways. A small sack was in a corner of the maze, and from it she removed a tiny squeaking creature.

"Do you know what this is?" she asked. "It's a guinea pig. And this is called a maze. The trick is to find the one way that goes out. Trial and error. Watch."

She put the guinea pig down at the beginning of the maze, locking the tiny gate behind the animal so it could not retreat. Instantly the guinea pig began scurrying along the narrow corridor. It reached a blank wall, retreated, tried another way.

Margaret watched the boy covertly. The frantic guinea pig scampered through an opening into a channel nearer the center of the maze and met a blank wall. The little animal shrilled protest and retreated to find another way. The boy began to show a little curiosity, and she thought she knew why. This game concerned escape and that was allied with wish fulfillment. Escape could fill certain emotional needs, finding a way out of a place in which things were confusing and out of control into another place where there was less tension and unnameable conflicts could be resolved. The boy could not escape in real life but he might be able to in a fantasy maze, where the twisting baffling passageways would lead eventually to a safer sanctuary.

The trapped guinea pig kept trying to find a way out, pushing on through obstacles and defeats and wrong turnings. The boy was watching closely now. Once he made a tentative motion, as if to snatch the guinea pig out of its perplexity. Then he drew his hand back.

As the guinea pig neared the exit from the maze, Margaret placed the open sack so the animal scurried into it. A poor reward for its effort—it was trapped again. As she was tying the sack, the little animal nipped vexatiously at her finger. She finished tying the sack before she looked at her finger. A speck of blood showed where tiny teeth had broken the skin.

"Did it hurt you?" a voice asked.

She turned. She gasped.

Miles insisted on hearing again, in detail, what he still found hard to believe.

"Is it possible that what you heard was a hallucination? Something inside your own head?"

She did not take offense. "No, I saw his reaction. He knew he'd made a slip, and was upset at having given himself away. He didn't mean to speak. It was a reflex when he saw I was hurt."

"A person with a severe learning disability usually breaks through with the simplest words. Usually 'food' or 'water.'"

Don nodded agreement. "There is no precedent for a person speaking for the first time in a complete sentence. A full sentence, conceived in response to a given situation, requires a basic understanding of how language works. Where could he have learned that?"

"I talk to him as much as I can," Margaret said without conviction.

"But did you ever say those exact words to him?" Don asked.

She shook her head. "Not that I can remember. He could have been deceiving us all the while," she suggested. "Understanding more than he let on."

"What would he have to gain by it?"

She shrugged. "He thinks of us as his enemy, so naturally he'd be cautious. He wouldn't give himself away. Also, he dislikes being tested and this may have been his way of resisting."

"What happened after he spoke?" Don asked.

"He lapsed into his usual silence."

Miles said, "The big question is, how could he have learned so fast?"

Margaret turned to Miles. "What's our next step?"

134

"We have to complete a number of tests to decide how much progress he's made."

"He won't cooperate."

"We know what he's up to," Don said. "He can't keep playing his game much longer."

"He can be pretty stubborn."

"We'll wait him out," Miles said. "Resume his lessons as if nothing unusual has happened. Continue using words but on the lowest level. A single phrase, continually repeated."

"What phrase would you suggest?"

"Something personal is best. 'I am Margaret.' How about that? A good beginning."

At the next morning's session, Margaret pretended that the remarkable event of the day before had not happened. The session was devoted to showing him objects and naming them. When he did not pay attention, she did not betray any sign of impatience. She knew now that his lack of attention was serving a purpose, enabling him to evade her.

Meanwhile she was observing him in a different way than before. Perhaps because his progress in learning had been so slow, she had continued to regard his physical appearance as the same. Now she realized that, almost unnoticed, there had been a definite change. His facial features were more open and accessible. His body had continued to fill out and was now sturdy-looking—not a boy's at all, she suddenly realized with pleasant surprise, but a young man's. It is possible to watch someone so closely you do not really perceive him, and that is what she had been doing until now. He was really a quite presentable young man.

Just before lunchtime, she began with Miles' suggestion: "I am Margaret." She accompanied the words with a gesture indicating she meant herself, but after a while she abandoned the gesture. She was certain he understood her and only obstinacy prevented him from acknowledging that he did.

She kept repeating, "I am Margaret," for a hundredth, a two hundredth time until she had the feeling

135

this was taking place in a movie—an interminable scene in which nothing important was going on but which would arrive at some significance before it ended. As time went on she caught him looking at her with an expression of annoyance.

Still she droned on, "I am Margaret." She could not stop now. There was never any sense in going only ninety-eight percent of the way.

The boy took hold of the arms of his chair as if he were going to lift it into the air and make it fly away with him. Abruptly he stood up, walked a few feet from the table, and stood with his back to her.

She began again. "I am—"

"I know you are Margaret," he said. "What is my name?"

His voice was a bit husky but nicely placed and had a certain resonance. A baritone.

Trying to control her excitement, she answered, "I haven't really thought about it until now. Is there a name you'd like to have?"

He turned to look at her. "Choose one."

The thought occurred to her: He's unique, the first of his kind.

"Your name is Adam," she said.

Adam

"From nothing else but the brain come joy, delights, laughter, and sports, and sorrows, griefs, despondency, and lamentation."

—Hippocrates

chapter 11

Looking back, I think Adam was showing consistent progress since his operation. The graph, despite occasional dips and discouragements, was always pointing upward. The only major element still missing was that he did not understand words and so lacked an impulse to communicate in words. We knew that language would represent a quantum leap, an achievement signifying the real possibility of intelligence.

As Miles explains it, human language is controlled in the temporal lobes of the neocortex, and the transfer of vocal language from the limbic system to the neocortex was an essential step in human evolution. The mastery of language required an essentially new brain system and not merely an improvement of the old vocal machinery for cries and calls.

This kind of epiphany occurred to the young Helen Keller when she held her hand under a water pump, felt running water, and connected it to the mark her teacher repeatedly made in her palm. In that dramatic moment she grasped the connection between the word and the thing.

When Adam's leap forward came, it was fully as dramatic and even more mysterious. *Did it hurt you?* In that incredible moment he revealed that he not only understood the connection between word and thing, but could put words together in grammatical order to make a meaningful statement, to reflect accurately a thought conceived in his mind.

What has happened since proves that we are witnessing a phenomenon. Every day Adam makes new and startling progress. It is as though a key had been turned in his mind and unlocked a treasury. No formal instruction is necessary. From morning to night everything he comes upon provides grist for his actively developing intelligence.

Yesterday I went into the library—he has moved upstairs and his cellar habitat is uninhabited—and found him reading a copy of my book on social customs among the primitive tribes in New Guinea. He asked me whether, in a modern society, it was possible for an individual to work out an entirely new pattern of life—in effect, to make a closed system of himself within that society. (Clearly, he has been giving thought to what his own future will be when he leaves us and has to make his own way.)

Don is anxious to tell everyone the results of what he calls "the Adam Project." He is impatient to get credit for what he has accomplished, and I don't blame him after his years of virtual exile from the scientific community. Miles, however, urges caution. He agrees that Adam's rapid mental development can only be attributed to the results of the surgery. But he is not sure that in other areas Adam's development is keeping pace. He cites, for example, that Adam has not displayed any real interest in anyone other than himself. This does not seem strange to me. Anyone who has undergone such an astonishing transformation would naturally be completely absorbed in the process. Miles also finds Adam refractory about obeying commands, and calls this a sign of disrespect for authority—an attitude counterproductive to making a real social adjustment. That point is arguable. It may be that there is little in our society that seems worthy of respect to Adam's rational mind.

Don is now writing a paper to submit to a scientific journal for publication. What's the use of waiting any longer? he asks. By publishing in a serious journal, he will avoid charges of sensationalizing the experiment. He asked Miles to coauthor the paper, but Miles refuses to make any definitive claim at this point. Since Miles will not publish jointly, Don says he will publish alone.

If that happens, I will feel free to publish my own account.

I would like to emphasize what a unique human being Adam is. He grew up in an environment in which he had no opportunity to learn in a way that we understand learning, no real chance to use his mind. In a sense, the innovative surgery on his brain gave him an opportunity to learn how to learn. Since then his progress has been spectacular.

It seems I am the only one who feels any alarm about that. I find the rate at which he is learning to be a bit frightening. Last evening, for example, the evening's entertainment was to be a game of Monopoly. The players: Jean Pierre, Miles, Don, myself, and Adam. The competitive aspects of the game are diminished because so much depends on chance. Nevertheless Adam won easily. Don was forced out first, then Jean Pierre, myself, and lastly Miles. Don grumbled—he is not a good loser—and remarked that chess was his game because there was less luck involved. Adam said he had watched Don play with Miles. Whereupon Don invited Adam to play with him.

I don't play chess because I don't like all the scheming, conspiracies, traps—the bewildering combinations. But as soon as they began to play, it was evident even to me that Adam was outclassed. Don kept picking up one piece after another until Adam was down to a queen, a rook, a bishop, and three pawns. The game appeared to be hopelessly lost. Quite suddenly, Adam made a startling move that began an elaborate checkmating combination. All of Don's early successes turned out to have been a part of Adam's overall strategy. Don was stunned. Adam suggested another game, but Don declined, and shortly afterward Adam went up to bed. He goes to bed early and sleeps late. Miles thinks that during sleep Adam's brain is busily storing up and reflecting on information he acquires during the day.

After Adam left, Miles and Don replayed the strategy by which Adam had won. It seems that this required keeping an incredible number of possible combinations in mind. Don remarked that Adam had to plan at least eight moves ahead. Miles agreed. This is proof of a very high order of analytical thinking.

Neither of them worries about the end result of all this. I think they consider Adam's development strictly in terms of (Miles) the neurology of the brain and (Don) the applicability of surgical technique to altering human intelligence. To a degree, Adam and what may be happening to him is irrelevant to their main concerns.

On the other hand, I have only wanted to restore Adam to normal human functioning so that he could find a place for himself in society. The significance of the project for me has been in the social and cultural area—the transformation of a primitive wild boy into someone capable of mastering modern social customs. But how will he function in a society that changes so slowly compared to his rapid development? Will he be satisfied with ordinary relationships—to people or, eventually, to a wife and family, or to an occupation?

Miles and Don are mostly interested in the results of their technical skill, but when I look into Adam's eyes I see—him. I am beginning to wonder if the person I see there will be my friend or my enemy, if we will draw closer together or further apart.

Margaret Denning went upstairs shortly before midnight. Don and Miles were still in the library discussing the implications of this new demonstration of Adam's ability.

As she walked along the second-floor landing toward her bedroom, she noticed a light beneath Adam's door. She knocked gently.

"Adam?"

"Come in."

She entered and closed the door behind her. Only a single small lamp was lit in the room, on a dressing table, and he was seated at the window staring out into the darkness.

She said, "Are you all right?"

"I made a mistake."

142

"In what way?"

"Dr. Swenson did not like to lose the chess game. He is angry with me."

"I think he was surprised that you won but he is not angry with you."

"I do not understand how other people feel about things."

"You will—in time."

"That is one skill I do not seem to acquire. It is not as simple as playing chess."

"No, it isn't."

"I want people to like me."

"They do—we all do."

"Do you like me?"

"Very much."

His expression remained puzzled. "Would you just sit with me for an hour each day and tell me about people and why they behave as they do? That would be the best lesson of all for me."

He was an extraordinary young man, and he understood his predicament: he was an outsider. She always had a strong feeling for that kind of person; she felt somehow connected to them. As a child in her parents' home in Vermont she had been close to Jean Pierre, and later at the mission her only real friend had been the Indian servant Ysabel. Part of Don's appeal for her had been the fact that as the son of a mestizo woman and a Norwegian missionary he too was an outsider. Everyone she had cared for had stood somewhere outside the magic circle of acceptance. Now she was back at the same old psychological starting place. No one is ever liberated from the past.

She said, "Do you mind if I ask you a question?"

"No."

"Can you remember how you felt before the operation? When you were still a wild boy?"

He turned his face to the window. "That life was very unpleasant to me. It's as though I had been terribly sick. Now that I am well I do not want that memory to come back."

143

"Tell me as much as you can."

"I knew that I was ignorant. I could not reach out of myself to anyone and no one could reach me. I was apart from everything and everyone."

"And after the operation?"

"My brain was awake but it was still ignorant. I wondered: How can I have thoughts of any value being what I am? As I began to improve mentally, I thought: Other people aren't so much smarter than I am. I will soon know everything they do."

"You were right. You're smarter than I am now. Smarter than Dr. Swenson or Dr. Kanter."

"All I have learned is how much more there is to learn."

She had to remind herself: her role as a scientist was to observe, not to participate. But she felt close to him at this moment, watching his growth and struggle to understand.

"Do you know they intend to examine you again tomorrow? To find out how much progress you've made since the last time."

"I am anxious to know that myself."

"Dr. Bristol is coming to the telephone, sir," the secretary said.

Don Swenson glanced at his watch. Miles and Margaret had taken Adam for an hour's drive in the countryside. They would be back in an hour. From the second-floor window he saw Jean Pierre at work in the yard with the power lawn mower. The loud whining of its engine reached him through the closed windows.

"Hello, Don?"

"Did you get the notes I mailed last week?"

"Quite amazing."

"There's been another evaluation test with the brain probe. That's why I'm calling you. I didn't want you to wait for my regular report. This latest test provides a possible—make that probable—explanation for what's been happening to Adam."

"Go on."

144

"The ordinary human brain is triune—three layers surmounting the spinal cord, hindbrain, and midbrain. In Adam a further evolutionary step seems to be occurring. So far it's only a kind of swelling of the neocortex, but in Miles' opinion this new brain forming will supersede the cortex just as our cortexes superseded the old limbic and crocodile brains. There are only minimal connections to the new brain so far— enough to account for some very interesting specialized capacities. But if the new brain keeps growing, well ..."

"Yes?"

"It isn't too much to say we might have a mutation on our hands. I don't want to talk about that at this time. I intend to write up a full report for a leading science journal."

Bristol said slowly, carefully spacing words for additional emphasis, "It would be completely irresponsible to let word about Adam leak out. And extremely dangerous."

"I've kept my part of our agreement. You have my notes and my commentaries. That's all you're entitled to."

Bristol lowered his voice. "I'm convening a special meeting of the Committee to discuss this problem. I'd like you to be there."

"I'll be there all right, and you'd better have some good reasons if you want to talk me out of publishing."

"I'm sure we can convince you. Call me tomorrow and I'll tell you where and when the meeting will take place."

Don Swenson replaced the telephone receiver. They would not just be discussing Adam's future at that meeting. They would be discussing his. And he did not need their approval or anyone else's for anything he did.

Shortly after eleven o'clock Miles Kanter retired to his bedroom. He undressed and got into his pajamas. Seated on the bed, resting one foot at a time across the opposite knee, he massaged his bare feet. At the end of a long day his arches hurt, his feet began to swell, and the tiny pieces of steel in his leg began to make their painful presence known. I'm getting old. Even in fairy tales old people don't live happily ever after. For one thing they have too many thoughts, too many memories.

I miss you, Lillian.

He got up and opened the portable phonograph. On the turntable was a record of piano études by Chopin. Using a steel nail file, he pried up the lid of the turntable and pushed it back, securing it with a short strap. Beneath was a compact recording machine. A glowing white light indicated that new material had been recorded and was ready to be played. The recorder was activated by the sound of a human voice or a telephone receiver being lifted anywhere inside the house. They had told him this method of eavesdropping was safer because an expert from the telephone company—or even someone posing as an employee of the telephone company—could make a sweep of the lines and discover a bug that had been installed. It all seemed a little ridiculous to Miles, like children playing at grown-up games.

He sighed and put on earphones, then lay back in bed with two pillows supporting him and began listening to the recording of Don Swenson's conversation with Ted Bristol, chairman of the Committee of Concerned Scientists.

How did he ever get mixed up in such a business?

When he first read in a medical journal about the surgery performed on a young man suffering from dyslexia, Miles wrote the surgeon a congratulatory letter. Dr. Donald Swenson and he then became friends at a distance, remaining more or less in correspondence until Swenson was called before a congressional committee with the resulting furor about a Russian scientist and a valuable microchip. Politicians were dipterous people, always buzzing around scientists. The very thought of Swenson as a spy or a traitor was ridiculous.

Miles knew about spies and traitors, for his wife had

been a teenager in Amsterdam before the Germans invaded. The Germans had hundreds of agents preparing the ground for invasion. Their military attaché in Berlin even warned the Dutch that the Nazis were smuggling Dutch army and police uniforms across the border to use when the invasion began in order to cause total disruption of vital services. Holland was so honeycombed with spies and traitors that the country fell in five days. Lillian and her family, being Jewish, were sent to various concentration camps. She never saw any member of her family again.

During that dreadful summer of 1940, while Holland and Belgium and France were falling in quick succession, Miles was leaving his home in Brooklyn to study at Johns Hopkins University to become a doctor. He had no other thought. The war was distant, an annoyance.

His family had emigrated from Germany before Hitler came to power—driven to escape from poverty more than from politicians. They remained poor in the new land of opportunity. During the Great Depression they lived in a rundown apartment building in a predominantly Jewish section of Brooklyn. All Miles' friends were Jewish and he grew up half-thinking of himself as a Jew. "Until I was sixteen," he said later in jest, "I thought all goyim had horns." His family sacrificed to send him to college at New York University, where he was such a brilliant student that he won a scholarship to attend medical school at Johns Hopkins.

Miles worked at odd jobs and studied day and night. What was Belgium to him? Or Holland? Only his mother's anguished letters during that summer reminded him that they still had relatives and friends in Germany who had not foreseen what would happen there. Miles had never known these people. He had never even heard most of the names that now suddenly cropped up in his mother's letters as if she were engraving a memorial tablet to their memory. The war was still very far away.

The war came closer when he got his draft notice.

He managed to win an occupational deferment in order to continue with his medical studies. Then Pearl Harbor was attacked, and suddenly America was in the war. He was drafted midway through medical school. On the final day he went to the billiard room and painted three balls with likenesses of Hitler and Hirohito and Mussolini and spent an hour knocking them about the table to work off his frustration.

He served four years in the Medical Corps, and he was with the first unit to enter the concentration camp at Auschwitz. That was a traumatic event, one of those that change the course of a life. He felt as if he was in a nightmare, falling, falling, simply falling into a pit with no bottom or sanity. He was too numbed to feel anger but simply wandered like a shell-shocked victim through horrific visions of inhumanity, his heart wrenched out of his chest by pity.

In his years in the Medical Corps he had seen terrible suffering, but none had seemed so personal to him. With wounded or dying soldiers he had a job to do, to save them or to limit their pain, and that took precedence over personal emotion. To the suffering of these survivors he could be nothing but a witness. He took photographs to help him bear witness.

One such photograph was of a man so wasted that his face consisted of nothing but bone and eyes. Miles tried to give him a sip of water but his throat muscles could no longer swallow. He stared up with an imploring look, as though trying to convey a message. He wore a single ragged garment on his skeletal body, and the knuckle-bones of his hands had broken through the stretched parchment skin. He died without ever uttering a sound.

Miles asked others in the camp if they could identify the dead man. None could. The dead man had lost all signs of identity. At last someone did remember, or thought he did, that the man's name was Kanter but could not recall a first name. In the brotherhood forged that brutal day, Miles vowed to strip himself of all his own illusions of identity—youth, doctor, son, soldier—

and became the dead man's link to a world that did not remember him.

When he returned home he changed his name to Miles Kanter. He became a Jew. In time his faith became his new identity—a fierce and gladiatorial force.

Years later, married to Lillian, he showed her photographs he had taken that day in Auschwitz. She recognized one starved scarecrow as her sister. It was one of those impossible coincidences that can only happen in real life, and it had the purposelessness of real life. They spent months trying to track down what became of her, but there was no record. She and the man named Kanter had vanished along wtih six million other victims. Fate left loose threads dangling; it did not arrange things tidily.

Lillian was a small, glossy, dark-haired woman with a mind of her own. He thought she was beautiful; she was convinced he had a "goldeneh" brain. "I like to do for you," she said, "so you can do your reading and thinking." She was absolutely certain that any day he would "be somebody," and people would recognize his superiority. He did not have to try to impress her, and that left him free to pursue his own path. He wanted only to live quietly and watch the turmoil of the world go by.

But the world did not leave them alone. Israel became a nation, and Lillian wanted to emigrate. "I am a Jew. Where should a Jew go if not there?" But he loved being an American. "Who were the soldiers who came to that camp and saved you?" he asked. Some American soldiers who came, she pointed out, must have been anti-Semites. "But they came," he replied. "It would be ungrateful to leave here. I was born here. This is my home."

1948 changed all that. When the Arab nations attacked Israel, he realized for the first time that the new nation could be wiped out. Another Holocaust would surely follow. The next year, as a full-fledged physician, he moved to Israel with Lillian. During the years that followed they had three children, two sons and a daughter.

In the 1967 Six-Day War, Miles served with the Medical Corps. He was wounded in the leg while crossing a wadi of pink smooth stone that curved up from the plain where Israelites of old had waited for Moses to come down from the mount.

There had been no sound, no movement except soft wind, and then suddenly in sunbright silence the explosion. Forty pieces of shrapnel lodged in his left leg. It was all remote and unreal lying alone on the hard-packed gravel track and watching the sun slide lower. He felt his own smallness against the vastness, the eternity of iron-red granite cliffs.

Before nightfall Miles was evacuated by ambulance. Minutes after the ambulance left the wadi, rain from the mountains rushed through the dried riverbed in a great torrent. He would certainly have drowned. He was convinced that his survival was a miracle, that God had a reason to grant him and Kanter another chance at life.

What reason could there be except to serve Him and the land of His chosen people?

Stern tests of his faith lay ahead. In the 1973 war with Egypt, during the surprise assault the Egyptians launched on the high holy day of Yom Kippur, he and Lillian lost their oldest son. Lillian never quite recovered from the shock and Miles buried himself in his work. Their daughter married and moved to England. Their youngest son went into business in Beirut and prospered. One day, crossing the street, he was shot by an Arab sniper and his body lay where it fell. The metal treads of passing tanks ground it into an unrecognizable smear. Another missing person.

Meanwhile Miles' reputation was growing. He wrote several books on the physiology of intelligence that drew wide attention. He began his experiments into NGF—the nerve growth factor. There were entreaties for him to return to the United States. He was promised money, the use of equipment and hospital facilities that

150

a small country could not provide. He was not tempted. His opinions had hardened since the death of his two sons. He and Lillian wanted to stay and help build Israel into a nation that would be forever secure from its enemies.

Not even his love could save Lillian. Death itself was not as frightening to him as knowing that someone he needed so much would die. He mourned her even while she lived. The last year was desperate. She lay in bed, a sheet covering the lower half of a body swollen with the tumor. The vitality that had characterized her every movement was drained. But she held on, even when powerful drugs being pumped into her body threatened to overwhelm her along with the alien devouring cells. She would force herself up out of unconsciousness and shake her small fist: "I have too much to do. You *can't* kill me! I'll fool you all...I'm going to live!"

He buried her on a hill beneath an olive tree with a fine view of the valley. When he looked at her a last time in the plain wooden coffin, he envied her: "Why can't life be as calm and peaceful as death?" Then, looking around at the valley and the hills beyond where enemies lived, he prayed no one would ever take any part of the land that was her last resting place.

Work was all that remained for him. He accepted an offer to return to the United States. It didn't matter where his body was; his heart was forever buried beneath an olive tree on a hilltop within sight of the Gaza Strip.

He entered a period of great success. His theory on regenerating nerve growth was tested, approved, acclaimed. He gained more recognition in two years in the United States than in the twenty-six years he had worked in Israel.

He met Don Swenson soon after he returned to the United States. This wraith-thin, coppery-skinned young man impressed him by the sheer intensity of his concentration on a task. The energy in him made him seem larger than he was. He appeared to be in a continual state of anxiety. There was always a thin luster of perspiration on his high-domed forehead, and his hand-clasp was a bit damp.

When Swenson invited him to make a thorough neurological examination and appraisal of the wild boy, Miles told him, "There's nothing I can do that you can't."

"A second opinion has been asked for. I'm asking you because if you disagree, yours is the only opinion I'll respect."

Miles chuckled. "One genius must help out another genius?"

He liked Margaret Denning at first sight. A fine specimen of womanhood, good-looking, with a friendly face and a full-lipped smile that made a dimple in her cheek. She had a strong character. He could imagine her enduring the discomforts of life in primitive conditions, crawling through bushpig tunnels or neck-deep in leech-infested swamps. Her movements had a shy grace compounded of artlessness and femininity.

He saw at once that Don Swenson was still in love with her. It took longer to discover how Margaret felt about her former husband. She was fond in a way that was not love. Kindness is not love, and neither is sympathy. Affection is not love. Sooner or later Don would understand that, but for the time being he did not.

The taped recording came to an end. Miles removed the headphones and carefully replaced them in the hiding place underneath the turntable. Then he rewound the tape, removed it, and took down a suitcase from the top of his closet. The suitcase had a false side containing a small powerful transmitter. The equipment also had a scrambler device. He put the tape onto the player next to the transmitter, connected a wire, and the tape began silently playing its message.

He got back into bed, glanced about the room, and got up again to push the lid down firmly on the turntable. There was no need to close the suitcase; it was closed, sitting on top of his closet and transmitting its message.

A crazy business, he thought.

chapter 12

On a hot sunny morning Don Swenson arrived in New York City and took a taxi from Grand Central Station to the glass-sheathed office building on Park Avenue. He was a little late because his train had not been on time. When he reached the eighth floor, he went directly to the office of the Committee of Concerned Scientists and the secretary waved him in.

In the conference room, Ted Bristol was seated at the head of a long oval table at which other members of the Committee had already gathered. In addition to Bristol, three of those seated at the table were familiar to Swenson. There was an aging scientist from California who had made one of the most important discoveries in modern chemistry. There was a pale scholarly spectacled physicist from King's College, Cambridge, who had worked with Robert Oppenheimer and contributed significantly to the development of nuclear energy—an achievement he now called "infamous labor." The third familiar face was an East German whose work on microbial genetics had corrected all that went before. The other four at the oval table, including an attractive auburn-haired woman of about Margaret's age, were unknown to Swenson.

Ted Bristol made the introductions. "Unfortunately, Rafael Campo is not able to be present. The Argentine Government has put him under arrest. But his lovely wife Juana, his coworker, is here as his proxy."

Juana Campo was ostensibly in New York to place her husband's case before the human rights council at the United Nations. The others present had arranged similar excuses to attend this extraordinary meeting. The Japanese representative was traveling under a false passport.

Ted Bristol told Don, "I've circulated copies of your

153

reports to all those present. But they haven't heard your latest news. Will you fill them in?"

Swenson quickly reviewed the data. Everyone was fascinated by the mysterious protuberance that had appeared on Adam's cerebral cortex and whether this signified the growth of a new brain. Ted Bristol firmly discouraged this line of questioning.

"We're not here to indulge in idle speculation. The problem I want you to consider first is, does Adam possess paranormal powers?"

Juana Campo leaned forward in her chair. "I am not convinced that the mental powers described are beyond the range of normal. We all know of persons who have developed prodigious abilities within certain narrow ranges. Idiot savants and others deficient in all-around intelligence often excel in one particular field. How can we be sure that Adam is not one of these?"

"That is a possibility," Swenson conceded. "Adam obviously has not been tested and observed in a broad range of situations. On the other hand, the progress mentioned has all taken place in a very short period of time. The unusual degree of neuron-electrical activity throughout the entire brain would seem to rule out his being an idiot savant."

Mrs. Campo brushed back a lock of auburn hair from her forehead. "I'd like to make another point. My husband, in his position as chief of the Laboratory of Brain Research in Buenos Aires, encountered many instances of extraordinary mental ability. He believes these individuals pay a price in some other area of their personality."

"For example?"

"Judgment and moral sense. One such person had a phenomenal IQ, but was a depraved criminal who had spent more than twenty years in prison. He had the emotional development of a four-year-old child. Unharnessed mental power can be as dangerous as an unguided missile."

A murmur of assent ran along the oval table.

"This would suggest," Ted Bristol said, "that tests

should be devised for Adam that will help us to learn more about this side of his development. We should know what his personality is like as well as the extent of his mental powers."

Put to a vote, this met with a chorus of ayes.

Karel Keyser, the East German representative, said, "My field is, as you know, microbial genetics. I would be interested in knowing more about the process by which a strip of DNA brain tissue was implanted in Adam's brain."

Don Swenson described how the genetic tissue had been prepared for implantation. The tissue was injected through a micropipette with a chemical to suppress the body's attempt to reject it as a foreign substance via the immunological system. Much had been learned about the crucial control system that regulates genes, and similar transplants of human genes had been successfully incorporated into developing embryos of higher primates where the actual site of the gene incorporation was not in the brain. But the method of implantation was the same and the transplant became a part of the permanent genetic endowment.

"I don't think it is necessary to give this group a detailed explanation of the powerful changes created in the human body by even a seemingly minor chemical change in a gene," Don said. "From the beginning it was clear to me that if genetic engineering could be extended to mammalian cells, the most exciting application would someday be to the human brain. My attempt succeeded somewhat beyond my expectations."

A sharp clattering burst of applause was led by Ted Bristol.

"Are there any other questions?" Don asked.

Keyser said, "Was the DNA brain tissue taken from a living donor?"

"The chairman is better able to answer that."

Ted Bristol said, "The tissue sample was obtained under a promise of extreme secrecy. I can only tell you that the person whose DNA tissue was used is no longer alive. I can also assure you that the removal of brain tissue was not the cause of death."

"Can you tell us if the donor was male or female?"

"No."

"Did the donor have any unusual qualifications that might account for the remarkable effect of the implantation?"

"I'm sorry. I can't say any more." Bristol glanced around the table. "We will move on now to a new topic. If further tests reveal Adam to possess genuine paranormal powers, how many of you believe that the discovery should be published in a scientific journal?"

A nearly unanimous chorus of nays.

One aye. "I don't see why not," Don argued. "The whole purpose of this Committee is to encourage the dissemination of scientific knowledge."

Juana Campo said, "There is a difference."

"You'd better explain it to me."

"We believe in sharing the knowledge that Adam may possess, not allowing Adam himself to become the property of any government. In that role he can be extremely dangerous. If any government in the world today could get its hands on Adam, they would use him as a weapon."

"This isn't a James Bond movie."

The Japanese representative said, "Perhaps I can make the point with a simple example. Many people believe that your country won World War II because they were able to break the Japanese secret military code. You knew what we were going to do before we did it. You even knew about the attack on Pearl Harbor, although you did not believe that until too late."

"What has this to do with Adam?"

"It took years of extremely difficult work by your very best cryptographers to break that code. How long do you think it would take Adam?"

Ted Bristol said, "The world is still divided into armed camps that will do anything, absolutely anything, to gain superiority over the other. I assure you that if

156

Adam has truly paranormal powers, he will become a military asset. One worth fighting for."

"This is the biggest medical story of this century. And you're saying I can't tell anyone about it."

"Not yet. Not until we've decided what should be done with Adam."

"And how long will that take?"

"We don't know right now. We must first find out precisely what Adam is capable of."

"You're asking a lot. I'm not sure I'm willing to make that sacrifice." Actually he was damn sure he was going to publish. But Bristol and his Committee could still be useful in helping him to cover all the angles in his report. "Let it pass for now," he said. "You indicated there's something more you want to know about Adam. What is it?"

"We need to know if he is going to be able to handle his newly acquired powers."

"Emotional maturity is very important," agreed the Cambridge physicist. "Some of the men who worked with Oppenheimer and myself in developing nuclear weaponry should not have been trusted with an air rifle."

"How are you going to find that out?" Don asked.

Ted Bristol said, "We will try to devise tests to discover what we need to know."

"Who's going to give him the tests?"

"You shouldn't have any trouble convincing your colleagues that this is a useful field of enquiry."

"Margaret Denning has the final word. How far can I go to clue her in on what we're trying to do?"

Bristol said quietly, "She is not to be informed under any conditions. She must not even know that our Committee is involved."

"Then she won't cooperate."

"You must persuade her of the necessity."

"It would help if I could tell her just what sort of test you're proposing."

"We'll start work on that immediately. As soon as we have something we'll send it to you."

"Where?"

"You will rent a post-office box under the name of James Adam in a town a few miles from Enosburg Landing. Look for an envelope that will bear the return address of *Modern Science Today*—a nonexistent publication."

"You've thought of everything."

"We try to. We are small and comparatively powerless. And we have very powerful enemies."

"I have one more question. Suppose Adam turns out to be all you think he should be. What do you propose to do about him?"

"Several plans are under consideration."

"And suppose he doesn't have the right emotional balance or whatever it is you're looking for. What then?"

"That would require other measures."

"You mean he might be too dangerous."

"At the right time we will address ourselves to that problem." Bristol turned to the others at the oval table. "This meeting stands adjourned. We will follow the usual procedure. Each member will depart at intervals of two minutes, and take the stairs to floors above or below this level. You will descend in the elevators from there."

Bristol explained to Don, "We assume that we are under surveillance because we're on the government's subversive list. They would like to know what people we meet, where we meet them, and what we are meeting about. We take what precautions we can."

Don was the last to leave. As he emerged into the corridor, Juana Campo was standing at the elevator on the eighth floor.

"You aren't following the procedure?" he asked.

"I was waiting for you."

Her auburn hair was stylishly cut and framed a face lightly tanned by the sun or Argentine ancestry. She wore a close-fitting beige linen dress that nicely complimented her figure.

"Any particular reason?" he asked as he pushed the elevator button.

"We are supposed to leave the building as inconspicuously as we can. What is less conspicuous than a man and woman together?"

The wall light glowed and the elevator doors began to open.

He smiled. "You're perfectly right. Do you have plans for the rest of the evening?"

"I am a stranger in the city. And quite alone."

"I have a remedy for that," he said, as they stepped into the elevator.

chapter 13

As he had done every day for two weeks Don Swenson entered a small rural post office, a mansard-roofed building that also housed a general store. He went directly to the box assigned to him under the name of James Adam. Through the glass door of the box he saw a small package wrapped in brown paper. When he removed the package, he saw that the return address was *Modern Science Today*.

It was early morning and the parking lot was nearly empty. Only one other car was there. He backed the Volvo out of the space defined by two white painted stripes, turned it around, and drove onto the road.

In the other car in the parking lot, a man crouching out of sight in the rear seat turned off a tiny movie camera that was pointed from a corner of the window. He picked up a microphone.

"Headed south," he said.

Don drove south along the same road he had traveled, stopping once again at the Enosburg Landing post office. The woman behind the counter handed him the mail for the Denning farm. There were advertising circulars, a supermarket throwaway, a copy of an anthropology journal, and two manila envelopes, one addressed to himself and the other to Miles Kanter. The manila envelopes contained mail being forwarded weekly from his and Miles' former addresses. He dropped the junk mail in a large trash can outside the post office.

Seated in his car, he opened the brown paper parcel addressed to James Adam. Inside, a sheaf of papers detailed various tests that Ted Bristol and the Committee wanted Adam to take. The tests were designed to evaluate Adam's emotional maturity. Don found nothing unusual until the final suggestion. Thinking about that one, he began to smile. He would have a

160

hard time persuading Margaret to go along, but he would certainly try. Of late she had been showing too personal an interest in Adam.

A small sealed envelope was enclosed with the sheaf of tests. Don opened it and read:

> Dear Don,
>   Here is the material we promised to send.
>   There is disturbing news. Shortly after Karel Keyser returned to East Germany, he was taken into "protective custody." He has been undergoing interrogation in Lichtenburg prison about his hurried trip to the United States. Our government, in concert with its allies, is working quietly through diplomatic channels to try to effect his release.
>   Meanwhile, you must redouble your vigilance. We presume that the East Germans will now know about Adam.
>
>   Yours,
>   Ted Bristol

Don recalled Karel Keyser at the Committee meeting—a soft fat man with a high-pitched voice who did not seem to know what to do with his hands; most of the time he sat with his hands folded in his lap or under his chin. Keyser was the kind of man who must have had a lonely childhood, always the last one picked when the kids were choosing up sides in a sandlot game. He was certainly not the kind who would stand up under interrogation. At the moment Don sincerely wished he had never become involved with Ted Bristol and his Committee, no matter how principled their motives.

As he drove away from the rural post office and headed back toward the farmhouse, a dusty tan Plymouth Reliant coupe stayed a discreet distance behind.

* * *

Four hundred feet above the ground the tiny model plane made a slow right-hand circular turn. The faint whining noise of its engine was a waspish sound. The tiny plane completed the turn in level flight, then pointed its nose up and began to climb.

On the ground Rory worked the controls on his transmitter, adjusting the plane's rudder and ailerons. The model plane reached its peak altitude and coasted along on balsa wood wings. Rory directed the plane to put its nose down and begin a slow descent.

He was distracted by a car that pulled up on a concrete path near the open grassy area where he was flying his model plane.

Rory sent instructions from his transmitter for a sharp course correction. The model plane responded beautifully, arcing into a sweeping turn that carried it away from the woods.

The car, a silver-gray Mercedes, stopped.

Rory changed the model plane's course, sending it over the nearby treetops. The whine of the plane's engine dwindled. Then there was an odd coughing sound in the motor.

Rory flashed a new instruction, and the plane peeled off to head back toward him. The engine sputtered again. The plane nosed down slightly. Rory put it into a steep dive to accelerate so he could straighten it out. The engine quit entirely and the plane started down in a steeper dive. Rory shouted as he ran toward it. There was a blue-red flash as the plane impacted; the muffled noise of an explosion came a split second afterward. Specks of debris from the disintegrated plane were hurled skyward and began falling slowly down.

Stunned, Rory watched until the tiny specks no longer stained the sky.

Two men stepped out of the Mercedes nearby.

One man was fairly tall and quite heavy, with a receding hairline. The other was of average height, with high red hair that rose in front like a rooster's comb.

162

The red-haired man carried a small transmitter in one hand.

Rory's anger burst out. "Lousy sons of bitches! *You* wrecked my plane!"

Sobbing, he flung himself at them. The taller, heavier man moved easily in front of the other and took Rory's charge head on. He held Rory in a grip like a grappling iron.

"Come now," he said in a surprisingly soft voice. "You don't want to get in more trouble than you're in, do you?"

The man's forearms were made of solid muscle. After a little while Rory gave up, breathing heavily.

"Trouble? What kind of trouble?"

The red-haired man said, "You have an FCC license?"

"What is this? Who are you guys?"

The red-haired man moved to confront Rory. "You were using a radio transmitter to operate a model plane. You need a license."

"I never heard of that." Rory had heard of it but he was not about to admit it. He blurted, "Listen, it's just a hobby of mine. Someday I'm going to join the Air Force and fly my own plane."

The red-haired man nodded, and Rory was suddenly free of the grappling irons that had been holding his arms.

"Better forget about that, sonny."

"Why should I?"

"The Air Force doesn't take anybody with a criminal record."

"A what?"

"The rules of the Federal Communications Commission say that using a radio transmitter and a receiver—like the one in your plane—is broadcasting. You were broadcasting without having a license to do it."

"I wasn't hurting anybody. I didn't even know I was doing wrong."

The red-haired man said, "Ignorance of the law is no excuse."

"Jesus! What are you going to do? Arrest me?" Rory had to fight back tears. "Mister, you don't realize what'll happen. I'll lose my job. My dad'll kill me. He don't even know I own...owned..." The crushing reminder of loss made it hard to go on, and to his shame he began to blubber. "What'd you have to go and blow it up for? I saved to get the parts for that plane. I built it myself. Now there's nothing."

"I'm sorry, but we can't be too careful. If you'd spotted us, you could have sent the plane flying away into the woods. Then we wouldn't have any evidence."

"You talk like I'm a criminal."

"Just a few weeks ago we brought down a model plane that had miniaturized aerial photo equipment and radio sensors. That evidence is going to send a certain foreign agent away for the rest of his life."

Rory's breath caught. "Hey, listen, you don't think that I...I wouldn't ever do anything like that!" New vistas of trouble unreeled in his imagination. "Who are you fellas, anyhow?"

The red-haired man reached into his pocket and produced a card-sized identification, which he flashed at Rory.

Rory's voice, incongruously deep, took on a hushed tone. "No wonder you're worried about spies."

"What's your name, sonny?"

Rory told him. "I should have known! You couldn't be just a couple of ordinary snoops. Not with equipment like that."

The tall heavy man with receding hair said, "We need to know your name and address."

"Rory Grandits. I'm okay. My dad votes straight Republican. My whole family's born here from way back. We fly a flag in our backyard, and my older brother fought in Vietnam. He even got a medal. You don't think I'd do anything against my country, do you?"

"Suppose you were asked to do it *for* your country?" the red-haired man asked.

"Well, that's different. I'd do anything. I registered for the draft as soon as I turned eighteen."

The two men were no longer unfriendly or accusing; in fact, they seemed downright friendly.

"Do you know how to keep your mouth shut, Rory?" the red-haired man asked. "Not to tell your best friend, even your own family?"

"Sure I do. If it's for something important." Rory was starting to feel better because it looked as if everything might turn out all right.

"We can use a bright young man like you. Would you be willing to take on a special assignment for us, Rory? Strictly in an unofficial capacity, of course. If you agree, we can forget all about those charges of broadcasting without a license."

Rory was dazed by the quick turn in his fortunes. "Work for the FBI!" he said. "Oh Jesus, would I!"

They had scheduled two days of tests for Adam. The first day covered familiar ground, the examination of cortical functions such as abstraction, memory, intelligence, and visual perception.

Less than a minute's study of electrical activity in the brain was sufficient to obtain valid results. Adam's neocortex, the seat of cerebral activity, was so fully activated that the accumulation of synapses was unlike any Don had ever seen. It was eerie to watch the computer screen light up with so many flashes of light.

Watching the screen, Don was reminded of the very first tests on the wild boy in which the cerebral cortex appeared as dormant and inactive as that of a crocodile. Now the smallest stimulus applied to the electrodes positioned on his skull caused tiny blips to march in progress across the computer screen. Clearly his brain was continuing to develop a hierarchy of nerve cells of amazingly complex functions.

Don thought it reasonable to suppose that this newly acquired formidable intellect might have caused a distortion, an abnormality in which there were points of disequilibrium—particularly emotional problems or phobias. Adam's amazing transformation from a wild boy should not have left him with attitudes as normal as everyone else's.

When he expressed this idea to Miles, the older man's eyes narrowed keenly. "You're not actually *hoping* to find problems, are you?"

Don recognized that he would have to be careful to disguise a streak of malice in his attitude toward Adam. "Of course not. But we have to know if his extraordinary mental powers are proving difficult to integrate psychologically. That's what these tests are about."

Miles nodded agreement with that. "There is something difficult to explain. As a wild boy, his mental life was largely determined by the limbic system. The neocortex was undeveloped—possibly impaired. There may have been some sort of lesion in the memory lobes that healed over. But now that his neocortex is fully developed he still has a traumatic amnesia about the early years of his life. It may be due to a psychological trauma in which he has forgotten experiences too painful for him to remember."

The following day the emphasis shifted to in-depth psychological testing, using a questionnaire for persons with exceptionally high intelligence developed by researchers at the University of California at Berkeley. This enabled them to probe Adam's reactions to various kinds of imagined situations.

The questionnaire showed a strong reaction to a situation in which he was cast ashore, like Robinson Crusoe, to live alone on a desert island. The graph of his emotional reaction to this almost shot off the chart.

"How do you explain this?" Miles asked Adam.

"I have a fear of isolation. That is very frightening to me. It may be from when I was a wild boy living alone in the jungle. But it was also how I felt when I first came here. I knew others were communicating in a language, and many things were going on of which I was unaware. That was my desert island."

"Did you feel you had a latent capability for understanding language?"

Adam nodded. "That increased my sense of frustra-

166

tion. It was very difficult to be in a room where everyone was chattering in a way I could not understand. I knew I was missing things that were important to know. I had a terrible need to learn. After my operation, as I began to gain an understanding of words, it was like having an interpreter with me who could explain things. Everything began to make sense. Does this sound foolish?"

"Quite the opposite," Miles said, smiling gently.

Margaret and Don and Miles were working late in the library, evaluating the results of the various psychological tests. Adam had gone upstairs to bed an hour before.

"As far as I can see he's passed with flying colors," Margaret said. "No hang-ups, no phobias, no hidden neuroses."

"There's one more test we haven't put him to," Don said, sitting back in his chair with a sly grin.

Margaret said, "I don't think we ought to go into that, Don."

"Why not?"

"Frankly, it's crude and tasteless."

Only the day before he had submitted a proposal that they arrange for Adam to have sexual relations with a woman.

He said, "Sexual feelings are among the most powerful that can be aroused in human beings. They're usually expressed quite differently by humans than by other species, including the higher primates. I think it's a valid way of getting important clues to Adam's emotional reactions."

"I disagree," Margaret said. "I'm disappointed that you even suggested it."

Don was perversely pleased. Her annoyance proved that he had touched a live nerve.

"I think you oppose the idea for reasons that have nothing to do with its validity."

"Such as?"

"Your puritanical upbringing."

167

"You don't have to be a puritan to turn down that kind of pornography," she said, removing herself to a cool distance. "No purpose would be served except sheer prurience."

He was driven to provoke her further.

"If I didn't know you better, I'd say you were interested in preserving Adam's virginity."

"That's ridiculous and you know it."

"Your attitude ought to be more objective, more professional." He added mockingly, "Is it that ole debbil sex that has you uptight?"

Miles said quietly, "I agree with you, Margaret, that the suggestion smacks of a live porno act. It's voyeurism. Pure voyeurism. Who can defend such a thing? On the other hand," he continued, with the air of a Talmudic scholar weighing a nicely balanced point, "discovering something about Adam's ability to deal with strong emotions would certainly provide important clues to how his brain operates. The primitive part of the brain, buried inside the cerebral cortex, is still very powerful. It still wants to take control. One little part of that primitive brain, the hypothalamus, causes anger, aggression, and what we call unreasoning fear, and only a millimeter away is the region of the brain that causes sexual desire."

"I'm afraid I don't see what you're leading up to."

"We know that a small current of electricity applied to the hypothalamus can change a personality. A rabbit can be made to act like a snarling, clawing tiger. Take away the current and it acts like a rabbit again. Strong sexual emotion is like an electric current that comes whizzing along from *inside* the brain. The cerebral cortex has all it can do to get things back under control. Sometimes it can't, and the primitive brain takes charge. That's when we say a person has lost his head—it isn't his head he loses but the controlling part of his brain.

"Adam's cerebral cortex is unusually developed, but we don't know how much control it has over the strong instincts centered in the old primitive brain. Will the cortex stay in control during highly charged stressful conditions? If the instinctual drives are too strong, considering Adam's abilities, that could become extremely dangerous."

A long moment passed. Don wondered how Margaret would respond to Miles' dispassionate summary. Although the facts were equally known to him, he couldn't have put it as well. Some unknown electrical current was stirring up his own hypothalamus, and threads of reasonable argument tended to gather into a knot of emotion.

Margaret said to Miles, "You mean you're in favor of the experiment?"

"If I could vote no and yes at the same time, I would."

Don pressed him. "You do think such a test would be useful?"

Miles nodded.

Margaret's eyes were bright with hostility. "You both go ahead and do what you like. I'll have no part in it."

She quickly left the library. Don heard her footsteps going down the stairs.

He leaned back in his chair with satisfaction. "You see how she behaves where Adam is involved. Isn't she jealous?"

"One of you is," Miles chided.

In his room Don was reading Eric Cassell's *The Healer's Art*. His gaze fell on a paragraph: *It is interesting that perhaps the most seemingly omnipotent of all physicians are the neurosurgeons, and theirs is the specialty in which nature's odds are most against them. In terms of curing, they are the least effective.*

Times change, Don thought. Our omnipotence has become real. The Adam Project proves that.

Don heard a knock at his door. He marked the page in the book and got up.

Jean Pierre said, "A young lady is asking for you. She only gave her first name. Elfrida. She said you'd know."

"Oh, yes. Thank you."

He went downstairs. Elfrida was not what he expected—a tall, slender woman whose blond hair was coiffed in a fashionable upsweep. She wore a pale gray suit and a mauve-colored blouse, and carried a burgundy leather handbag.

"They told me to ask for Dr. Swenson," she said.

She had a slight accent. Swedish or Norwegian, Don thought.

"You name is Elfrida?"

"You can call me Elfie," she said, pale lips parting in a slight smile.

"You're a most attractive woman. But I did specify someone young."

"I'm twenty-six."

She was on the downhill slope of thirty.

Elfrida put one hand on a hip and turned to give him the full benefit of her figure in profile. She had a full bust despite her slenderness. "I could pass for younger if I tried. But I like to be honest with customers."

"That's the point. I'm not your customer. It's a young man, and he's only seventeen."

Elfrida nodded understandingly. "I'm marvelous with that kind. You need experience with someone like that."

"Actually, this is in the nature of an experiment."

Suspicion put a sharper edge on her voice. "I draw the line at any rough stuff."

He decided she would do.

"What happens—and how it happens—is entirely up to you. My friend and I will only be observers."

She stared at him for a moment. "If you want a show, I can supply a male partner."

"You miss the point. It's the young man we're interested in."

Elfrida shrugged. "Okay."

"You'll need a few simple instructions."

"That's one thing I *don't* need."

"I didn't mean that kind of instruction."

He had taken the precaution of ordering nurse uniforms in four different sizes, and one was right for Elfrida, whose slender figure was disguised within its

170

starched limits. After trying to fit her into nurse's shoes, however, Don gave up and let her wear her own shoes. It was unlikely Adam would know the difference. His only acquaintance with nurses had been at the hospital at a time when he was not a particularly acute observer.

Don repeated his instructions for a last time, and then brought Elfrida to Adam's room. As she knocked, he ducked through the door of the adjacent room. A two-way mirror had been purchased and installed by Jean Pierre on an afternoon when Don and Miles and Margaret were taking Adam for a drive, an outing that had become part of his daily schedule. Jean Pierre was told that the mirror was necessary in order to keep a closer watch on Adam's activities when the young man thought himself alone.

A half-empty glass of Scotch was on a small table beside Miles.

"Margaret is right, you know," he said. "This is pornography."

"Scientific prurience," Don corrected him, smiling. He took the empty chair.

A bathroom door opened in the adjacent room and Adam emerged with shaving lather on his face, responding to the knock. He opened the door. Elfrida entered in her nurse's costume, carrying a small medical kit.

"Shoes," Miles commented sourly.

"Nothing we had fit."

"My name is Elfie," she was saying to Adam. "Dr. Swenson wants you to have a complete physical. He's too busy to give it to you, so I'm helping out."

"I haven't finished shaving," Adam said.

"There's no rush."

Adam returned to the bathroom. Elfrida put her black kit down on the nubby white coverlet of the bed. In a minute Adam came out of the bathroom, latherless. During the past months, Don realized, Adam had become a strikingly good-looking young man. The tiny nicks that once marred his face had healed and his

171

complexion was free of acne or pimples. He seemed to have molted and grown a shining new skin.

"Take off your shirt, please," Elfrida murmured.

Adam unbuttoned his sport shirt and removed it. He wore nothing underneath. His torso was slender and muscular.

"Sit down right over here," Elfrida said, indicating a place on the bed.

She took the blood pressure unit from the kit and put the cuff on Adam's arm as Don had shown her.

Miles said, "She isn't even reading the dial."

Elfrida had squeezed the bulb and released it. She immediately began to unwrap the pressure bandage. As she did, she let her fingers drift slowly up Adam's arm to his shoulder.

Adam watched her with a mixture of appraisal and curiosity.

"You're a very good-looking young man," Elfrida said. She bent over to kiss Adam's bare chest. Adam was staring at the back of her head where the nurse's cap perched like a wary gull.

Adam knows what's going on, Don decided, and he doesn't mind. He's normal and doesn't appear to suffer from any sexual inhibitions or hang-ups.

Elfrida moved over to caress Adam's nipples with her tongue. She looked up at him. "You're so nice," she whispered huskily.

Don was recalling his own first sexual experience. Everything had moved smoothly to a disastrous conclusion. In his eagerness he ejaculated prematurely. *Was that it?* the girl asked, giving him the kind of look he wished had been directed at someone else.

It would be interesting to see how Adam would perform when the moment arrived. Sexual failure could result in emotional confusion, guilt, anger, or might even unleash aggressive impulses.

Elfrida stood up and with a sweep of her hand removed her nurse's cap. Unbuttoning her uniform, she wriggled out of it. She wore a lacy black bra supporting

172

large smooth well-shaped breasts. Her only other garment was a garter belt.

Don felt a warming response in his libido. A psychiatrist had once interpreted Don's first traumatic sexual experience as one reason he had become a compulsive womanizer. He had to keep proving his potency to any available woman. But for every psychiatric opinion there is an equal and opposite opinion, Don thought, and he did not need to look to the past to explain the simple fact that he found attractive women irresistible. Nor did he see why this compulsion to bed down other women diminished in any way his special feeling for Margaret.

Elfrida had moved close to where Adam sat on the bed. She put her arms over his shoulders and drew him toward her.

Suddenly Adam pulled back.

"What is it?" she asked.

He turned and looked directly at the mirror.

Elfrida saw where he was looking and misinterpreted its meaning. "Why not?" she said. "I like to watch too."

She removed her bra and garter belt. Then, posing nude in front of the mirror, she unzipped Adam's trousers. She took his penis in her hand—it was stiff and hard—and rubbed it against her crotch.

"We're going to have fun."

Miles slumped in his chair, his chin resting almost on his chest, his eyes closed.

Don felt the palms of his hands turn moist. "I think he's looking at us," he whispered.

Miles opened his eyes. "There's no way he can see through the mirror."

The steady directness of Adam's gaze was unsettling.

"He senses that we're here," Don replied.

Elfrida was saying, "Come on. I want you to." She went down to her knees on a level with his rigid penis. Her pale lips opened hungrily.

Adam pushed her aside. She rolled over onto the floor, writhing and moving slender legs while her hips

173

made circular movements. She moved her hand down her abdomen to her crotch. "I'm ready," she moaned. "Come on. Do it."

Adam looked directly into the mirror. Don thought: If the mirror was not between us, our eyes would meet.

Miles whispered, "You're right. It isn't possible, but you're—"

Adam picked up a chair and smashed it into the mirror. There was an explosion of shattering glass.

Elfrida screamed.

chapter 14

made circular movements. She moved her hand over her abdomen to her crotch. "I'm ready," she mou...
Come on. Do...
Adam looked directly into the mirror. Don...
it his mirror image, and said, but there was no pa...

Margaret decided it was time for Adam to choose his own apparel. She had been ordering his clothing from a catalogue store.

She told Miles, "It will be a new experience for him. He needs new experiences. We'll see how he conducts himself with salespeople and what sort of choices he makes. I've given him a budget and I want to see how well he does with that too. I'll get a better idea of how well he can function on his own."

"Has he mentioned what happened yesterday?"

"Not a word."

"He was pretty angry."

"I don't blame him. I hope you're not going to tell me his reaction proves his primitive brain was taking over. That's nonsense. Anyone would have acted as he did with the same provocation."

"How could he know we were watching? That's what interests me. He couldn't see us or hear us or smell us. He couldn't touch us or taste us. That takes care of the usual five senses."

"He had an intuition."

"Not the way we usually use the word. It wasn't a hunch. He *knew*. Human beings have ways of knowing of which we are just becoming aware. Ways that are different from verbal and analytical consciousness. We don't understand yet how we come by such knowledge, but it has a long history in our evolution. Rational thinking didn't show up until much later, probably less than half a million years ago. In Adam's case, this power of knowing is more advanced than in other people."

"And he's been keeping it from us?"

"Is that surprising? He's repeating his previous pat-

175

tern of not telling us when he begins to function on a higher level."

Riding in the car with Adam, Margaret was recalling Miles' words. They arrived in town and she parked in the public lot behind the savings bank.

"Where are we going first?" Adam asked.

"An army-navy store."

"Am I to dress like a soldier?" he asked smiling.

She smiled back. "Not if I can help it."

They got out of the car. Adam was attired in a yellow open sport shirt, casual slacks, and white sneakers. He moved with easy lazy grace. Quite a change from the wild boy. She was reminded of Locke's sock. Can we say that a sock, which has been mended and remended until it is finally all patches containing none of the original material, is the *same* sock? Does identity endure, or is there a succession of different selves? Little or nothing of the wild boy was left in Adam.

A few minutes later in the store she watched him try on a light blue Windbreaker jacket. He stood in front of a mirror with side panels and ran the zipper of the jacket up and down. Watching him, she was reminded again of the incident with the prostitute. It was a stupid thing to have done. His violent reaction was understandable. She wished that somehow the topic would come up so she could assure him that she had disapproved of the idea.

Adam came over to her. "Do you like this?"

"If you do."

He nodded. "I think so. How much is the price?"

"It's on the tag." She had made up her mind not to become involved in his decision-making.

"I'll take it."

Within an hour they had bought several more outfits, a sweater, some more slacks, a pair of moccasins, a corduroy shirt.

He said, "I do not wish to go over the budget."

She took four fifty-dollar bills from her purse and gave him the money. "See how close you came."

The cashier was a tanned blue-eyed young woman

in a blue T-shirt and candy-striped trousers. As she rang up the total, she gave Adam a frankly admiring glance. Adam looked embarrassed, and Margaret wondered: Can he tell what the girl is thinking?

The total was three dollars under the budget. Margaret put the change in her purse. As they were leaving the store, she told him, "You did very well. You can shop for your own clothes from now on."

"You are kind to me."

She reached up and put her hand to his cheek.

They walked slowly toward the parking lot.

He said unexpectedly, "I was not angry because I was being tested. What made me angry was being spied on."

"I wish there were a proper way to apologize for that. They will not replace the mirror, and there will be no more spying."

"To the others I am an experiment. Not to you."

"We are all fond of you, Adam. Truly." She had a feeling that she was like one of those divers taking off from the high cliffs at Acapulco, starting on a wild plunge down an abyss to where rocks grew like carnivorous teeth. "But we are all curious about how much progress you are making."

His head tilted to one side as he looked at her. He knows what I am going to ask, she thought.

"Did you know they were watching you?"

"Yes."

"How did you know?"

"A feeling. It formed in my mind."

"In the store, with the girl cashier just now, did you get a feeling of what she was thinking?"

He looked unhappy with the trend of the conversation. "A little. She was foolish. She is very young."

"She's older than you."

They reached the car, and Adam put the packages into the rear seat. As he turned to her, his smoky green eyes glowed with a cat's lambency.

He said, "I don't know how old I am."

— * * * —

When Jean Pierre locked up for the night he noticed that the key to the kitchen door was missing. The key was always in the jar marked *Cloves* on the second shelf of the cabinet near the door. Margaret must have forgotten to put it back after the groceries were brought in that afternoon. He would ask in the morning what she had done with it.

He did not need the key to lock up. He just turned the lock. Then he made certain all downstairs lights were out before going up to the second floor. He turned out a dim hallway light on the landing and climbed to his own apartment on the top floor. A small living room, a small bedroom, a private bath, a place for everything and everything in its place. He didn't have to go running around like a centipede with a hundred broken legs looking for something he needed.

Like the bottle of cognac. Jean Pierre always had a glassful before going to bed for the night. It helped him to sleep soundly. Other people counted sheep, but he had raised too many sheep for them to make him drowsy. He worried too much about them. He was relieved when Mr. Denning, Margaret's grandfather, began selling them off. There had been a fence around the property, but the dumb critters would somehow find a place in the fence where they could jump through and then the neighbor's dogs would fall on them and cut them up.

One time he had found a sheep torn up so bad he had to shoot it. That was not a chore he was partial to. Not at all partial. If he could have found the dog that did it, there would have been two shootings that day.

He sipped cognac to the half-empty mark before he turned out the overhead light. He didn't want anyone to know his late habits. With the lights out they would think him asleep. The farmhouse was totally dark. Only a sliver of moon illumined the yard. He was sipping the last of his cognac when he saw the reflection of a light from inside the kitchen. The light made the yard a little brighter for a second.

Then darkness returned.

Jean Pierre felt uneasy. The overhead kitchen light

178

would have lit up a whole rectangle in the yard and showed the bars of the windows. This was merely a quick probing; a light beam.

He moved quietly in his stockinged feet to look down the staircase.

A steady light beam was moving up the stairs. Then the beam was swallowed up inside the library on the second floor.

Probably Adam was sneaking around the house again. Jean Pierre still thought of him as the wild boy. He had never trusted him the way the others did. You couldn't take the wildness out of him any more than you could take the hump out of a man's back.

Jean Pierre descended halfway to the second-floor landing. The beam of light was moving around inside the library. He crept down to wait beside the door. He waited until the light beam went out. A minute later a denser shadow came out the door.

There was a strangled cry of surprise as Jean Pierre locked his arm around the crook of the intruder's neck. A flashlight dropped, rolled in an aimless semicircle on the floor, and stopped.

Someone turned on the hall light.

Jean Pierre was holding a young man who was trying vainly to free himself.

"What's going on?" Margaret was standing beside the switch she had turned on. She was wearing her robe.

"I catch a damn thief!" Jean Pierre said.

"I can't breathe!" the young man cried in a deep voice.

"Rory!" Margaret said. "What are you doing here?"

"Make him let me go!"

From inside Rory's short leather jacket a large notebook worked loose. Jean Pierre pulled it free with one hand.

"My journal!" Margaret said. "What could he possibly want with it?"

Rory was sagging lower in the punishing neck grip. His face had a purplish-red color. He whimpered.

"Let him go," Margaret said.

Jean Pierre released his hold. Rory bent over, doubling at the waist before slumping to his knees. "Jeez!" he said.

"I'm waiting to hear what you are doing in my house," Margaret said. "How did you get in?"

Rory did not answer.

"Search him, Jean Pierre."

From a pocket of Rory's leather jacket, Jean Pierre removed a miniature camera.

"That's mine!" Rory said sullenly. "I didn't steal it!"

Margaret examined the camera. "We'd better call Sheriff Hamilton."

"They damn well put him in jail," Jean Pierre said with satisfaction.

Rory blurted, "I was looking for *him*!"

"Who?" Margaret asked.

"You know." Rory stared at her with a hangdog defiance. "You still got him around here somewhere. He didn't disappear like you said."

"So you broke into my house with an expensive foreign-made camera and tried to steal my journal. That doesn't make sense, Rory."

Adam, Miles, and Don appeared on the landing.

Adam said, "I can find out the truth if you want me to."

"Who's this guy?" Rory demanded.

"I call the sheriff now, okay?" Jean Pierre volunteered.

"Wait a minute." Margaret nodded to Adam. "Go ahead."

Rory stood his ground defiantly as Adam moved close to him. Every muscle in Rory's body seemed anxious to move back. "Don't you hit me," he warned in a sepulchral croak.

Adam merely raised his hand. Rory seemed to rock back on his heels. When he returned to a level stance, his head was as rigid as if held in a brace and his eyes were very wide and staring.

"Why did you come to the house tonight?" Adam asked.

"They told me to." Rory's voice sounded as if he were talking from a great distance.

"Who told you?"

"The men."

"How many?"

"Two."

"Who were they?"

"They're from the government. FBI. They were tryin' to find out about the wild boy. The one who lives here."

What was happening mystified Jean Pierre. He had heard about hypnosis but did not believe in it. Mumbo jumbo. He had once seen a woman hypnotized onstage by a professional hypnotist, but he dismissed the crazy things that had happened as part of the act.

"Can you describe the two men?" Adam asked.

Rory's forehead wrinkled with concentration. "One had red hair. The other was big and kinda baldy."

Adam turned to Margaret. "Can we go into the library?"

Inside the library Margaret turned on the light. Adam guided Rory to the large round table where Rory sat down as stiffly as a wind-up toy.

"Pencil and paper, please." Adam placed the paper before Rory, the pencil vertically along its edge. "I want you to picture these men very clearly in your mind. And I want you to draw exactly what you see."

Adam placed the pencil in Rory's grasp. Obediently Rory began making scrawls on the paper. The scrawls vaguely resembled a human face.

"He doesn't know how to draw." Adam drew up a chair and sat beside Rory, took the pencil into his own hand. "Start again and think hard about those men."

Rory seemed asleep although his eyes remained wide open. Adam put Rory's hand on top of his own and began to draw velvety lines, thin here, broad there, carefully shading in certain areas. A face emerged, heavy-jawed, with a thick neck and receding hair. Every line, every detail was photographic. Adam's fingers
181

continued moving, putting in another line on the face, making a tiny elongation of the mouth, adding a mole.

A few minutes later he drew another face to go with the first. The second face was long and narrow and had a high comb of hair rising in front, a suggestion of freckles.

"Is this the one with red hair?" Adam asked.

Rory nodded. His eyes were open so wide that Jean Pierre thought the whites were bulging from the sockets.

"What did the men tell you to do?" Adam asked.

"Put the thing in the telephone."

Don picked up the telephone from the library table. He unscrewed the mouthpiece and removed a circular ring that had been screwed into place beneath it.

Jean Pierre's head began to ache.

"Anything else?" Adam asked.

"Take pictures."

"Did you?"

"Only thing I found was her notebook. I couldn't photograph all the pages. So I took it."

"I call the sheriff now?" Jean Pierre asked.

Don said dryly, "This isn't a simple police matter. If those men are from the FBI, there's more to it."

Miles said, "They're not from the FBI."

"Then who are they?" Margaret asked.

"I don't know."

Jean Pierre's headache was getting worse. "What we do with this fella?"

Miles turned to Adam. "Can you make him forget what happened with those two men?"

Adam nodded.

"What's the point of that?" Margaret asked.

"It will give us time to check. If they're not from the FBI, some real FBI men will want to talk to Rory."

"I'm not sure we want the FBI in on this," Don said.

"We have no choice," Miles answered. "This whole thing is getting too complicated for us to handle alone."

The next morning at McNamen's Food Market, Rory was busy until ten o'clock. Then he drove off in the van to make his deliveries. He completed his last delivery at noon. His next stop was the Friendly Ice Cream Shoppe, where his girl Marian was a waitress. They kidded around for a while. He told her he was going over to the park and test his new model plane, a B-52 Stratofortress.

"It's got J-57 turbojets and everything. Those babies carry regular bombs and nuclear."

"Maybe you'll take me for a ride in it someday," Marian said.

Rory liked her because she had a swell sense of humor.

"Anytime you say, honey," he came right back. "How about a movie tonight?"

"I don't know."

"It's the new Robert Redford."

"Okay."

"Just keep in mind, honey, he ain't gonna come down off that screen and ask you to marry him."

Always leave 'em laughing, he thought as he went out. Before he reached the luncheonette's parking area, a man stepped away from the side of the building. He had a long narrow face with a high comb of red hair.

"Hello, Rory."

Rory thought he must be a customer at McNamen's but he knew most of the regulars.

"Hi."

"Do you like your new model plane? The B-52?"

"Neat." Word certainly did get around, Rory thought. He had told only a few close friends about his new acquisition.

"How did everything go last night? Did you do what you were told?"

"Sorry, mister, if this is a joke I don't get it."

The man's lips thinned. "I'm in no mood to play games."

"I don't know what you're talking about."

The man took his arm in a tight grip.

"Did you get into the house?"

183

"What house? Lemme alone, will ya?" Rory tried to pull his arm free.

"If you're trying a double cross, you'll be sorry."

"Mister, I never saw you before in my life."

"The camera," the man hissed. "The phone tap. What did you do with them?"

"I ate them."

The slap stung his face.

"What the *hell*?" Rory stared at the man unbelievingly as he felt the sting on his face. A man and two women came out of the luncheonette, busy in conversation. Rory looked toward them, thinking to call for help.

The grip on his arm tightened further.

"I wouldn't if I were you," the man said.

"Jesus! What are you picking on me for? Are you nuts?"

The three people, chatting, were still coming toward them. Suddenly the grip on Rory's arm slackened.

"Just remember," the man said, "to keep your mouth shut."

Rory was quiet as the others got into a Dodge Mirada in the luncheonette parking lot. The two women were laughing at something their companion said. They were close enough for Rory to hail if he wanted to. But he watched them drive away. The red-haired man was scary and there was no telling what he might do.

"So you decided not to go through with it," the man said. Freckles stood out on his pale face. "You won't get away with this. That I promise you."

He turned and walked away. Rory watched him go around the side of the building. A minute later a silver-gray Mercedes emerged and sped out of the parking lot.

Rory stood still, wondering if he should go back in the luncheonette and tell Marian what had happened. Maybe even call the sheriff about his strange encounter with the red-haired man. But there didn't seem much point. There wasn't anything anybody could do, and the sting in his cheek reminded him that he had not

184

cut a particularly heroic figure. He just hoped no one, especially not Marian, had seen him get his face slapped like that.

He had two hours before he had to go back to relieve old man McNamen for lunch. Time enough for him to try out his new model plane. Queer that the red-haired man had known about that. But everything about the red-haired man was pretty queer.

For just a moment Rory was puzzled about his new model plane. It was pretty expensive and he wasn't quite sure how he had come to be in possession of it. The question floated around in his mind without making a connection with an answer. The answer was there somewhere, but for the moment it slipped his mind.

He got into the van, started it up, and drove slowly west on Ethan Allen Highway, headed toward the park. He turned on the radio. Rick Springfield was singing one of his good ones. Rory beat on the wheel in time with the music. A few minutes later he drove the van into the small parking area adjoining the open grassland.

As soon as the B-52 Stratofortress model was airborne, Rory maneuvered it into a steady climb. It climbed high above the trees. Then he brought it around and back in a steady bombing run. Nearing the target.

Bombs away!

The model plane, freed of its imaginary burden, veered up and away. Up, up—to where the gigantic mushrooming atomic cloud would present no danger.

Up, up...

He was annoyed by a buzzing sound from the hand transmitter. He shook it, shifted the dial back and forth, but couldn't get rid of the buzzing. He opened it to check the batteries. Everything seemed normal.

When he looked back, the Stratofortress was still ascending, headed out over the treetops. Immediately he flashed a signal to turn.

The Stratofortress held its course, ascending as

though all its J-57 turbojets were at full thrust. Rory again commanded the plane to turn.

Up and up.

He cursed and began sending other instructions. But he was no longer in communication. The plane sailed on and on, climbing and dwindling into the distance.

The silver-gray Mercedes was parked almost at the edge of the open grassland.

Rory stared at it, expecting the red-haired man to emerge. Why would the man follow him? The windshield of the Mercedes was the kind that darkened against the sun glare, and he could not make out anyone inside.

Then a side window rolled down halfway and something flashed out. Rory tilted his head to follow it.

Because its speed was constant, the long, finned cylinder seemed almost suspended in air. Its engine gave a high-pitched whining sound. Admiringly, Rory watched the rocket until he realized it was headed toward him on a collision course.

He took a step or two to the side, then broke into a jog, looking back. The rocket altered direction to follow him. He ran faster, his heart pumping. The rocket accelerated. With peripheral vision he saw it closing in on him like a giant angry hornet. Suddenly he dropped flat down on his face in the grass.

The rocket zoomed low. He felt its heated passage on his head and neck.

Somebody get me outta this!

The whining sound of the rocket passed over him. He rolled over, got up and raced toward the woods. He had gone no more than twenty feet when he heard a swift accelerated whine. The rocket returned, passing between him and the trees.

He took a step back, then another, turned and ran in the other direction.

This time he headed for the side of the parking area where he had left the van. Before he reached it the rocket reappeared, flying almost level with him a short distance away. He saw its powerful sleek curves and stubby wings.

He cut sharply right, then left again, but the rocket followed him with only a second's delay. Some crazy son of a bitch was getting his kicks! Now the rocket was surging up beside him. He could almost touch it with his left hand.

His van was only a dozen feet away. There was no time to open the door. He fell hard and rolled quickly beneath the undercarriage. He scraped his hands on the concrete and jolted his head on the undercarriage. Dazed, he lay still while a small trickle of blood moved down his forehead and splattered on the bridge of his nose.

From his hiding place beneath the van he could see the silver-gray Mercedes parked across the way.

"Hey!" he yelled loudly. "What are you trying to do, you stupid pisshead?"

There was no answer.

Quickly he rolled out of his hiding place. He had planned his move carefully. The van concealed him from the Mercedes across the way. He flung open the van door and jumped into the driver's seat. An instant later the ignition key was in and the motor revved up. He jammed down on the gas pedal. The van lunged forward and he spun the wheel.

As the van turned he saw the rocket—dead ahead and coming at him on a ballistics trajectory. His chest muscles constricted with terror.

BASTARD!

The rocket zoomed in shrilling like a train whistle. It crashed through the windshield.

Combustible chemicals in the payload went off at impact. The front of the van was engulfed in flames.

With scorched, shock-paralyzed hands Rory kept trying to turn the wheel as he pushed down on the gas pedal.

Flames hit the gas line. The explosion raced back to the tank.

He never heard the roar of the explosion that killed him.

Miles found the man he was looking for without difficulty. Neatly attired, an attaché case under his arm, Yarosh was standing at the far end of the railway platform looking at a poster ad for Caribbean holidays.

"It would be nice," Yarosh said as Miles came up to him, "just to get away from everything and lie in the sun."

"Israel has a warm climate."

"I can't wait to go back. I've been here four years. Too long."

They sat on a bench under the protection of a wooden overhang. No one was on the platform. The next train wasn't due to arrive for fifty minutes.

Yarosh unlocked his attaché case. The case was attached to his wrist with a chain and steel band.

"Do you speak Yiddish?" Yarosh inquired.

"What a question."

"Some people in our country consider it the language of the Diaspora," Yarosh said, effortlessly switching into Yiddish. "Something of which the Jews had to divest themselves, along with the Exile."

"I never spoke a word of Hebrew until I went to Israel to live," Miles replied in Yiddish. "I could barely read a sign in Hebrew. I had to have a rabbi teach me. And now I'm afraid I'm forgetting everything."

"That's too bad. Hebrew is beautiful."

"Beautiful, but it lacks enough ordinary words for conversation. It's for writing, with dictionaries. But why are we speaking Yiddish?"

"An extra precaution. There are lip readers who with binoculars might pick up a conversation at a distance. I have something for you."

From the attaché case Yarosh removed the sketches Adam had made of the two men. "These are very exact. We had no trouble identifying the man with the bull neck as Hans Diederich. The one with red hair is Otto Strauss. They work for East German intelligence."

"The KGB?"

"Everyone makes that mistake. Eastern European countries have their own intelligence agencies. They are not just paws of the Russian bear. Strauss and Diederich have been working in this country. They are good operatives. Long on technology, short on understanding human nature. You take Strauss, he's by far the brighter of the two. An expert in miniature rocketry, but with a rather simplistic view of people. He thinks everyone can be bought or intimidated."

"You don't agree."

"People who are bought or intimidated do not remain loyal. There is always someplace they can sell their services for more, or they can be intimidated by someone who is more frightening."

"Did these men have anything to do with the accident yesterday in which that boy was killed?"

"It was not an accident. In some way they found out he was no longer to be counted on."

Miles made an abrupt gesture of rejection. "I want no more of it. I'm not meant to be a spy. What for?"

"To keep a watch on Adam," Yarosh said mildly.

"What do you want to know? He's learned more in a few months than an ordinary person will learn in a lifetime. Does that sound absurd? It's true. I don't believe even he has the power to control what's going on. It will keep happening. There you are. A full report. The last you get from me."

Yarosh replied calmly, "Your description of how he got those sketches was interesting. That talent would be extremely useful in our line of work. So far, however, nothing proves that Adam is unique. There are chess wizards, lightning calculators, and hypnotists—even mind readers. What we're looking for are abilities that transcend anyone else's. The kind that might be worth the effort and risk involved in seizing him and hiding him from the rest of the world."

"Such games are not for scientists."

"Swenson has been keeping Ted Bristol and his Committee informed. They are watching Adam. So are

Diederich and Strauss. Others will soon be involved. The KGB. The Chinese. Would you rather see Adam in their hands?"

"If big powerful countries want to destroy each other, they don't need my help."

Yarosh smiled. "Sometimes we feel the same way. We are a small nation, surrounded on every side by enemies. And with very few friends. Israel wishes only to survive. We do not wish to destroy anyone. If Adam's future were in our hands, the world would not move closer to war."

"What are you suggesting?"

"Our interests are close to those of the United States, but they are not identical. In fact, we have had some surprises lately. We sincerely hope it is a temporary disagreement among friends, but we are increasingly worried about our own security."

"So you'd like me to give up spying for this country and do it for you."

"You don't have to choose now. Just continue working as you have. In that matter you have no choice. The Security Bureau needs you more than ever. But the time may come when you wish to choose. In that event, contact me directly. Call this number."

"Everyone spying on everyone else. It's a crazy business."

"It's a crazy world," Yarosh said.

In the morning Jean Pierre asked for the day off, muttering something about visiting a friend. Margaret knew where he was going. He got onto his motorbike, a plain no-frills machine that had no automatic starter or gears and a maximum speed of under twenty miles an hour. He made a tight circle in the yard, avoiding ruts while getting up momentum to move slowly out onto the road.

Margaret went into the barn. Adam loved to do chores around the farm, and this morning he was to milk the cow. He placed the stool and positioned the bucket beneath the cow's udder. Before he began the milking he touched the cow's plump body with his hand reassuringly. Thereafter the cow never moved, not even to switch its tail. Some form of communication was going on. There were always things going on with Adam that she could not interpret fully, and some that she was missing entirely.

Adam began to work the cow's teats. She watched until the bucket was three-quarters full and the spattering milky stream from depleted teats had dwindled to a trickle.

Then she said casually, "Those math problems I gave you to solve yesterday were taken from doctoral examinations at Princeton University."

"How did I do?"

"None of the doctoral candidates scored more than ninety percent. Your score was perfect."

"But you are not pleased."

"I had looked up the answers. They were in math symbols, but I did see them. I wonder if you might have been picking up my thought projections."

"I didn't need to."

"But you could have."

"Yes."

"The other day when we were shopping you told me you get a 'feeling' about what people are thinking. Are you getting clearer pictures now—ideographs?"

Adam's fingers kept working the cow's teats. "I wish you would not question me this way."

"I want to know how far your ability to read minds has progressed. Do you see other people's thoughts as pictures or in words?"

"Not in words. Not in pictures. Symbols would be nearer."

"How about abstract thoughts? I am thinking one now." She thought: Honesty is the best policy. "What did you get?"

Adam stood up, lifting the almost full bucket. "Nothing."

"You're not telling me the truth."

"I am. When I wish to I can shut off my mind."

"Then it's a power you control at will."

"I would not like to talk about it anymore."

They walked away from the barn over ground that was soft from recent rains. Her shoes made squishing sounds. Adam walked so lightly that he seemed to leave no mark on the soggy turf.

That evening Margaret was reading in her room and listening to the rushing sound of heavy rain splashing from the gutters and beating against windows and walls. A strong wind was blowing, and loose things were rattling everywhere. It had been raining for some time. When she looked out the window small lakes had formed in the backyard and were lapping at the barn door and the chicken house. Adam, wearing a storm hat and long green slicker and wading boots, was carrying logs and feed bags to barricade the entrance to the henhouse.

She got up and dressed hurriedly in boots and raincoat and a plastic cap pulled down over her hair. She helped Adam to drag logs through water that was already ankle-deep. No rain could have caused this, she thought. The creek must have overflowed its banks. Unknown to her, the ground at one place near the creek had split to let a cascade go racing through and over rain-soaked ground no longer able to absorb moisture.

When she returned for more logs, she had to plant her feet carefully against the swirl and pull of the current. A darkly gleaming log bounced down from the top of a small pyramid. She barely got out of its way. It floated beyond her, turning slowly in foot-deep water.

Lightning broke with a blinding flash overhead and the resulting clap of thunder was simultaneous. The sound had physical force; she was staggered by it. As she stepped back, a vicious swirling torrent caught her and brought her to her hands and knees. She was rolled over and carried along by another powerful surge. She tried to force herself up; her raincoat had torn and was hindering her. She scrabbled with her hands for support, but the ground was no longer in reach. Her fingers grasped at nothing.

Flash flood!

She rolled over, came up sputtering and coughing, gasping to get air into her lungs. Desperately she flailed her arms to gain balance against the pummeling current, got her feet under her, and took lunging steps in the direction of the flow. The ground was a quagmire and her boots stuck. She fought to free herself but the wrenching effort turned her toward the oncoming flood. She was knocked over and lay on her back half submerged. A heavy log rose on a surging wave. She raised her arms to protect herself. A numbing shock struck her arms, pushed them aside, and a jarring blow struck her chest and drove her underwater again. She saw darkness splintered with light; she was drowning.

Suddenly she felt herself lifted out of the water. Adam was her rescuer; she clung to him, clawing and struggling to pull herself up.

He put his mouth close to her ear. "Can you walk?"

She nodded dazedly. Holding her tightly about the waist with his arm, he half-carried her back to the house.

Jean Pierre rolled over soddenly in bed. He touched the corpulent nakedness of the woman sleeping beside him. "Eh, Pierre?" she said drowsily. She thought that he wanted her again.

The alcohol which had first given him a warm feeling of relaxation was now making him restless. He reached out and took her large fleshy buttock in one hand. Françoise was a woman of the right proportion and quality. They had been lovers for eighteen years. They were both good Catholics and she had married in the Church and had a husband who was still alive and three children who were grown up, so there was no possibility of marriage.

Usually he could fall asleep holding her buttock, which gave him a sense of capaciousness and abundance. But tonight sleep would not come. In moments he rolled onto his back. The air in the room was thick and muggy and pressed down on him like warm wet

193

feathers. His skin prickled with perspiration. A flash of lightning lit up the bedroom, followed a moment later by rolling rumbling thunder.

Françoise woke up and put her hands to her ears. The frame walls shook. They were on the second floor of the building, and the feed store was beneath.

"A bad one," she said.

"One hell of one," he told her, and thought of the ground at the farm soaked through with previous rains. If the creek kept rising, everything would be flooded.

He sat up. "I have to go."

"It's late. And there's a bad storm coming."

"Those people at the farm don't know what to do." He had worked for city people before. A woman had rented the farm from Margaret's father after he left. Along with truck and dairy farming, they were still raising a few sheep. She came to him in the middle of one night to plead, "Jean Pierre, come quickly. The poor little ewe is in terrible pain." He got up, on the coldest night, and went to the barn to find that the ewe was just having a lamb, the way nature meant her to. The woman insisted on helping the "poor thing." The woman ran up with a towel to wipe off the newborn lamb because she was sure it would freeze. She didn't care that she was removing the smell so that the ewe mother couldn't identify her lamb. Later the ewe mother would butt her own lamb and try to get rid of it. City people!

His motorbike was parked inside the front door of the feed store. He revved it up and started. He was five minutes under way when the rain came down in torrents. The bike wobbled in the strong wind, its engine chugging. The headlight was weak and he could barely make out the puddles rapidly forming on the dirt road. The bike splashed through, sending up fans of spray.

He hit the brake on the way down a hill, but the bike started to wobble and then toppled over in mud at the bottom. He had trouble starting the stalled engine. He had to dismount and walk the bike up the hill.

By then he knew he had made a mistake to set out on this journey. But going back was as difficult as going

194

forward. He got the engine started again but he was unable to see more than a few feet ahead. The road was slippery, and he fell and hurt his knee. He got up, spitting back at the rain. His trouser was torn at the knee and he could see blood that thinned out as the rain struck it.

He gunned the engine and the bike lurched along an asphalt road that led to the bridge. When he got there the river was swollen and water was pouring over the bridge. Part of the guardrail had broken. Some damn flood! He could make it across if he kept the bike at full throttle and steered hard against the current washing over the bridge.

He stamped on the pedal. The engine sputtered, coughed, and died. He could not start it again. The engine was soaking wet so there was no ignition. He laid the bike carefully down on its side and started back.

Françoise would certainly tell him what a fool he had been. But the thought of the warm dry bedroom and her richly welcoming body urged him on. If he kept putting one foot down after the other, he would be all right. One who had the patience to endure was always all right.

A car loomed as a black indistinct shape out of the rain, its headlight beams shimmering as if shining underwater. He lifted his arm to signal, at the same time stepping aside in case the driver did not see him or decided to pass him by.

The car stopped and its rear door opened. A man with oddly slanted eyes regarded Jean Pierre coldly. He spoke in a single hissing breath: "It is such bad weather. Please get in."

He was holding a gun aimed directly at Jean Pierre's heart.

Outside the farmhouse the rain continued with diminishing force, and occasional gusts of wind still rattled doors and windows.

Margaret was relaxing in a warm tub. She was feeling much better. Now that the danger was behind her, she could view the hectic events of the evening in a new perspective. It had been an adventure. No one was hurt and Adam had proved himself in a crisis.

Someone knocked on the door of the bathroom.

"You okay?" Don asked.

"Yes, I'm fine."

"I was just checking up. Good night."

"Good night."

She lay back in the warm bath, laving her thighs. Don always said a warm bath put her into an erotic mood. An important part of their relationship had been sexuality. She had not allowed a man to make love to her since. How long ago? No matter. She did not count the time in weeks or months, but in frustration—which has a calendar of its own.

She thought about Adam. A charming young man with the inexplicable magnetism of strangeness. When he was older few women would be able to deny him anything.

She had never wished anything more for him than to become a normal human being, but he had quickly bypassed what most people would consider normal. The saddest thing is that he cannot, or will not, confide what he feels. I am sure he could do so eloquently. I would hold his secrets safe.

Heat seemed to emanate from the region of her bruised chest and rise into her cheeks. There had undeniably been an extra titillation for her these past weeks in the possibility that (if she were not wise enough, on guard enough, aware enough that he was too young) something more might be added to their relationship.

As she got out of the bath and wrapped herself in a large white fluffy towel, she advised herself strongly to think of something else. She thought of the fireplace in the living room. An excellent idea.

The living room was deserted; logs and kindling and paper were ready in the fireplace. She lit a match to the crumpled paper and watched the flame sprout several tongues. At the liquor cabinet she chose an outsize goblet and filled its bottom with brandy.

Sitting on the sofa in her bathrobe, she sipped brandy and watched the fire leaping.

"I didn't know you were here."

Adam was in the doorway. He wore open-necked blue pajamas and a gray bathrobe.

And then, unbidden: I have to be careful, for he can read minds.

She said, "I thought you were asleep."

"I was thirsty."

There was always a gallon jug of well water in the refrigerator. Early memories still showed themselves in his new persona, and his craving for fresh water was one of them. When he was about to drink crystal-clear well water, his lips pursed with expectancy—like a connoisseur about to sample an exquisite vintage wine. Sometimes he would hold up a glass of water to admire its speckless purity against the light. She believed his fascination with fresh drinking water derived from early unpleasant memories of tepid tropical water defiled by mud and insects and vegetable matter.

"Come in and sit by the fire." A foolish invitation, which she amended quickly. "On one condition."

"Yes?"

"You can stop reading other people's thoughts. Would you mind turning off now? I don't want to be around anyone perceptive at the moment."

He entered the room. His feet were bare. He liked to walk in bare feet. Another throwback to an earlier time.

"You are afraid of something," he said.

Her small laugh sounded brittle. "Do you have to ask? Can't you read my mind?"

He looked puzzled. "You asked me not to."

"So I did. I appreciate that, Adam."

He sat down cross-legged on the floor and looked into the fire. His expression was not readable. It isn't fair. He can read my mind at will and I know nothing of what he is thinking.

197

"Why do you hide things from me?" she asked.

"What things?"

"You know."

He answered quietly, "Because I do not want you to worry."

"I do worry sometimes. Tell me. If you could stop the whole process right where you are, would you?"

The shaman crying: No more. No more. Not good!

"I don't think so."

"I can sense that we are growing apart. You're drifting away from me."

He seemed about to say something, then did not.

She compelled herself to go on: "What I mean is that this may be one of the last times we can meet as equals."

"As equals?"

"As a woman—and a man." You damn fool, she accused herself. Putting it in words left her no avenue of retreat. Words continued to force their way out: "You said I was afraid of something, and I am. I'm afraid of losing you." She pushed back a loose tendril of hair. She knew how rosy she looked in the firelight, fresh from her bath. This doesn't mean I expect anything to happen, she told herself. A certain amount of fantasizing is allowed; one part of herself was tantalizing another part, that was all. "Come here and sit beside me."

He hesitated before doing as she asked. In a mysterious way she was now able to control his movements. She put down her brandy glass on the table, and firelight reflected in the brandy.

"Do you think I'm attractive?"

"Yes."

She wanted to please him with how she looked. It had been a long time since she had wanted to please a man in that way.

In the darkened living room the flame in the fireplace was consuming the logs. She felt heat being transferred to her body, altering the nature of her perceptions. The warmth of desire permeated every cell of her body. She was rapidly losing her ability to resist temptation.

The yellow flame danced, and she wanted to lie in its soothing light and let her naked body become illuminated. She wanted to immerse herself in flame and let it pour over her as warm water had in her bath.

She moved closer, advancing toward him without shame or timidity. He did not need special powers to read her intent. Her lips brushed his cheek, a touch so light he could barely have felt it. She kissed the hollow of his throat and let her lips glide along the underside of his jaw.

Slowly, an insistent voice warned; she did not wish to frighten or alarm him. Her fingertips caressed his hair and then moved down to make little circular motions under his earlobe. Suddenly his lips were demandingly on hers, with his own urgent message. He fumbled with the belt of her robe and it fell open, revealing her bare breasts. His hand took her full breast and gently rubbed her nipple.

She flinched.

He stopped, looking at the dark red bruise beneath her breasts.

"I'm sorry."

She lay back, her heart throbbing uncontrollably. He was coming closer and closer until his lean body flowed over her.

"I don't want to hurt you."

Take me. Hurt me if you must, but take me. I don't care about anything else.

"It's all right. *Really.*"

She was lost in the surge and swell of a need she could no longer contain. Her arms pulled him down. She was holding tight to him but her whole body was loosening, relaxing. She felt his full power. Darts of excitement began to shoot up her spine. As their bodies joined, she was imagining and experiencing his love at the same moment; it was bewildering and marvelous. His lithe body pressed her down and she felt his hardness stroking her. Her heart beat closely against him. She pushed upward to meet him as he rolled between her thighs.

199

Sheer yearning overwhelmed her. She closed her eyes, shuddering, as the delicious madness began. She was drowning in sensation. Consciousness flickered low, sinking down in rapid spirals.

A cry was rising in her throat.

It was all so perfect, so right, so...

At the door to the living room Don Swenson watched the leaping play of shadow and firelight. He raised one hand to his throat and held it in a tight grip.

A moment later he turned away and noiselessly climbed the stairs to his room.

chapter 15

Aunt Tillie's Antiques had gone out of business, and the small off-the-main-street frame building was vacant. The front door was closed with stout crossed planks, the windows taped over, and a faded *For Sale* sign was plastered to a side wall.

The building had no tenant, but was not unoccupied.

In a rear room with blacked-out windows, a portable electric heater glowed brightly. Jean Pierre's sodden clothes gave off wisps of steam that rose toward a large bare light bulb positioned above a plain wooden table. He sat across the table from a thin, older, saffron-faced man. Another man was on guard at the door. A third was positioned near the blacked-out window.

A gold tooth flashed when the thin older man opened his mouth. "You must not be afraid. We wish to be your friends."

"You bring me here with a gun to be friends?"

The thin man's voice was soft, almost disembodied. "I apologize for the inconvenience. When you hear what we have to say, I hope you will forgive us."

Jean Pierre recognized the patronizing tone and did not like it. These slant-eyed people were treating him as a simpleminded Canuck. It was bad enough to hear that tone from other people, but from this, this... Oriental, it sounded worse.

"I think you look for somebody else." He could speak better English but fell naturally into patois with these foreigners.

"We know who you are. We have been observing you for some time."

"If you know me, what is my name?"

"Jean Pierre Baptiste Robespierre Leclerc."

By damn. He'd never told anyone his full name.

"Okay. That's who I am. What you want?"

201

"To employ you."

Nothing that had happened tonight fit that idea.

"I don't need job. I look after farm."

The gold tooth flashed. "This will be very well paid. You will be able to own your own farm."

Jean Pierre was not an ambitious man, but he had a peasant's greed for land. Because he lacked money and land was expensive, his greed was impractical, so he had forced himself not to think of it.

"What I got to do?"

"A young man lives at the farmhouse where you work. We would like to know more about him." Thin lips quirked. "We rely on your cleverness to keep your eyes open and report what you see. To keep your ears open and report what you hear."

"That is all?"

"That is all."

Jean Pierre made a downward-dipping motion of his hand. "How much you pay for this?"

"A thousand dollars a week."

This was so much money that Jean Pierre's worst suspicions were aroused. They were trying to make a fool of him. They were probably spies. If he did what they asked, he would be hanged or put into the electric chair.

He decided to bargain. "Canadian dollars?"

The thin Oriental gave him a sharp look. "American. You can even be paid in gold."

"American dollars okay."

The thin older man gestured to the one standing guard at the blacked-out window. "We will drink on it. You like to drink, is it not so?"

The man left the room to return with a bottle of Canadian whiskey. Jean Pierre took a full-sized slug from the bottle. The fiery liquid felt good in his throat and right down to his stomach. You like to drink, is it not so? They were playing him for a fool all right.

"Now tell me what to do," he said.

The thin Oriental explained how he must report to them. Once a week at a certain hour he would step into a telephone booth and leave an envelope containing his report. He would leave and return a few minutes later to the booth to find another envelope with his money.

"I don't write good," he told them.

"Use your own words. We don't employ you as a writer. We want information." The thin Oriental was watching him carefully. "If you have something for us that is important, you may call a number from that same telephone booth at any time. We will get the message."

"What is the number?"

"In time." The voice remained low and melodious, but Jean Pierre heard something new in it.

"Can I go now?"

The thin Oriental man nodded gravely. He turned and spoke to the other two in the room. The man on guard at the door opened it, but not until the other turned out the light.

On the drive back, the atmosphere was distinctly less friendly. Jean Pierre could not recall a point in their discussion in which everything had begun to go the other way. But he was sure now they did not trust him.

It was raining heavily.

"Would you like us to take you to the farm?" asked the thin Oriental. "Or to where you left your machine?"

"The farm," Jean Pierre replied, and somehow this was the wrong answer.

The slanted eyes in the saffron face confronting him held a strange glimmer. "I hope you are not thinking that you will go back to your friends and tell them of our conversation."

"That would be crazy."

"Yes, it would," the thin Oriental said in a soft reflective monotone. "But I think this is precisely what you intend to do. It is so very difficult, learning to judge men. One has to watch for little things. A man accepting employment that will betray his friends does not bargain for pennies. Canadian dollars or American. That is for other types of bargaining. Is it not so?"

Jean Pierre felt a small thrill of fear. "I will do as you tell me."

"One must, in the end, trust one's instincts. There are no facts to put together to form a truth. It is a question of very delicate choices. One must depart from the path of logic in order to—I believe the Americans say, play a hunch. Not a strong hunch, but one which fits the situation as one understands it. One must do so because nothing else is left to rely on. One's choice may be wrong, but it is better to be wrong than sorry."

Jean Pierre did not understand what the Oriental was saying, but he knew that this man intended to do him harm. He had to act quickly to save himself. The men in the car had guns, but even as he warned himself about that he was in motion. He went for the thin man because he was nearest and the leader.

Jean Pierre got his hands on the skinny throat, and that cleared his own body of fear. He could wring this little neck in seconds.

The thin man was not as frail as he looked. He struggled like a caught hen and pulled Jean Pierre down into the space between the front and rear seats. His thumbs groped for Jean Pierre's eyes. Jean Pierre tightened his strangling hold. The thin man's gold tooth flashed as he gasped for breath.

At that moment the man in the front seat turned and hit Jean Pierre with the side of his hand. It was a small-wristed hand that one would not believe capable of delivering such a blow. Jean Pierre felt as if his head had been decapitated. His vision dimmed. Through a spinning gray spiral he tried to keep his strangling hold, but there was no strength left in his arms. Everything was swimming away from him in great noiseless strokes.

The hand struck again.

Darkness came down like a shield over Jean Pierre's eyes.

Don Swenson put up a pot of water to boil. Then he broke an egg on the edge of the frying pan and began

204

to stir up a scrambled egg for himself—forgetting to put in the butter. As he was stirring up the egg, he remembered that he had put out an orange to be sliced and forgotten to slice it.

He was nervous and preoccupied and depressed. He looked at his watch, wondering when Margaret would wake up and how he would act when he saw her. He had no right to be accusatory. He had no rights with her at all, not any longer. The divorce decree had made that too painfully clear. *The parties shall continue to live separate and apart for the rest of their lives. Each shall be free of interference, direct or indirect, by the other.*

From the first he had been sure that their lives were bound together, that neither could ever go separate ways again.

He had asked for a divorce only because he expected her to refuse, dispute, plead with him, and amid tears and threats and recriminations demonstrate once and for all that he was as necessary to her as she was to him. That stratagem had clearly not worked.

To others he appeared in control of himself, but his emotional history seemed to him one of continually varying emotions and moods: now full of hope, now despairing, now sure of his work's worth, now ready to abandon work, now passionately in love, now rejected and bitter. How was he to deal with the loss of Margaret's love? He might learn to live with it, but never to cope with it.

When he received Margaret's cable asking him to meet her at the ship's dock, he thought fate was giving him another chance. He was living with a young woman at the time, but he had never deceived her or told her he loved her. The joy had already gone out of their simple physical mating. The day he received Margaret's cable, he informed the young woman (her name was Elizabeth) that she would have to make other arrangements. Not for him the lingering sentiment, the rueful backward glance. Margaret's message was a summons to life.

A ship's horn was sounding on the fog-shrouded harbor as he reached the dock. When he glimpsed her on the deck of the *Malmö Explorer* he was shaken by the joy and cruelty of reawakened desire. She was the only woman he had ever truly loved.

From that moment his central need was to possess her again. She had put him out of her heart, but there was enough in their past that he could exploit to win her back. He was chained to her by a desire that surprised him by its genuineness and intensity. He wanted to explore all the facets of his renewed passion, discover the contours of it, penetrate to the heart of it, know it in all its extremes.

He sat down at the kitchen table in the farmhouse before a plate of scrambled eggs and toast. Last night's experience had been nerve-tearing; in the dark, watching the yellow blaze of light from the fireplace, he imagined her wide eyes steady with attention on Adam's face as their bodies linked, remembering how her head fell back in sensual abandon and her body began to turn and twist as though to rid itself of a burden. As the first strangled cries were torn from her throat, "Ahhh...Ahhhhhh," the gorge rose in his own throat, choking him, and he was compelled to leave.

Now, sitting calmly in the kitchen in sane morning light, he realized that last night he had been quite irrational, a naked ape ruled more by primitive neural structures than by his thinking forebrain. He was in control again, capable of reevaluating his priorities. The success of the Adam Project was no longer most important to him. Most important was getting Adam away from Margaret by whatever means he could.

A forkful of scrambled eggs was halfway to his mouth when he heard a car stop outside the house. He put the fork down carefully on his plate and left the kitchen. Through the window of the living room he saw a chauffeur opening the rear door of a White Cloud sedan.

He answered the knocker. The woman who entered was wearing a chamois-colored, fringed suede poncho, matching suede trousers, and knee-high copper-brown boots.

"Miss Margaret Denning, please," she said as she came in.

Margaret entered the living room. "What brings you back, Miss De Wein?"

"Perhaps this will explain."

She handed Margaret a letter. Margaret looked at it while Don was helping Cornelia De Wein out of her poncho.

Margaret handed the letter to Don. The letter was on the official stationery of the Boston Museum.

> *Dear Miss De Wein:*
>
> *You have long been a valuable and esteemed contributor to the funding of the Division of Anthropology and Archeology of this museum. I feel sure that you will want to assist in the important, ongoing work that is now being done with the so-called wild boy of New Guinea. This project, under the guidance of famed anthropologist Margaret Denning, is now moving toward a successful conclusion.*
>
> *What the Museum is proposing to do is make a film based on this attempt to educate and train the boy so there will be an imperishable record for the future. This can only be carried out by generous contributions from individuals like yourself.*
>
> *We will need to gather material from many different sources, including a photographic journey to the Mondugami pygmy tribe which captured the wild boy. The film will balance anthropological concerns with film-making techniques and the cataloguing of primitive behavior, both among the pygmies*

> *and, specifically, in the story of the wild boy. The story of the boy's change from a primitive to a completely modern man is a truly inspirational theme.*
>
> *We solicit your help. I can assure you that the disbursement of any monies you contribute will be my solemn responsibility.*
>
> Yours very truly,
> James Halas

Margaret turned to Cornelia. "You came all this way on the basis of this letter?"

"I began to wonder if the boy has actually undergone a transformation."

"I'm afraid Mr. Halas has a tendency to exaggerate. I told him we were making progress. I certainly didn't anticipate that he would exploit it in this fashion."

"I'd like to judge for myself."

"Frankly, I don't think that would..."

"He's outside," Don volunteered. "Clearing up after the flood we had last night."

Margaret gave him an accusing look.

Cornelia moved to a window that gave a view of the backyard, where Adam was dumping loose twigs and branches into a heaped-up pile. Watching her, Don was dry-mouthed with excitement. If Cornelia was sufficiently impressed by Adam's progress, her imagination might again be captured by the improbable idea that Adam was her long-lost nephew.

Her voice had a small catch of surprise: "Is this the same boy I saw before?"

"The same."

"It hardly seems possible." Cornelia turned to Margaret. "You are to be congratulated."

"Thank you."

"Does he have a name?"

"Adam."

"Adam. How nice." Cornelia opened her handbag, took a monocular from its slipcase, and affixed it to her right eye. At that moment, Adam looked directly at the window from which he was being observed.

Cornelia's fingers holding the monocular began to tremble. "I must meet him! I must talk to him!"

Margaret said, "That isn't part of our program."

"You don't understand. He bears a definite resemblance to my brother. A *definite* resemblance!" Cornelia was making no effort to control her impatience. "I want to see him up close. I want to question him!"

Margaret appeared to be caught short by Cornelia's eagerness. After a moment she replied, "Not unless I have your promise that you won't say or do anything to upset him."

"Yes. Yes!"

Margaret asked Don, "Will you tell Adam someone is here who is anxious to meet him."

Don went out and gave Adam the message.

Adam's hands were dirty from his yard work. "I'll clean up." He stopped to wash his hands at the water hose. Before he entered the kitchen he stamped his boots to shake off mud particles.

Don was making an effort not to show the hostility he felt. He had been struggling in vain to accept the fact that Adam and Margaret were lovers. It was a feeling of pressure, as though a heavy weight was pressing down on his chest.

They stopped in the doorway to the living room. Don watched Margaret for a reaction that would show a changed attitude toward Adam, but there was no clue in her expression. The strongest response came from Cornelia De Wein, who drew in a sharply-taken breath as soon as Adam entered the room.

She said, "My brother's eyes were green. A slightly different shade." She was looking at Adam intently. "Do you remember me at all? Do I seem in the least familiar to you?"

Adam shook his head.

"We may have known each other in the past, when you were only a small child."

"As a small child I did not know anyone."

209

"I'm sorry, Miss De Wein," Margaret said, "that's all of this I'm going to allow."

Cornelia ignored her. "How did you get your name?" she asked Adam.

Adam nodded toward Margaret. "She gave it to me."

"It is possible that someone else gave you another name a long time ago. Does the name Jacques mean anything to you?"

"Jacques?"

"Sometimes petit Jacques. Does that seem familiar?"

Adam's attitude turned wary. "No."

"I'm cutting short this interview," Margaret said.

"Please go away. Leave us alone," Cornelia said with a dismissing gesture. "Do you recall anything of your childhood?" she asked Adam.

"Very little."

Cornelia was still searching his face. "I mean when you were very young. Only three or four years old. Please try to remember. You were alone in the jungle. Ask yourself: How did I get there? You couldn't have survived as a helpless infant. There had to be someone to help you, look after you."

"There was no one."

"You had parents. They were with you. You were only a little child at the time. Everything can't have gone. Even little children have memories." Her tone was insistent; she seemed to be stressing each syllable.

"I do not remember."

"Your father's name was Philippe. I will show you his picture."

With trembling fingers she removed a small snapshot from her handbag. "There. Do you see the resemblance?"

Adam looked at the snapshot impassively.

"You loved your father very much," Cornelia said. "And he loved you."

"May I see?" Margaret asked, and Adam handed her the snapshot.

"The resemblance is quite marked, isn't it?" Cornelia asked. "The father and the son?"

Margaret studied the snapshot. "I'm afraid I can't agree."

Cornelia greeted this with incredulity. She took the snapshot and showed it to Don. He saw a man and a small boy standing on a lawn at the brink of a wide pond. His hopes fell. Adam had a slight resemblance to the boy in the photograph, but not much to the father. The notable likeness was between Philippe and Cornelia: the same patrician good looks bordering on arrogance.

"It's possible," he said.

"There. You hear? It's perfectly plain to anyone with eyes." Cornelia returned the snapshot to her handbag with a flourish of vindication.

"Dr. Swenson only said it was possible," Margaret pointed out. "Adam doesn't seem to remember you at all."

"The wild boy I saw before did not even recognize himself as a person. He was not an individual in the true meaning of the word. Little Jacques was a person. I think he is living inside this young man."

As the meaning of what Cornelia said impressed itself on Don's mind, he felt a fresh surge of hope. He thought exultantly: She will take Adam away with her.

Cornelia persisted: "You must have certain memories," she said to Adam. "Things buried in your subconscious. Have you ever flown in a plane?"

"No."

"Ah, then you are afraid of flying. Do you wonder why? Is it something you have forgotten, an accident? A plane crashed in that jungle where you were found. You may have been on it. Your terror would have been so great that it could block everything out of your mind."

Adam turned to Margaret. "I have a lot of work to do. I am leaving now."

Cornelia said with a note of triumph: "I believe you are my nephew, my dear brother Philippe's lost son."

"Does that matter?" Adam asked.

Cornelia blinked, then smiled. "Charming. It is natural that you should feel that way because you have

211

no experience of the real world. If you did, you would realize how very much it matters."

"It's been very nice to meet you, Miss De Wein."

"You can't go. Not until we've completed arrangements."

"What arrangements?" Margaret asked.

"I am prepared to accept that he is Philippe's son."

"You don't have much to go on."

"I have the evidence of my own eyes, the logic of where he was found, his age, my intuition. He is the legitimate heir to the De Wein fortune."

"And I am his legal guardian."

Their glances locked.

Don watched the conflict of wills, knowing the reason for Margaret's resistance and certain she would not prevail. Not even Margaret could keep Cornelia De Wein from having her way.

Cornelia's expression subtly hardened. "I will adopt him; he will be someone of consequence. One day he will take control of a great business empire—one that I have been managing since the death of his father. It will become his by right of inheritance."

"That may not be what he wants."

"How is he capable of making such a judgment? How can he know what is best for him?"

Don said to Adam, "What Miss De Wein is offering you is a very rare opportunity. If you go to live with her, you will have every possible advantage."

"But I will have to leave here."

"Yes," Cornelia said, "but you can continue to see your friends as often as you like—for as long as you like."

"I choose to stay here," Adam said.

Cornelia said sharply, "You cannot make such a decision."

"As far as I'm concerned," Margaret answered firmly, "he just made it."

"I will take you into court and prove you are an unfit guardian. You have been using this innocent young man in a controversial experiment. You will be fortunate if you do not go to prison. But whatever happens to you, this young man will become what he was born to be—a De Wein. With money enough to do whatever he wants."

Although Don was on Cornelia's side in this struggle, he resented her. Even her voice, the cultivated superior voice of those who are used to devouring the less fortunate, offended him. She was like an Etruscan shrew that has to eat its full body weight every day. Margaret and Adam were on today's menu.

"Will I be able to give it away?" Adam asked suddenly.

"Give what away?" Cornelia asked.

"This money you speak of."

"You could if you wanted to. But that will not happen. My brother Philippe also had radical ideas at your age." She turned to Margaret. "I see what kind of influence he will be subject to if he remains here. I will take him away as soon as possible."

"You can try."

Don watched Margaret with interest, her strong bones, her clear eyes, her thick springy hair. He admired the way she was doing battle in a lost cause.

"Goodbye for a while," Cornelia said to Adam. "Depend on it. I will be back shortly."

Adam said quietly, "You pretend you are trying to preserve a dynasty, but that is only a small part of your reason."

Cornelia looked a bit startled. "We will have a nice long discussion about such things when the time is right for it."

Adam said, "You do not feel safe. That is why you are here now. You have powerful enemies that you fear may take power from you."

For a moment Cornelia seemed disoriented; she glanced at Margaret as if to assure herself the attack did not come from her.

"This is ridiculous!" she said.

Adam went on: "Your associates don't like what is happening to the diamond market. They blame you for

213

letting Israeli cutters build up a stockpile of precious stones. They blame you for Zaire, the largest diamond-producing country, breaking away to form its own syndicate."

"You've been reading lies in the business journals. I have no reason to fear…"

"Now there are the Australians. With their newly discovered diamond mines they can dominate the world market."

"Those reports are exaggerated. Besides, this has nothing to do with you and me." She gave a bright false smile. "If you are trying to make me angry it will not work. I have no reason to be angry with you, dear Jacques."

"Having someone to carry on the De Wein name would help you to retain power. The family dynasty would not end with you."

"You are a parrot reciting what you do not understand," Cornelia said with a shade less conviction.

"You need an ally, and who better than the son of Philippe, the man you loved better than anyone."

"You presume."

"Did Philippe's wife know?"

"What? What are you saying?"

"You were forced to have an abortion. The genetic risks were too great for a child born of brother and sister."

An exclamation broke from Cornelia's lips. As she picked up her handbag she spilled half its contents onto the floor. Then she seemed uncertain of what to do.

Adam stooped to pick up her things from the floor.

"Don't touch them! I don't want you touching anything of mine!" She stooped to pick up her own things, including a snapshot of Philippe and his son. She held the snapshot to her breast for a moment before putting it back into her bag.

She stood up: her mask had slipped to reveal a thoroughly dismayed and frightened woman. The abrupt reversal left Don with a sharp sense of frustration.

She said to Margaret, "You've made him a monster
214

as unfit to live in this world as he was before! I want nothing to do with him or you—ever!"

She snatched up her poncho from the armchair and flung it over her arm. Her back was stiff as she went out the front door.

Moments later the White Cloud sedan departed, so swiftly one might have thought it was fleeing a house haunted by an accusing ghost.

Inside the living room the telephone rang.

"Miss Denning? This is Sheriff Hamilton. You'd better come to the hospital right away."

"The hospital?"

"It's the man who works for you. We found his body floating in the river an hour ago."

Don accompanied her to the hospital, and Sheriff Hamilton led the way through stone-walled basement rooms to the morgue. An attendant in a short white coat was having lunch at a small table outside the door. He got up quickly, wiping his mouth with a handkerchief. Sheriff Hamilton showed his badge and said whom they had come to see.

The attendant pulled out a flat slab from a wall niche. A sheet was covering the body. The feet were uncovered and a tag was attached to the big toe.

The attendant pulled back the sheet from Jean Pierre's face. He looked as composed as though he were sleeping. But no sleeping person had ever lain so still. Margaret turned away, refusing to acknowledge this last encounter with the friend of her youth. She was overwhelmed by images out of her past: Jean Pierre's strong arms lifting her, placing her on the back of the old ram, guiding her.

She said, "That's him." Her voice was unsteady, and the words had a slight echo in the white-tiled morgue room.

Don said, "It must have been an easy death."

The attendant slid Jean Pierre back into his resting place. As they were leaving, the attendant returned to his lunch.

"What happened?" Don asked the sheriff.

"We found his motorbike where he'd left it on the riverbank. My guess is that he tried to cross the bridge on foot and was swept away." Hamilton seemed to be testing his words before uttering them. "He'd been drinking. And it was during the storm. The worst of it."

They left the morgue room; the door closed with finality.

"Where was he going—do you know?" Margaret asked.

"Françoise Pelletier, who runs the feed store, said he was visiting her when the storm broke. He decided to return to the farm. She tried to talk him out of it but he wouldn't listen. He said you'd need him."

Margaret said quietly, "I did." She swayed a little against Don's supporting arm.

chapter 16

The cemetery was on a rise of ground with a lovely view of town. There were only a few mourners at Jean Pierre's funeral. His brother came down from Quebec and Françoise wept copiously.

Jean Pierre had made no provision for a funeral, so Margaret paid for the religious ceremony and the interment. She watched the coffin lowered into the ground with a feeling that she was emptying out contents from her past. In this same cemetery her mother lay under a single headstone. There must be a governing purpose that decides the course of life, she thought, and makes sense of it. Was it loving or amassing riches, raising a family or serving a cause, mortifying the flesh or simply living as Jean Pierre did? Perhaps all were different facets of the same hard core.

What I spent I had.
What I gave I have.
What I kept I lost.

On the way back from the cemetery they stopped at the post office. A letter from Boston Memorial Hospital informed them that a truck would arrive in two days to pick up the electroencephalograph that was on loan to them.

Don said, "I'd like to run a final test with the equipment. Just to find out what's going on inside Adam's head. We haven't tested him in several weeks."

At four-thirty that afternoon she met with Don and Miles to examine the test results.

It's future shock, Margaret thought. A penny-arcade machine updated for modern science. Step right up, ladeez and gennelmen. Our machine will reveal beyond a doubt just how in-tell-i-gent you are.

Adam was first to break the stunned silence: "Fascinating," he said, putting down the last of the brain

217

scan photographs. "There's been considerable growth in that small swelling on my cerebral cortex."

Don muttered, "To say the least."

Margaret could tell from Don's and Miles' reactions how seriously they viewed this new development. It was physical proof of the incredible progress Adam had been making over the past few months. In that short time he had retraced practically the whole of human evolution, from man's earliest ancestors to men who have mastered a complex language, from men who did not know how to control a fire or operate a wheel to the kind of intelligence needed to control and use nuclear energy and walk on the moon. She would have thought that sort of progress farfetched a little while ago.

"An unusual chemical process appears to be taking place," Miles said in a voice that was not quite under control. "The insertion of the DNA strip has caused a synergistic reaction. The new brain formation is producing small proteins, which in turn set off vastly increased electrical activity. Some unknown hormones are also at work, undoubtedly including ACTH and vasopressin. In animals, these two hormones greatly improve the ability to retain or recall memories. In humans it is probable that they help the brain to create new functions of intelligence."

"More than intelligence is involved." Don looked at Adam. "Right after we attached the electrodes you asked, 'What was that sound?'"

"Yes."

"Neither Miles nor I heard anything. But I tested the electrodes afterward on an extremely sensitive recording machine. There *was* a sound. It registered at three hundred kilohertz."

Margaret asked, "What does that mean?"

Don replied, "Human beings can hear in a narrow range from as low as 29 hertz to as high as 19 kilohertz. Dogs and rats and bats hear much higher frequencies, and other species hear much lower frequencies. Three hundred kilohertz is a range inaudible to all known species."

Adam said gravely, "I learned some time ago that I was hearing what others could not."

"If we were able to hear in that range, we'd be overwhelmed with the incredible number and variety of sounds. We'd go mad trying to sort them out. Obviously, you've worked out a way to handle it."

"I suppose I have."

"How do you *see* things lately?" Miles asked him.

Adam answered reluctantly: "In slow motion."

Margaret thought, Adam has been keeping secrets again. In addition to his phenomenal mind he's developing extraordinary physical abilities.

"When did you first notice this?" Miles asked. "About things slowing down."

"About a week ago. I was on my way to the kitchen to get a snack. The pendulum clock on the stairway landing began to strike midnight. When I was returning, after I'd had my snack, the clock was still striking. But it seemed to me at least twenty minutes had passed."

"What was your reaction?"

"I thought the clock was wrong. When I understood it was me, I didn't wish anyone else to know."

"How did you conceal it?"

"I slowed my own reactions to stay at a comparable pace."

"Why?"

"I do not wish to be different."

Miles gave an expressive shrug of the shoulders. "I'm afraid it's too late for that."

"When do you think it will stop?"

"I don't know."

None of us knows, Margaret thought confusedly. There was no answer that logical, rational, analytical thinking could provide. What was happening to Adam had not happened to anyone before. Any attempt to predict his future was sure to founder in bewilderment. *No one knows.*

219

"One thing's sure," Don said at last. "It's going to be very interesting while it lasts."

If he meant to lighten the general mood, he failed miserably.

Later that night, after Adam retired to his bedroom, Miles suggested a long walk to clear their heads. They left the farmhouse. The darkness on the narrow road was relieved only by the light of a gibbous moon. They walked a quarter of a mile in silence broken only by the chirping of crickets and the rustle of a breeze in the treetops. Margaret was becoming uneasy.

Miles stopped. "It's safe here. Even he can't hear us at this distance." He was whispering. "What do you think we should do?"

"Do?" Margaret asked.

"About Adam."

"What about him?"

"A decision must be reached quickly. We can't cope with him any longer."

"I'm afraid this is all beyond me," she said. "I don't understand the problem."

Miles' avuncular face had settled into worried jowls. "Think of it this way. Our minds are like telephone banks handling maybe four or five digits. We make enough combinations out of them to function on what we call a normal level. Adam's mind is operating with eight or nine digits. That enables him to perform an incredible number of new combinations—to perform in a way that our limited minds cannot imagine."

"You're discussing Adam as though he were a machine."

In the ordered world of machines every cause has an effect and every effect a cause, and the same causes achieve the same effects. How neat. Every question with an answer. Rational machines do not understand that only the shallowest forms of thinking are rational. When number and catalogue and categorize every hidden corner of the human brain, will they be able to understand the mystery of the human mind? If we could

220

only stop looking for signs, if we could open the inner eye of wisdom and really see . . .

Miles said, "The point is, we don't know what may be coming next. If Adam is developing paranormal powers, he should be monitored under very careful conditions."

"I agree," Don said.

Margaret looked back at the farmhouse. A light was shining in the upstairs window of Adam's bedroom.

She said angrily, "There's nothing wrong with him. He isn't a freak. He's as human as we are."

"Exactly what are you suggesting, Miles?" Don asked.

"It's time for someone at a higher level to take control. I think the government is better equipped to deal with him."

"The government?" Margaret asked. "You mean the kind of men who carry their authority in titles, in briefcases, operating through what they call channels? Why are they better qualified to take charge of Adam?"

"They might put his abilities to better use."

"To do what? Build a better bomb? I'm appalled to think of the use they'd make of him."

Don said, "Margaret's right. I'd rather turn him over to the Committee of Concerned Scientists."

"Can we trust those people?" Miles asked.

"They don't have an ax to grind. The Committee has altruists and Scrooges, atheists and devout, left-wingers and right-wingers, homo- and heterosexuals. It consists of scientists of every race, religion, and nationality. Their only common interest is in advancing the cause of science throughout the world."

"I have no intention of turning him over to anyone," Margaret said firmly.

Don said, "We can't let our personal feelings decide what's best for him. We have to think this through carefully and do the sensible thing."

"Who is to decide what's sensible?"

Miles said, "I confess that for the first time Adam has begun to frighten me."

"*He's* been frightened for some time," Margaret replied sharply. "You heard him. 'When do you think it will stop?'" She looked at them both challengingly. "This is no time to put him in the custody of anyone who won't care about him. As far as I'm concerned, Adam will stay right where he is—with us—as long as he wants to. *Indefinitely*!"

She turned and started back along the road. A faint mist was clinging close to the ground. The farmhouse was dimly illumined by a penumbra of light from the downstairs windows. Upstairs, in the bedroom where Adam was asleep, the window was dark.

She did not look back to see if anyone was following her.

At two o'clock in the morning Don Swenson watched flickering black and white images on the small television set in the living room. The movie was *In Old Chicago*, with Tyrone Power and Alice Faye and Don Ameche, and had to do with an Irish family at the time of the great Chicago fire.

The room seemed to brighten as Chicago began going up in flames. This is how great disasters begin, Don thought. Mrs. O'Leary's cow and a little neglect and the next thing you have is a catastrophe.

The fire he was watching on screen reminded him of the one that had cast leaping shadows and yellow light over a scene he wished he could forget. Meg was in love with Adam; that was why she was so unwilling to have him leave. The truth spoke through her words in a kind of contrapuntal message.

Yet she had felt something for him once. Her feeling could not all have vanished. How many times he had wanted to go to her and say simply: We'll get along much better this time, we'll get along fine; give me another chance. Everything he might have said was stifled by a mixture of pride and regret. He was afraid he would hear only a fond refusal, evoke only pity. He had had enough people feeling pity for him. For a time he had wallowed in it like a sow in muck.

He asked himself: Would he change what happened

to Adam even if he could? The answer was no. Adam was the path along which man must evolve, continuing a process that had begun with a flow of negentropy from some cyanide molecule three and a half billion years ago. The brain was not flesh; it was a mystery. Aeons ago strange creatures swimming in primordial oceans had brains with the same basic divisions as the human brain today. But the reflections of the brain's activity that are called mind were entirely different. The human brain had evolved and specialized, layer after layer. Now Adam had taken a further evolutionary step. He was the culmination of a cycle, perhaps the beginning of a new era in which human intelligence would turn toward the farthest reaches of space and pick up previously unrecorded impulses from nonhuman intelligences.

Don would not change that if he could.

But that was no reason to forgive the way Adam had wrecked his plans. The solution to that problem, however, was simple.

The television screen was making a kind of gobbling sound. The movie was over. Chicago had burned out.

He turned off the set. It was two-thirty and everyone was asleep.

He removed his shoes and went quietly upstairs in stockinged feet. The library was in darkness. He did not risk turning on a light but groped his way to the center. He found the table, the telephone cord, then the telephone.

The die is not cast until I pick up the telephone.

It is Margaret I mourn for.

As he removed the receiver a small dial light went on. It provided enough illumination for him to dial the chairman's private number.

The telephone rang several times before a sleepy voice answered.

"Ted? This is Don Swenson. The situation here has turned critical."

* * *

In Miles Kanter's bedroom a beeper signaled him that a recording was being made. He listened to the playback of Swenson's conversation with the chairman of the Committee of Concerned Scientists. Ted Bristol agreed that Adam should be taken into custody by his Committee, and promised to make arrangements immediately.

As soon as the playback ended, Miles placed a call on the suitcase transmitter. He gave a brief message and connected the recording to the telephone.

He looked at the electric clock in his bedroom. It was fourteen minutes to three o'clock.

Margaret spent a restless night. She knew she had allowed her decision about Adam to be influenced by the fact that the relationship was precious to her. She thought: He will outgrow me and become involved in all kinds of things that I won't even understand. But I don't care. At this moment life was being wonderful to her. She appreciated it more because there had been times not too long ago when life had been absolutely awful to her, when she almost hoped she would not live one more moment. On her trip to Mondugami she had been subject to terrible fits of loneliness, and during the difficulties and frustrations of her sojourn in the pygmy village there was not one person to sympathize or understand. She could have thrown a bottled message out into the Pacific addressed *To Whom It May Concern* with absolute certainty that no one would have been concerned.

Now there was Adam. She had come through the bad time. Life was meaningful again—it was rich.

In her haste to avoid the possibility of a separation from Adam, she had been peremptory with Don and Miles. Their questions were reasonable. Adam himself was troubled: *When do you think this will stop?*

If only she could discuss his problem openly with him, but they had never had an intimate conversation. He had not asked a single question about her life, and she knew nothing about him except how he made love.

224

Their relationship needed time to flower into mutual trust.

Perhaps he would understand how much she cared if she spoke to him with the voice of her heart. Love is a universal language, a method of conveying the most profound human emotion. Love can bring forth a harmony of communication that has no parallel in the rest of our lives.

She sat up because in another instant she would not have been able to breathe. Lying abed was like lying in her own coffin. Nails were being driven through the coffin lid into her flesh. She went to the window and looked out into the darkness. When she returned to look at the clock it was five-thirty. How could the night pass so slowly? Her thoughts returned to the long amorous night in which she and Adam had lain in each other's arms. She had never known anyone so tender and direct, with such strength and simplicity. His lovemaking had a sweet consoling power. She turned on the lamp and put her feet into slippers. Erotic images kept invading her thoughts. There was no use trying to go back to sleep. She went to the closet for her robe and, as she was putting it on, she realized that she had not chosen the comfortable blue flannel but a flimsy white peignoir that would provide no warmth at all. Feeling foolish, feeling a bit rattled, she imagined Adam seeing her in the peignoir.

At the door she stopped. A distant thrumming of which she had been faintly aware now intruded fully into consciousness. She returned to the window. The sky was slightly brighter now but she could see nothing.

As the thrumming became louder, she got a better sense of direction. Looking to the extreme right, she glimpsed flashing blue-and-white lights. A helicopter was descending just beyond the barn!

She hurried out into the corridor. Don was coming out of his room, which faced the other side of the building. He was fully dressed.

She said, "It's a helicopter. It's landing here."

225

"I didn't expect them so quickly."

"Didn't expect who?"

"The men from Ted Bristol's Committee. They're coming for Adam."

She stared incredulously. "You sent for them?"

"Yes."

Her swinging hand struck him across the face. "You bastard! I'll never trust you again. Never!"

Thunderous hammering shook the front door.

"I have to open it," Don said, "before they break it down."

All she could do was to warn Adam. She ran.

Don hurried downstairs, calling, "All right! All right!" The moment he opened the door five men wearing black turtlenecks and dark tight-fitting trousers poured in. Their leader, a slender man with hollow cheeks and slicked-down hair, was carrying an M-16 at the ready.

"You won't need that," Don said.

"Where is he?"

"He won't understand. He won't know what it is. It'll only lead to trou—"

He was brushed out of the way. The men took the stairs like mountain goats. When Don reached the landing they were pushing open doors on opposite sides of the corridor.

"Last bedroom on the right!" he shouted.

He got there a moment after they did. Margaret was a stationary figure amid a swirl of movement: men searching the closets, under the bed, opening the window.

The leader with the M-16 turned to Margaret. *"Where is he?"*

Those seemed to be the only words he knew. Even the harsh inflection of his voice was the same.

Margaret looked at Don with a bitter derisive smile. "He's gone," she said.

chapter 17

Adam was awake when he first heard the helicopter. He had been lying awake in his room thinking about the conversation he overheard between Margaret and Don and Miles. What Miles said was true; the situation was now beyond their ability to cope. The time had come for him to go out on his own and to survive in a hostile environment—as the wild boy had.

In the sky a pearly light from the east arched up toward purple banks of cloud. From his window he stared intently to where the last stars still bloomed like flowers. The helicopter was a distance away, coming toward the farmhouse. Adam pulled on clothes over his pajamas, let himself out the window. He was a mile from the farmhouse before the helicopter touched down.

From the sheltering edge of a small copse, he watched the black-clad men run from the helicopter to the house. A few minutes later they hurried back to the helicopter and it took off. He moved deeper into the thicket of small trees and bushes, and sat down with his back to a sapling, hidden in shadows. The helicopter flew low past his hiding place and veered off to search another area.

Several animals approached him: a raccoon, a pair of squirrels, a jackrabbit. He smiled and held out his hand, and trustfully each came to be petted. *I think I could spend my life with animals.* Once in a while a deeply intuitive mind leaps from the periphery to the center where all knowledge is one. Walt Whitman made that leap, intuiting that the purposes of animals are closer to the real simplicity. Mammals and birds and social insects devote themselves without question to fulfill a plan of whose scope they have not the faintest inkling.

Adam slowed down his heartbeat and respiration

227

until his body was in a receptive state of serenity. He appeared to himself to be sitting alone in a great amphitheater, watching on a gigantic screen the evolution of life through geologic time. Each era succeeded another in an impossibly speeded-up procession. The earliest forms of cellular life became more complicated and were succeeded by reptiles (a crocodile slithered swiftly into yellow-brown water), then the dinosaurs came, followed by a man creature, standing erect, struggling to separate himself from other species. Then came man in the modern era. The next leap would be to life in the future, but the screen dimmed as Adam struggled to hold it in focus. The effort destroyed his receptive state, and the vision disappeared.

Day had come.

As he turned, a girl seated on a fallen log was watching him. He understood at once that he had summoned her image from his memory. His ability to control the physical world with his mind was steadily increasing.

Amelia looked sad and reproachful. He crossed to her and took her hand in his. I have not forgotten you, he said.

At that moment, in an institution a hundred miles away, Amelia sat up in her bed. Her hand gathered the bed sheet into wrinkles as her attention became fixed. She was receiving his message.

Margaret went through the motions of making breakfast. A few minutes later Don appeared and said good morning. She did not reply.

"Are you willing to talk about it?" he asked.

"I don't know what there is to talk about."

He came over to where she was pouring coffee from the percolator. "I was surprised by how they handled it. Those men moved in like a squad of mercenaries. It wasn't what I expected at all."

She filled her cup and sat down at the table. He poured from the percolator into another cup and joined her.

He said, "Miles wanted the government to take charge. I thought Ted Bristol's Committee was a better choice."

"I didn't agree with either of you. Neither did Adam. I believe that what he did is called voting with your feet."

"I'm sorry. I thought Ted Bristol had more sense."

"You acted on your own in calling him in the first place. You didn't consult me."

"No matter what, you couldn't keep him here much longer. It was getting too hard to pretend he isn't the unique human being that he is. And there's no recognized procedure, no assigned place for those who are too intelligent to live among their fellow humans. No institutions exist for their kind."

"It's just impossible for you to be honest. You did it for your own selfish reasons. No one else's."

"You might be a little more charitable. I've been sitting on the biggest medical news story that ever happened. I could have written a paper that would have made my reputation. But I didn't write it." She was right. It was impossible for him to be honest.

"Go ahead and write your paper. Do anything you damn please." She took a sip of black coffee. "I want you out of my house today—this morning."

Miles came into the kitchen.

"Someone's coming," he said.

"I hope these aren't more of your friends," Margaret said to Don.

Don recognized them as soon as they got out of the car. Ted Bristol's stocky figure was joined by the stylish, attractive Juana Campo, looking like an exotic bird in this rural area. They were followed by Dr. Albert Maynard, the Pulitzer Prize-winning scientist-author of *Cybernetics and Human Intelligence*.

Margaret confronted them at the door.

"We've come about Adam," Bristol said.

"I don't know where he is."

Bristol looked inquiringly at Don, who was standing slightly behind Margaret.

"Your men were here earlier," Don said. "Adam got away."

Bristol looked puzzled. "No one from our Committee has been here."

Don caught Juana Campo's eyes and with a slight motion of the head she confirmed it.

Don said, "Let them in, Margaret. It seems we've got a lot to talk about."

The sat in the living room with their visitors while Don described the arrival of the helicopter and the squad of black-clad men who had searched the house.

Bristol said, "The Security Bureau."

"What's that?" Margaret asked.

"The Bureau was specifically created to safeguard America's scientific secrets. In a sense they operate outside of our government. They are not subject to the freedom of information or privacy laws, and no statutory charter defines the limits of what they can do. They're beyond the control of the democratic process."

Juana Campo said, "The important thing is that they did not get Adam. We must find him before they do."

Dr. Maynard said, "Meanwhile, it would be very helpful if we can have all your research—the notes, tapes, the results of your various tests. We need to know as much as possible about this young man."

Dr. Maynard made the mistake of presuming they could count on Margaret's cooperation. Don did not have time to warn him.

"I have no intention of giving you anything," Margaret said.

Ted Bristol looked surprised. "Now that the Security Bureau is in the picture," he said, "we must work together to keep Adam out of the wrong hands."

Margaret replied, "I haven't decided who the right hands are."

"This whole question is a little ridiculous," Don pointed out. "None of us knows where Adam is."

The sun was rising toward the zenith as Adam emerged from the copse. He began walking along the road at a carefully controlled pace. Everything around him seemed to be in very slow motion—a flight of geese headed southward were fixed in the sky. After a while he heard a car engine some distance behind him, moving in his direction. A few minutes later a small pickup truck passed and stopped ahead on the road. A grizzled graying man opened the door on the passenger side.

"Hop in."

Adam smiled pleasantly. "I'd rather walk."

"Ain't no place to walk to. Not for eight mile."

"I don't mind the exercise."

Don't see many strangers walking around here. The last time a stranger was wanderin' through here it turned out he was a lunatic from the state hospital.

"Where you headin' to?"

Adam had decided the best place to find privacy was among millions of people.

"New York City. But first I have to stop to see a friend."

"Well, okay, young feller, if you don't want a ride."

"Thanks anyway."

I'll call the sheriff from Thompson's gas station.

The messages were coming through to Adam clearly. By picking up and interpreting brain waves, particularly the alpha rhythms, and adjusting his own alpha rhythms to a particular frequency, the messages appeared as though from a radio transmitter in a kind of alpha Morse code.

The pickup truck went a hundred yards before the engine sputtered and gave a whooping sound. Steam burbled out of the hood. As Adam caught up, the man was lifting the hood.

He scratched his grizzled gray head. "Dang engine. Don't see anything wrong with it."

"Let it cool. It'll start in about an hour."

"You know engines?"

"I know this one."

Talks queer enough to be a lunatic, that's for sure.

"I'll be seeing you," the man said.

"I don't think you will," Adam told him.

231

Whiteoak Sanitarium was a collection of long white barracks-like buildings surrounding a large main building. The barracks-like buildings housed the medical staff, nurses, and facilities for treating patients. In the six-story main building the upper floors were for the patients' living quarters. On the ground floor were a reception area with visiting rooms, and administrative offices.

Adam entered the grounds between a pair of white stone columns that marked the entrance. The reception area of the main building was enclosed in glass walls on three sides, and behind a counter a plump woman in a nurse's cap and white uniform was working.

Adam said, "I'd like to see one of your patients."

"Are you a relative or a friend?" She was already starting to look through her card file.

"A friend."

"Sign the register." She turned around a large imitation leather-bound book.

He signed his name as Adam Denning, adding the time of his visit, the patient he wanted to see, and the reason (personal) in the indicated columns.

The nurse looked up a card in the files. Adam picked up a current of suspicion running through her mind.

"You say you're a friend of the patient?"

"Yes."

Her card indicates that she can only have visits from her family. And you look pretty young, and not very well dressed either.

"I'm afraid you'll have to wait. Take a seat right over there."

He sat down by the window and the nurse picked up the interoffice phone. The mouthpiece curved upward to keep her voice from being heard. Adam heard her perfectly.

"I've got someone here who wants to see a patient on the restricted list. Says he's a friend. I asked him to wait in case you want to question him."

She put down the interoffice phone to answer an incoming call. Before she finished the conversation

Adam slipped out of the chair and went rapidly up the stairs. On the second floor was a wide corridor lined with doors on either side. All the doors were closed and one or two had a signal light burning above the door. At the end of the corridor there was a nurse's station. A nurse came out and went into one of the doors that had a light burning. She paid no attention to Adam.

Amelia, he called silently.

In a room on the fourth floor, Amelia was sitting in a chair cross-legged, with knitting in her lap she had not touched for hours. Her eyes blinked, then her gaze fixed on the door to her room. She kept staring at the door until the knob slowly turned.

Adam came in. Amelia stared at a tall good-looking young man she had not seen before. She looked down at her knitting. Something tugged again at her mind and she looked up. The tall good-looking young man had moved very close to her.

Her hand was resting on her knitting wool and he put his hand over hers.

"Remember," he said.

Her eyes opened wider. "You're...not...the...same."

"I've changed. You will too. It will be much easier for you because I will be there to help."

His hand touched her forehead. A new kind of quiet, more peaceful, came over her. She closed her eyes while he gently stroked her forehead, his other hand still holding her hand. She began to breathe deeply. The ball of knitting slipped off her lap and she was hardly aware of its soft fall.

"Come," Adam said. "We will go together."

Downstairs in the reception area Amelia's parents were just arriving for their regular weekly visit. The nurse at the counter was busy talking to a hospital security guard. He was a burly man, with a touch of premature baldness and heavy meaty hands.

"What name was that?" the father asked. "Are you talking about my daughter?"

The nurse said, "A young man came to see her a few minutes ago. He said he was a friend of hers."

"She has no friends."

233

"I told him to wait and called the guard. The next minute the young man was gone. He slipped out while I was calling."

"Who is he? What did he want?" Amelia's mother asked. Now that she no longer had to care for Amelia on a daily basis, her maternal feeling had returned strongly, fortified by guilt.

"I asked him to sign the register."

The father looked at the register and slammed the flat of his hand down on it. "Denning! The name of that crazy woman doctor."

"Oh my God," the mother said in a choked wail.

The nurse turned to the guard. "You'd better check the patient's room."

"We'll go with you," the father told the guard.

As they emerged on the fourth floor, Adam and Amelia were coming toward them, walking hand in hand. Amelia was looking at Adam and did not see them.

"There she is!" the father said. "That's my daughter!"

"Who's the young man with her?"

"I never saw him in my life."

"Stay here," the guard warned. "I'll handle this."

When Amelia saw the guard coming, she became frightened and tried to remove her hand from Adam's. Adam held it tighter.

"Let her go," the guard ordered.

Amelia stopped, unable to move.

"I'm telling you one last time," the guard said.

Adam looked at him.

"Let her go," the guard said, his voice shaking. He glanced uncertainly at Amelia's father.

"He's got no business with her," the father said.

"Oh my God!" the mother cried. "Who is he? What does he want?" She ran to Amelia, interposing her own body between Adam and the girl. "Leave her alone!"

The guard shook his head slightly, as though to rid himself of a temporary dizziness.

"Come on now, buddy," he said. "I don't want to have to get rough." He sounded nervous.

234

"We're leaving," Adam said. "We don't want any trouble."

The guard placed a heavy hand on Adam's shoulder.

His hand was flung violently back though Adam had not moved.

The guard's fists knotted and he stepped forward. His legs lifted off the floor until he was poised horizontally in midair. He began to fly rapidly backward.

The mother screamed.

The father ran down the staircase shouting for help.

Adam held out his hand to Amelia. Her shoulders and arms and torso shuddered. Then she began to sink down slowly along the wall, her fingers scrabbling at the plaster.

The guard struck the far wall of the corridor feet first. He fell to the floor. He scrambled up, reached for the gun in his holster.

Another guard raced up the staircase, followed closely by Amelia's father. The guard's gun was drawn and he was holding it in both hands.

"Freeze!"

His hands jerked up suddenly. He managed to pull the trigger but the bullet chunked into the ceiling.

"Hold it right where you are. Or I'll..." He was trying to force his hands down to a level position again.

The other guard pounded back along the corridor. He snapped off a shot on the run before he shrieked and dropped his gun. The gun lay on the carpeted floor, turning a dull orange with heat and slowly melting.

"Jesus God Almighty!"

"I'll be back," Adam whispered to Amelia. He ran down the corridor in the opposite direction.

Amelia lay slumped against the wall and a powerful electric shock seemed to convulse her body. She cried out through tightly clenched teeth.

Her father went to her. "Are you hurt?"

She lifted one hand, staring intently at the middle finger. She kept staring at it.

Her father said, "What is it? Is anything wrong?"

235

Amelia's eyes rolled up until the whites were showing. She fainted.

Visitors were arriving in a steady stream at the parking lot and the driveway was lined with waiting cars. Adam cut sharply to the left, leapt a hedge, and ran along the back of a long low barracks building.

When he was a distance from the hospital he sat down to examine the stump of his middle finger. The top joint was missing and blood welled from it. That last shot had severed it.

The pain was severe. Adam ordered his body to increase endorphins and enkephalines, the natural opiate-like substances that relieved pain, and to begin producing antibodies to fight off infection. He bent his gaze upon the stump, constricting blood vessels there until the bleeding stopped. He commanded the healing process to begin.

He resumed his journey toward the highway.

chapter 18

Don Swenson finished packing in his room. He snapped the suitcase shut. Nothing remained except to say goodbye.

Miles had a first-floor bedroom so he would not have to be constantly climbing the stairs. Don decided to say goodbye to him first. He went downstairs and, from the connecting foyer, he heard a voice inside Miles' room. It was Margaret and she sounded angry. Then he clearly heard a man's voice that did not belong to Miles. A cool prickling of flesh on his arms alerted him to why the other voice sounded familiar.

When he knocked the voices in the room stopped and he heard quick movement inside.

After a short delay, Miles asked, "Who is it?"

"Don. I came to say goodbye."

Miles opened the door. He looked flustered.

"I thought I heard Margaret in here with you," Don said.

"I was listening to the radio."

On a low table near the bed was a portable phonograph player with a closed lid. Don crossed the room toward it. He opened the lid. A Chopin record was on the turntable inside.

"You're being very rude," Miles said. "Please leave."

There was a fraction of an inch gap between the turntable and the bottom edge of the case. Don lifted up the turntable.

Miles said wearily, "You shouldn't have done that."

Recording equipment was hidden inside. Don turned it on. He listened in silence to Margaret ordering him out of her house. He listened until the recording ended.

Miles was watching him, his hands at his sides.

"How does it work?" Don asked. "Do you have bugs planted all through the house?"

"It isn't necessary. This can pick up a sound in any room."

"You've been spying on us." He had been irrationally hoping for some other explanation. "How long has this been going on?"

"Since they asked me for help."

"'They'?"

"The people you heard of."

"The Security Bureau? A nice lot of friends you have."

"No worse than yours. We all know what Adam can do. The important question is, which side will he do it for?"

Don removed the tape canister from the spindle with a vague idea of showing it to Margaret in case she would not believe him. He closed the phonograph lid. "What now? Will you tell them what's happened?"

Miles put his hand into his jacket pocket. "Naturally. They will have to think of something to do about you."

"What they think of may not be very nice."

"I have no choice." Miles took his hand out of his pocket with a gun in it. "Don't make the mistake of thinking I won't use this."

"Would you really?" Don asked and hurled the tape canister. It struck Miles high on the forehead and staggered him. Don was on him before the gun went off. The explosion seemed to take place within his eardrum. Then the chair broke beneath their combined weight with a sharp splintering noise.

They rolled on the floor with Don holding Miles' wrist. The reverberations of the explosion were still hammering in Don's ear. Miles tried to wrench his gun hand free. He almost did before Don brought his fist down heavily. Miles' hand released the gun as his fingers opened. Don picked up the gun.

Miles lay unmoving. One eye was quickly becoming a dark red blur.

The door opened.

Margaret stood in the doorway, amazed.

* * *

Adam heard the siren a long way off and stayed out of sight. The police car sped past, its siren fading in the direction of Whiteoak Sanitarium.

A hundred yards away on the main highway, cars were moving swiftly. Adam waited in the nearest lane as a car moved toward him.

I don't trust hitchhikers. Don't you dare stop.

The car slowed and stopped a short distance beyond the place Adam was standing. He caught up to the car and got into the rear. The woman, on the passenger's side in front, turned around to give him a disapproving glare.

"We can only take you as far as Turnbridge. You'll have to get another ride from there."

"That will be fine."

The car quickly regained highway speed.

"Where you coming from?" the man at the wheel asked.

"Visiting someone."

The woman asked, "Someone who lives around here?"

"She's at Whiteoak Sanitarium."

Birds of a feather.

"You ask too many questions," the man said.

"Do I ask too many questions?" the woman asked Adam.

"No."

"As usual," the woman said, "you don't know what the hell you're talking about."

"Knock it off," the man said.

"What have you got in your hand?" the woman asked.

Adam opened his partly clenched hand. The wound was almost healed. Skin was forming around the very tip of his middle finger.

"How did that happen?"

"An accident."

"Can't you leave him alone? You're embarrassing him."

"Am I embarrassing you?" the woman asked Adam.

"No."

"If an accident happened to you while you were riding in our car, we'd be responsible."

239

"We're going to Brattleboro," the man said. "We can take you that far."

"Thank you."

The woman said, "You'll have a better chance of getting a ride in Tunbri—"

Adam looked at her.

There was a silence for a space of three seconds.

She said, "As long as we're going to play good Samaritans we might as well go whole hog. We'll take him where he wants to go."

"Huh?" the man said.

"Where's that?" she asked Adam.

"New York City."

"New York City!" the man said.

"I could do some shopping. They've redone Bloomingdale's again."

"Do you know what you're saying? Do you know how far—"

"Be human once in a while. Try it. It won't hurt you."

"This is crazy," the man said. "It's nuts!"

"We're going to New York and that's final. Why are you always quarreling with me?"

"I heard a shot," Margaret said. She was looking at Don as if not fully recognizing him.

Don couldn't think of a way to explain, then he did. He picked up the tape canister from the floor, put it on the spindle, and she listened.

"He was recording us." Margaret glanced at Miles as if she expected him to deny it. "Why?"

"He's a spy for the Security Bureau."

"You killed him for that?" she asked.

"I just knocked him out. He'll come to in a minute."

"Who fired the shot?"

"It was an accident." Don showed her the gun in his hand. "It's his gun, not mine."

The tape was still running with their quarreling voices.

She shivered. "Please turn that off."

He did.

She said, "It's a nightmare. We're living through a nightmare." With an effort she kept control. "Are we going to call the police?"

"If we bring them in, the nightmare will get worse."

"You don't expect to keep this a secret?" She shook her head with disbelief. "It's too late."

Don and Miles had been pursuing their own paths, their own interests, while she cared only about Adam. She was in love with him, but what was all-important to her was that Adam be given a chance to fulfill his destiny. She could not hazard a guess as to what that destiny might be.

Miles groaned and rolled over. He sat up, frowning and staring at them with his one good eye.

Don leveled the gun at Miles. He said to Margaret, "Get a wet sponge and a scarf. Quickly."

She returned in a minute. Don handed the gun to her. He put the sponge in Miles' mouth and tied the scarf to hold it in place.

"Kneel down facing that chair," he told Miles.

Miles kneeled.

"There should be a necktie in that closet," Don told Margaret.

She opened the closet. A suitcase was on an upper shelf. A few ties were draped over a large hook on the side of the closet. She brought a necktie to Don, who used it to tie Miles' hands behind him.

"How long do you intend to keep him here?" she asked.

"I think the cellar is a better permanent residence." He looked up. "Did you hear a car?"

"It just stopped outside."

Someone was coming to the front door.

"Whoever it is, don't answer."

"Suppose it's Adam? Or someone with news about him?"

There was a knocking at the front door.

Don said, "See who it is. But get rid of them as fast as you can."

241

She turned, moving like an automaton. For the first time Don realized that she was in shock. He put the gun carefully against the side of Miles' head.

"We're going to be quiet, aren't we? Church quiet."

A moment later he heard Margaret open the front door.

"Oh, it's you, Sheriff Hamilton. Come in."

Adam paused at the south corner of Forty-second Street and Eighth Avenue, waiting for a light to change. He was surrounded by a ceaseless clamor, and he sorted out the sounds he wished to avoid hearing. Before the light changed he had diminished the noise to a manageable level.

To stay in the city he needed a place to live and a way to earn his living. He had no idea of how to go about finding either one. He did not know where to look or how to conduct himself in order not to arouse suspicion. His ignorance of ordinary everyday problems was nearly total.

He had no luggage, no extra clothing, no cash, no credit cards, no Social Security number, no driver's license, no means of identification. He was a nonperson in this great bustling noisy metropolis. He would have to be very careful not to draw attention to himself until he could establish a new identity and merge into the anonymous multitude.

The light changed and he crossed the street. Two heavily made-up women, wearing bushy fake fur jackets over hot pants that showed long legs in net stockings, regarded him curiously. One was dark-skinned and her voice had a musical lilt: "You look tired, baby. You like to rest in my bed?"

"Thank you," Adam said. "I'm really not that tired."

"Wise guy!"

The other woman sidled up. "You don't want her, mister. She kinky like hell." This woman, as dark-skinned as the other, had a pronounced Caribbean accent. "I have a nice clean place. You like it, hey?"

He ought to be good for fifty.

242

"I have no money."

"Forty dollah?"

Adam shook his head and walked on.

"Cheapskate!"

A block farther Adam stopped before garishly lit windows revealing an arcade in which mostly young people were playing video games. The store was crowded, and a bald pockmarked man wearing a leather apron with pockets in it for change was presiding over the ceaseless surge and flow of customers.

A small sign in a corner of the window read *Help Wanted. Part Time.*

Adam entered. A boy about fourteen was manipulating the controls of a video game called Space Sleuth, in which a space vehicle had to survive hazards en route to various clue-stations. If the vehicle reached all the clue-stations, it would enter through gates that led to the solution of the Ultimate Mystery.

The boy was moving the knobs rapidly in a frantic hopeless attempt to evade predators closing in on him from three sides. The predators were about to devour his spaceship when suddenly all three vanished from the screen in little bursts of light.

The boy shot a quick bewildered glance at Adam. "Did'ja see that? What'd I *do?*"

Adam smiled.

The boy turned back to the game and sent his spaceship out again on a zigzag journey toward the next station. Adam meanwhile was distracted by a television set in a corner that was tuned to a news program. He was looking at a slightly blurred close-up photograph of himself on the television screen. There was enough background detail to deduce that the photograph had been taken outside the farmhouse in Vermont, and the blurriness suggested it might have been taken with a telephoto lens.

The television sound did not penetrate through the noise in the arcade but Adam had no difficulty hearing what the voice-over was saying:

"Tonight's final story is an unusual human drama.

This young man, an amnesiac, was last seen in a small town in northern Vermont. What makes this story unusual is that he needs prompt medical attention, within hours. This and other television news shows are showing his photograph as a public service, in the hope someone will see him in time. If you see him—and this is very important—*do not approach him under any conditions*. He has suffered an accidental dose of extremely high-level radiation that is dangerous to anyone with whom he comes in contact. Anyone with information as to his whereabouts should contact local police immediately."

Adam left the arcade and with an unobtrusive sideways movement rejoined the throng passing by on the sidewalk. The news story was ingeniously designed to serve several ends: to enlist the aid of the public in locating him, to prevent anyone from rendering any assistance to him, to preclude any opportunity for him to tell his side of the story.

His pursuers would soon discover where he was. The quarreling couple who had driven him to the city would get in touch with the police as soon as they heard; they would probably panic about having been exposed to radiation.

The traffic on Forty-second Street was constant. Cars were maneuvering for position and honking impatiently. It seemed to Adam that one or two persons stared at him as he passed. He walked on quickly and turned at the next corner. He intended to follow a route that would avoid the main avenues. There was no longer anonymity to be found in crowds of people; they were all potential enemies.

A policeman was coming toward him.

"You, there."

Adam began to run.

"Wait a minute!"

As the policeman rounded the corner, no one was in sight. It didn't seem possible the young man could have vanished so quickly. Probably just another young drifter. From a distance he had looked a little like the young man whose photograph was being shown on all the television news channels...

Adam realized now that his plan to live and work in the city was impractical. What alternative? He had to get away entirely, out of the country, to a place where no one would know who he was, or care. He could not manage that by himself.

He did not even know anyone he could turn to for help.

Except Margaret.

Near the corner there was a partially enclosed telephone booth but he would be visible to anyone passing on the sidewalk. He looked ahead down the dim-lit side street. A dingy cafe was open. He walked to it quickly, and inside the door was a telephone booth. There were only a few customers in the cafe. A waitress was wiping off the counter.

As Adam went inside, the waitress looked up briefly. He ducked into the telephone booth. The instruction panel said to deposit a dime and wait for the dial tone, but he had no coin to deposit.

He stared intently at the telephone box for a moment. There was a slight jingle as a coin dropped. The receiver hummed. He dialed the operator and gave Margaret's number at the farmhouse.

"Deposit a dollar seventy-five," the operator said, "for the first three minutes."

"I don't have money."

"Is this a collect call, sir?"

"Yes. A collect call."

"Will you speak to anyone who answers at this number?"

"Miss Margaret Denning, please."

"And who shall I say is calling?"

"Adam."

"Just Adam?"

"She will know."

The operator dialed a number. Moments later Adam heard the telephone ring.

chapter 19

Sheriff Hamilton's yellow slicker had powdery-looking marks where light raindrops had hit.

Margaret's mind raced in confusion. "What brings you here, Sheriff?"

"That young fellow you've got living here has got himself into some trouble."

"Trouble?"

"At a place called Whiteoak Sanitarium."

The sheriff removed his slicker and Margaret hung it in the guest closet. She thought of Don and Miles in the room at the end of the hall.

"What makes you think it's him?"

"He signed the visitors' registry Adam Denning. Denning's your name. And he was trying to visit a patient at the sanitarium. Amelia Quigley. Her father's the one tried to press kidnapping charges against him."

She had the same feeling she had during the flood, of being swept away; then suddenly she found herself on firm ground. There was no way the sheriff could know that Adam and the wild boy were the same.

"You're wrong, Sheriff. Adam Denning is my nephew. He's living temporarily with us."

Sheriff Hamilton examined her with half-lidded eyes. "What happened to the boy who was here?"

"We weren't able to do anything for him after all. He had to be put away."

She could almost watch the slow progression of this through his mind.

"That don't explain why he should want to visit that girl at the sanitarium."

"I think I can explain that. Adam wants to be a doctor. He and Dr. Swenson got into the habit of discussing medical problems. Dr. Swenson told him about Amelia Quigley. They discussed at some length whether

her problem was caused by a psychological disorder or by a genetic deficiency or a specific form of brain damage. Apparently, Adam decided to try to see her and find out for himself."

Sheriff Hamilton sorted this out before he nodded. "Makes sense. Description I got of him sure didn't fit. When your nephew shows up here, I still want to talk to him."

"Any particular reason?"

"He had a fight with a hospital guard. Guard took a shot at him."

Margaret stifled an exclamation. "Was he hurt?"

"Couldn't be too serious," Sheriff Hamilton said. "Not from the way they say he took off. But he and I need to have a little sitdown."

"I'll give him the message."

"Appreciate that."

The sheriff was at the door when the telephone rang, a shrill startling intrusion.

"I have a collect call for a Miss Margaret Denning. From Adam."

Margaret's hand holding the receiver began to tremble. "Will you hold on just a minute, operator?" She put her other hand over the mouthpiece. "A business call, Sheriff. You can let yourself out."

"Sure can."

She waited until the door closed after him. Then she took her hand off the telephone. "I'm Margaret Denning, operator."

"Will you accept charges?"

"Yes, yes! Adam! Are you all right?"

"A few minutes ago they had my picture on television."

"Your picture?"

She held the receiver tight to her ear as he explained.

She released a long-held breath. "Of course they made it up in order to find you." She thought a moment. "It will take most of the night to drive to the city. Can you find a place to stay until morning?"

"I will try."

247

"We'll meet in the main reading room of the public library on Fifth Avenue and Forty-second Street. As soon as it opens go there. It will be almost deserted. When we arrive we'll have worked out a plan. Be especially careful tonight."

She went back to the room where Don was standing guard over Miles.

"That was Adam," she said. "We have to leave. At once."

"Where?"

"New York. What can you do about Miles? There's no time to waste with him."

"Just give me a minute. And we won't have to worry about him anymore."

She felt resolve flowing into her entire body: her hands, her arms, her legs. She could do whatever had to be done.

She met Don's eyes. "All right. Get it over with."

As Adam stepped out of the booth, a young girl in jeans and a red parka was talking in a whisper to the waitress. It's him. The one on television.

Adam left the cafe quickly. He turned up Eighth Avenue, keeping close to the buildings and away from the streetlights. Storefronts were locked up for the night, with iron grilles over their windows. In the middle of the block was a small theater, without a marquee, flush at sidewalk level with other buildings. Inside the small lobby were photographs of nearly naked women in seductive poses. A sign advertised: *Nonstop Sex Action! Beautiful Girls!* A bored-looking cashier in a glass booth was buffing her fingernails.

Look! It's him!

He had picked up the thought from somewhere nearby. Hurriedly he made his way to the corner and ran down the dark street toward Broadway. At the corner, on his right, was a new office building. He looked through a glass wall at a spacious marbleized lobby and twin escalators that were now motionless. He tried the door but it was locked.

Inside the lobby a short stocky watchman got up from a night stand and slowly approached the entrance. He did not open the locked door, but his voice came clearly over an amplifier:

"Anything I can do for you?"

You know me very well, Adam thought.

The watchman smiled widely. "Oh, it's you, Mr. Harrad. Just a minute."

He unlocked the door and Adam entered the lobby. The watchman carefully closed and locked the entrance doors behind him.

"Going to put in some late hours, are you?"

Adam nodded.

The watchman led the way to the night stand. There was a register book open.

"I have to ask you to sign in, Mr. Harrad."

Adam looked at him.

The watchman seemed confused for a second. Then he said, "It isn't necessary. I'll sign in for you."

You did not let anyone in, Adam thought.

On the board of building tenants, Harrad and Associates, Business Consultants, was on the thirty-second floor.

A light was glowing above an elevator door in the bank of elevators. Adam took the stairs. He reached the thirty-second floor as the elevator reached the ground floor.

The tenant leaving was a silver-haired plump man. He said cheerily to the night watchman, "You can lock up now, Harry. I must be the last to leave the building."

"That you are, sir. It's been a quiet night. No one coming or going."

Miles opened his eyes and saw the ceiling of his room. The departing Volvo's headlights brightened a corner that was in shadow.

The injection Don had given him should work very quickly to cause unconsciousness. Obligingly, he had feigned an instant effect, toppling over onto the floor. Don removed the gag and sponge from his mouth so he

249

wouldn't choke to death while unconscious. Then they both left immediately to go to Adam.

He stood up with his hands bound behind his back. He forced himself to walk with a dizzying effort. He moved waveringly out of the room. A comical figure. A drunk. What a party.

He reached the door of the bathroom outside his room in the foyer. He held on to a diminishing chink of awareness. The shadows were growing longer, blacker, turning into velvet wings. One drug-activated cell was transmitting its message to another cell, releasing a chemical at the interface where the two cells met.

Sleep.

He lurched into the bathroom and over to the shower. Hoisting his body up and back, he turned on the water with his bound hands. Cold shock on his head and cold wetness pouring down his neck. The shadows retreated a little.

Into the living room.

He was breathing heavily, as though he had run a long way.

Time to rest. To sleep. Inexorably, shadows length-ened again across his mind.

He saw something out of the corner of his eye, just beyond the range of vision.

Pain, Lillian said. Pain is the antidote.

He saw her now at the extremest periphery of sight. A misty blurred figure. Yes, she knew about pain.

He reached the fireplace, gasping. His foot stumbled against the box of long fireplace matches and the box tipped over and one or two matches spilled.

It took time to work it out, ten seconds, before he held a match between his fingers at his back. He struck it against the scraping edge of the box and felt the scorching heat. Moving his fingers with great effort, moving slowly, very slowly, he brought the flaming match toward the necktie twisted into a bond around his wrists.

Pain blazed like a bright sun. He could even smell it. His wrists hurt in a way he had not known even when he lay on the dry wadi waiting for death. He had felt mostly numbness then. This was knife-sharp, direct and undeniable, true pain. The shadows blew up. He thrust the dark ribbons aside, like a shredded curtain.

He tugged at his wrists until they came free.

Back to the room. Get transmitter and tell hardfaced men in black uniforms with guns. Pain was fastened like an adhesive to his burned wrists. He remembered the black-clad men racing into the house. Cold warriors. My country 'tis of thee. *Über alles.*

If I should forget thee, O Israel.

Lillian.

My sons, my sons, would God I had died for thee.

A number. A number given to him to call. The numbers had a rhythm that danced in his head. Nines and sevens.

Adam mustn't fall into the wrong hands.

I haven't made up my mind whose *are* the wrong hands.

Dear Margaret. He forgave her. He forgave Don too.

Shadows were creeping back. He saw them like an afterimage on his eye retinas. He turned away from the room with the suitcase and the hidden transmitter and went unsteadily into the living room.

He reached the telephone. Hurry up. Dark mists were rolling in from a secret weather center in his head.

Isosceles is a Greek philosopher who was equal on both sides.

Concentrate!

Nines and sevens in rippling rhythm. His finger swung independent of control in the dial.

Shadows surged. He remembered gripping the edge of the table. Then he was lying with his cheek on it and looking directly into the mouthpiece of a telephone.

Something had wakened him.

He heard it again. A voice.

"Yarosh speaking."

He formed his mouth around a name. "Miles."

Miles to go before I sleep.

"Miles Kanter? I can hardly hear you."

251

With a tremendous effort he formed his mouth around two more words: "Adam... called."

Black tide coming in, merging, flowing over him.

"New York. They're driving to... meet him..."

Far away, not a voice any longer but the sound of a distant drummer: "Go on, Miles!"

Miles did not hear. He was profoundly asleep.

The small trailer was parked in an area that the Kiwanis Club had donated to the town as a recreation center. There was a children's playground, with slides and swings, an obstacle course, and a climbing mountain of old automobile tires. Beyond the large asphalt parking lot was a hedge-protected artificial pond where in summer the children of town residents could swim in three-foot-deep safety.

The recreation area was deserted in winter. The trailer was parked in the center of a wide half-moon of open space that was occasionally used as a ball field. Anyone who saw it there would think it was the temporary home of a caretaker.

It was much more. Inside the trailer was a two-room electronic listening post. In one room Martin Holcomb, in charge of field operations, was tapping out his daily report on a computer terminal linked to the giant computer nicknamed Gert at the Fort Meade headquarters of the Security Bureau.

A quick-moving man came into his office from the adjoining room of the trailer.

"The Volvo just left the farmhouse. We're tracking it."

Martin Holcomb pushed a button on his desk. On the wall screen an area map appeared. A small red dot was moving along Route 105 to Route 89, the main north-south highway.

He watched until the red dot turned onto the highway.

"Headed south." He picked up the telephone that put him in direct communication with Fort Meade and asked for Commander Richards.

As he waited, the red dot continued moving south on Route 89. The Volvo was being tracked by sensors attuned to an inaudible signal sent out by a small capsule attached to its undercarriage. The capsule had been attached during the early morning visit by the Security Bureau forces to the farmhouse.

Commander Richards came on the line. "Yes, Martin?"

"The Volvo left the farmhouse two minutes ago, heading south."

"Any reason for this?"

"None I know of, sir."

"Check Mother Bell."

A highly placed official at the telephone company had been assigned to keep a record of all incoming and outgoing calls from the farmhouse. The commander believed in backup systems. If one factor in a situation failed, an alternative was ready.

In moments Martin had a printout of the evening's two telephone calls before him: Adam's call to Margaret Denning, and Miles Kanter's aborted call to Yarosh. He read the transcript to the commander.

"We should have been informed earlier of Adam's call. Yarosh has not informed us of the call from Dr. Kanter?"

"No, sir. Not yet."

"With our Israeli friends cooperation is not always a two-way street."

"Apparently not, sir."

"Yarosh does not have one essential piece of information," the Commander said. "According to the phone transcript, Miles Kanter did not complete his message. Therefore, Yarosh has no choice except to follow Dr. Swenson and Miss Denning and hope they lead him to Adam."

"Shall we lay on our own tracking team?"

"That won't be necessary, Martin. We have the advantage of knowing exactly where Dr. Swenson and Miss Denning are headed. We just have to wait for

Adam to show up at the Library. Remember, it's Adam we're interested in. Not the other two."

Martin twined his fingers together, the balls of his thumbs strongly opposing each other. "Yes, sir. I understand that."

"Make sure you have enough men to do the job. There must be no mistake. Whatever means are needed, whatever force is called for."

"Yes, sir."

"And send someone to the farmhouse to see about Dr. Kanter."

Jean Pierre was summoning her into a dark pit, raising long arms wrapped in white cerecloth. She stood at the edge of the pit looking down at him, at the open mouth in a ghastly bloodless white face with empty eye sockets. As she tried to move back, the ground crumbled beneath her and she began sliding into the pit. Jean Pierre's long arms rose to embrace her.

"Wake up, Meg."

She was huddled in the shadowed corner of the Volvo's front seat. Don was at the wheel.

"You were making moaning noises in your sleep," Don said.

A passing road sign said *Fairfax*. They were still in Vermont, only half an hour from the farmhouse.

"I've been worrying about Adam's telephone call," Margaret said. "Someone may have been listening."

"I don't think so. They didn't need phone taps. The equipment Miles had could pick up a conversation from any room. It could even pick up what was said on the other end of a telephone."

"Let's not talk about Miles." She sat, her head bowed. As the Volvo raced through the night her thoughts were of Adam and the strange fate that was reserved for him.

Finally she said, "You're right. Ted Bristol is Adam's best chance."

"What convinced you?"

She replied faintly, "Logic."

254

Don looked at the rearview mirror and frowned. "Hello, I've seen that car behind us. Twenty miles back."

He pressed down on the accelerator and gradually increased speed. The Volvo was traveling seventy-five miles an hour when, at the next turn, a heavy growth of trees on the right obscured his rear vision. He completed the turn and looked again at the rearview mirror. He counted slowly to eight, and the yellow headlights reappeared.

He removed his foot from the accelerator. The yellow headlights moved closer, then fell behind, remaining at a distance of a quarter mile.

"We're being followed. Probably since we left the house. Is there a way to get off the highway?"

"Up ahead there's a turnoff to an alternative route."

"They'd just follow us. I'm looking to lose them."

She thought for a few seconds. "There's a small overpass bridge and a culvert."

"That may do it."

"You'll see it in a few miles."

He steadily increased speed until the car was going eighty miles an hour. The yellow headlights dwindled to barely visible dots. They passed the turnoff to the alternative route south.

"Coming soon," Margaret said. She pointed. "There!"

He turned off the lights and slowed down abruptly. The stone bridge was a lighter hue in the darkness. He drove across and swung to the right, bumped jarringly down the descending ground. Below the bridge was the culvert. The car hit it with a drenching spray. He drove through, found the ascending ground, and quickly cut off the engine.

He counted to eleven before the car with yellow headlights roared past. They heard its racing engine above the pelting wind. He quickly turned the key in the ignition. The engine whined, but did not catch. He pumped the accelerator, turned the key again. The whine became a cough, a sputter; the engine caught.

He drove up to the other side of the bridge, crossed the road divider, and sped back toward the turnoff to
255

the alternate route. As he drove he kept watching for yellow headlights. On the other side of the road a black Cadillac whizzed by. No other car appeared.

Just beyond the bridge over the culvert, the black Cadillac pulled off the road. Its star-bright headlights probed the empty blackness ahead.

Yarosh turned to the driver. "That was them going by in the opposite lane. They must have spotted the Mercedes following them."

"Shall we go after them?"

"They'll go south again at the turnoff. That road rejoins the highway in about ten miles. We'll pick them up then."

"What about the Mercedes?"

"Strauss and Diederich were useful while we could follow them and stay out of sight ourselves. Now they're just in our way."

The driver turned out the headlights. In the darkness the black Cadillac was nearly invisible.

A minute later a silver-gray Mercedes with yellow headlights came racing back along the highway. There was a stuttering series of explosions from the Cadillac. One yellow headlight of the Mercedes went out. The other headlight's beam swung wildly as the car veered, careening to its right. The Mercedes went over the bridge at the culvert and crashed and rolled down the incline to the edge of the stream. Seconds later the yellow lights seemed to come on again, bathing the car and its interior in golden luminescence. The canary conflagration wavered higher against the darkness and the wind.

chapter 20

Harrad and Associates had a glass entranceway that revealed a comfortable-looking anteroom with a black leather couch. The door was locked. A moment's concentration released the lock and Adam went in.

The large room had no windows. Under a ceiling of fluorescent lights desks were placed within right-angle cubicles to give an illusion of privacy. The walls of the cubicles were only five feet high. Each desk had a small computer terminal linked to a computer elsewhere in the office. Each also had a small bookcase. A few contained a standing houseplant, further cramping a tiny space but providing a small personal touch.

Adam leaned over a cubicle wall. A cork bulletin board was festooned with company news and a copy of a printout. From this he discovered that Harrad and Associates was engaged in advanced computer systems work for several large corporations and the United States Government. Copies of the printout were in all the cubicles.

A short corridor led Adam from this area to William Harrad's private office furnished in luxurious dark woods, its walls covered in a maroon cloth. On one wall were several plaques acknowledging the contribution William Harrad and his company had made to the United States defense effort.

On a large mahogany desk was a contract authorizing Harrad and Associates to undertake a review of control systems for information transfer currently in use by various intelligence agencies. The contract was signed by the Secretary of Defense and bore William Harrad's sweepingly self-confident signature. Adam noted the date; the contract had been signed only twenty-four hours before.

Next to the contract was a half-finished handwritten

letter in which William Harrad informed the Secretary of Defense that he would undertake the assignment forthwith. He suggested a long list of signals that might be appropriate for his office as identification, pointing out that all communications from intelligence agencies involve certain risks and therefore require fail-proof controls.

A steel door leading off from Harrad's private office bore a sign: *Restricted Area.* This door was closed with a four-sided cylinder safety lock. It was the work of a moment for Adam to open the locked door.

He entered a small rectangular area completely dominated by a large computer in three conjoined cabinets. The floor of the room was cement, and the computer was bolted into the floor. The cabinets that formed the machine looked like refrigerators of varying heights.

Clearly this central computer for the office was large enough to perform demanding tasks. Adam regarded the machine with interest and respect. There was a similarity between this large computer, with its immense fund of knowledge, and a human brain. Human nerve fibers were basically electrical conductors; so was the computer's electrical wiring.

His electronic rival confronted him with its blank gaze of infallibility. A creature of silicon and wire and microcode confronting a creature of carbon and blood vessels and brain. In operation, the computer's wiring circuit would move information at a speed of 186,000 miles per second. By contrast, the nerve fibers in a human body could travel only 100 yards in the same time. Furthermore, the computer's storage house was systematically arranged and the material was instantly accessible, while in the human brain information was stored here, there, and everywhere, accessible only by the association of ideas.

A Darwinian struggle was looming between two rival forms of intelligence. In a world where truly "thinking" machines existed, man needed to increase vastly his own ability to reason. The struggle would no longer be with competing species of life but with his own inanimate creations. Man had to evolve more quickly than his machines—or perish.

Adam decided to accept the challenge.

He unlocked the machine and turned on the switch. He recalled to mind the list of identification codes suggested in William Harrad's half-finished letter, and began to punch in the codes. A four-digit code, WHAA, for William Harrad and Associates, proved to be the right one.

PROCEED, the screen replied.

He asked the computer how many other computer data banks were accessible to it. The computer replied there were seventeen such machines. He asked for a complete list. Among the names instantly printed on the screen, one caught his interest: the computer's data line accessed the Security Bureau's computer. Undoubtedly, there were stringent controls at the other end in addition to the basic requirements of identification authorization and enforcement.

The Security Bureau's computer would try to close off paths to an unauthorized person and to defend itself against attack. There would be an elaborate set of protective measures and various levels and techniques for encryption, using the same basic algorithm, but protecting different levels of classified data.

But there was no such thing as total security. A single item had to travel many different routes and appear under many different nodes during its life cycle. Each stopping point was an opportunity for an interception, a point of vulnerability.

He punched out the authentication algorithm on the computer console and requested access to the Security Bureau's data base. The computer at the Security Bureau answered instantly:

PROCEED.

CLEAR INFORMATION TRANSFER TO HARRAD AND ASSOCIATES.

PURPOSE OF TRANSFER?

TESTING COMMUNICATION LINK.

AUTHORIZATION.

CONTRACT SIGNED YESTERDAY WITH HAR-
RAD AND ASSOCIATES. AUTHORIZED REVIEW
AND ASSESSMENT ADEQUACY OF CONTROLS.

After a second's hesitation, his computer screen
flashed: PROCEED.

INQUIRY DATA BASE. WHO MAY INQUIRE?
WHO MAY MODIFY? UNDER WHAT CIRCUM-
STANCES? WHEN?

The computer terminal dutifully printed the name
of persons at the Security Bureau authorized to enter
data into the system. A password and identification
were required for each user. He inquired if electronic
encryption was in use to scramble a message during
transmission and thereby maintain the computer's in-
tegrity. It was; in fact there were different levels of
encryption.

Whatever a machine could encode, however, could
be decoded, given sufficient time and the will to do it.
The more complex, the more chances for backdoor entry. Different audit trails meant to document personal
responsibility had the secondary effect of opening passageways for an attack.

The contract between William Harrad and the Secretary of Defense must allow for a test of auditing and
security controls in order to develop detailed control
guidelines. So there must be a clear and enforceable
authorization for appropriate access. Harrad could not
be expected to fulfill his responsibility without being
given proper authority.

ACCESS TO FILE FOR REVIEW OF PROCE-
DURES.

PROCEED.

SEND DATA ON DR. DONALD SWENSON.

The computer blinked, then gave back a physical
description of Dr. Swenson followed by a listing of his
academic credits.

Adam interrupted with a question: REASON FOR
LISTING?

SUBJECT SURVEILLANCE. CATEGORY 19.

PROVIDE DATA CATEGORY 19.

CODE RED AUTHORIZATION NEEDED.

In order to find the algorithm for Code Red, Adam asked for a record of the Security Bureau's encrypted messages for the past forty-eight hours. A very long list appeared on the teleprinter. Working with this data, he picked those messages requiring the higher degree of encryption. He set about discovering a pattern in these, and quickly worked back to discover the necessary algorithm.

The computer waited, humming patiently. Adam punched out the new authentication algorithm. Then he repeated:

PROVIDE DATA FORM CATEGORY 19 ON DR. DONALD SWENSON.

The computer lights blinked.

DONALD SWENSON CONVEYED IMPORTANT DEFENSE SECRETS TO SCIENTIST OF THE USSR DURING CONFERENCE AT GREENBRIER, WEST VIRGINIA. INVESTIGATION COULD NOT ESTABLISH SWENSON'S MOTIVE. HE HAS BEEN IN CONTACT WITH COMMITTEE OF CONCERNED SCIENTISTS WHO BELIEVE ALL SCIENTIFIC KNOWLEDGE SHOULD BE SHARED WITH OTHER COUNTRIES. (SEE THEODORE BRISTOL FILE #664.) SURVEILLANCE OF SUBJECT BEGAN 4/14/83. CONTINUING. DATA FROM SURVEILLANCE INDICATES SWENSON ENGAGED IN SECRET PROJECT. OSTENSIBLE PURPOSE: TRAINING AND EDUCATION SO CALLED WILD BOY. (SEE MARGARET DENNING FILE #781.) ACTUAL PURPOSE BELIEVED CREATION OF HUMAN WITH SUPERINTELLIGENCE. SURVEILLANCE INCREASED 8/19/83 TO COVER SWENSON AND MARGARET DENNING. ATTEMPT TODAY (11/17/83) TO TAKE CUSTODY OF SUBJECT OF EXPERIMENT FAILED. SWENSON AND DENNING REGARDED AS HOSTILE TO BUREAU'S CUSTODY OF SUBJECT. INSTRUCTIONS FROM HIGHEST REPEAT HIGHEST AUTHORITY TO USE ALL FORCE

NECESSARY TO GAIN CUSTODY OF THEIR SUB-
JECT. (SEE MILES KANTER FILE #1004.)

Adam punched out an instruction on the computer:
TERMINATE DATA ON DONALD SWENSON, MAR-
GARET DENNING, AND MILES KANTER.

The computer lights blinked.

UNAUTHORIZED.

The computer would not obey because some advanced method of access control prohibited obedience
to instructions that were either too wide-ranging or
which violated a carefully defined standard of reason-
ableness.

The word UNAUTHORIZED stared at him from the
screen.

Quickly he tapped: CANCEL PREVIOUS IN-
STRUCTION. ERASE SWENSON FILE ONLY.

He awaited the result.

REPEAT CODE RED AUTHENTICATION.

The computer was cross-checking in order to reduce
or eliminate the possibility of error.

He tapped out the Code Red identification, and ordered again: ERASE SWENSON FILE ONLY.

REASON FOR INSTRUCTION?

OBSOLETE DATA.

DOES INSTRUCTION INCLUDE CATEGORY 19?

YES.

The screen went blank for a few seconds. Then the
single word flashed: CONFIRMED.

Adam repeated the instruction for all data on Margaret Denning and then Miles Kanter.

IS THERE ANY OTHER REFERENCE TO CAN-
CELED FILE SUBJECTS? he inquired.

YES.

NAME CATEGORY.

NATIONAL DEFENSE SECURITY.

NEW CLEARANCE REQUIRED?

YES.

Adam thought for a moment. To gain access to this
top-secret category would require still higher authentication. Even if he obtained the code for such authen-

tication, an order to the computer to erase a reference in that file might awaken a Pandora's box of further safeguards designed to protect such top-secret data. There had to be another way to accomplish the same end.

Once more he searched the record of encrypted messages, tested each, and discovered three that did not correspond even to the Code Red authentication. He set about discovering a pattern in these three. The mathematical calculations were intricate and abstruse, but finally he had what he believed was the proper decoding signal. He punched it out on the computer.

E PLURIBUS UNUM.

The computer's lights blinked. PROCEED.

The next minute would answer the question: Could the machine reason as a human being does? Was it capable of lateral thinking or programmed for mere logical progression of thought? Was it able to draw on all its memory cells with the sublime indifference of the human brain?

Information had to travel through the human brain in a network of processes and combinations and circuitry that no one was able to chart. What was astonishing was the capacity of human memory to find what was needed in that incalculable network. To retrieve information from a computer, one had to know how the information was classified and filed or there was no way of discovering its existence. A computer cannot find its way around in its own memory as a human being does, from any number of starting points via any number of routes.

He tapped: RECLASSIFY FILES ON DONALD SWENSON AND MARGARET DENNING AND MILES KANTER AS PROJECT NUMBER THREE.

CONFIRMED.

As he hoped, it was easier for the computer to reclassify data than to order it eliminated.

PROJECT NUMBER THREE TO RECEIVE HIGHEST SECURITY CLASSIFICATION.

CONFIRMED.

263

REVEAL CONTENTS ONLY ON INSTRUCTIONS FROM HIGHEST REPEAT HIGHEST AUTHORITY.
CONFIRMED.
INSTRUCTIONS FROM HIGHEST AUTHORITY TO REQUIRE ELECTRONICALLY ANALYZED SIGNATURE.
CONFIRMED.
Two final steps were needed to remove forever this particular memory file from recovery.
CANCEL RECORD OF CLASSIFICATION. TRANSFER FROM NATIONAL DEFENSE SECURITY TO PROJECT NUMBER THREE.
CONFIRMED.
ERASE RECORD THESE TRANSACTIONS.
After a second's delay the computer screen inquired: DOES INSTRUCTION INCLUDE ARCHIVES?
ERASE ARCHIVE RECORDS ALSO.
CONFIRMED.
Adam turned off the computer console. The data had not been destroyed, but no one would ever locate the data under the new classification. He sat back, his hands behind his head, smiling. It had been an interesting struggle with a worthy antagonist.

As he emerged into the reception area, a woman in a shapeless brown dress, short socks, and low-heeled heavy shoes was about to plug in an upright vacuum cleaner that stood nearby.

"I didn't know anybody was here," she said. "I have to get the work done."

"You go ahead," Adam told her. "I'm leaving now."

She stared at him, as though she had not understood a word. Then she shrugged. The humming of the vacuum cleaner began as Adam left the office.

chapter 21

The main reading room of the library was empty. Rows of polished yellow oak tables confronted chairs attendant on them like scholars. In the wide room with its immensely high ceiling, shelves of books stood along the side walls. He chose several heavy volumes of an encyclopedia and carried them to a table. He began to read, unaware how fast he was riffling the pages. Two men entered and sat down at either end of the long table where he was absorbed in reading.

Adam sensed the vibrations of danger before he picked up their thoughts. By then the two men had moved and seated themselves directly on either side of him.

One man said, "Please try to understand that we're your friends. We want to help you."

"What have you done with them?" Adam asked.

The man looked at him as if he were speaking gibberish.

"Dr. Swenson and Margaret Denning," Adam said, "were supposed to meet me here. What have you done with them?"

The other man put his hand on Adam's arm.

"It won't help trying to play games. We know who you are."

The man had excellent self-control, for he did not cry out as his chair rose swiftly into the air. The other man's chair also rose. Both men gripped their chairs tightly as they rapidly escalated. The only sound was from the librarian, who screamed and ran out of her office behind the counter.

The two men's ascent stopped near the roof of the fity-foot-high ceiling. By then Adam was no longer at the table where he had been seated.

At that moment Margaret and Don were climbing the stairs between the guardian stone lions at the Fifth

Avenue entrance of the library. A guard was stationed near the door, and as soon as they were out of earshot, he picked up a walkie-talkie to issue a brief message.

Margaret and Don hurried up wide marble steps to the second floor, and again to the third floor. As they reached the door to the Manuscript Room, Margaret caught Don's arm. She directed him into the Manuscript Room.

"We said the main reading room," Don objected.

Inside the Manuscript Room a long glass display case ran down the center of the room and smaller glass display cases were against each of the walls.

"Adam?" Margaret whispered.

His reflection appeared in the glass between two volumes of the special Balzac exhibition.

"I'm sorry we're late," she said. "We were followed."

The door opened and two men swiftly entered the room. They wore the black Security Bureau uniform and were carrying peculiar-looking guns with long thin barrels. Adam's reflection vanished.

"Back against the wall, please," one man said while the other closed the door.

Margaret and Don moved back to the wall. They watched the men searching the room. There was no place for Adam to hide but he was no longer to be seen.

"Is this where you're supposed to meet him?" one man asked.

Margaret felt a swelling exultance like incipient laughter. "I don't know what you're talking about."

"We'll wait," the man said, holstering his weapon.

"What kind of gun is that?" she asked.

"Fires a harmless pellet. Something to help him sleep."

A walkie-talkie the other man was carrying rustled with preliminary sound. Then: "Cartwright?"

"Here."

"He plastered two men to the ceiling in Room 315. We're using ladders to get them down."

"We've got Swenson and Denning here."

"Bring them to the Fifth Avenue entrance."

Downstairs they were escorted to a man in a business suit standing at a lectern near the wide revolving doors.

"May I ask what you are doing here?" the man asked, in the perfunctory tone of someone who already knew the answer.

"We came to see the Balzac exhibition," Margaret said.

"Do you have any identification?"

Margaret produced her Social Security card and an instant-cash card from her bank. Don showed his driver's license and his Blue Cross.

"All right. You can go."

They left the library, walking down the steps between crouching stone lions onto Fifth Avenue.

"How do you explain that?" Margaret asked.

"Either they have no charge they can hold us on, or they hope we'll lead them to Adam."

"What then?"

"I'm not sure I understand what you mean."

"They'll try to capture him, right? Try to make him into a weapon for our side."

"I suppose so."

She studied him and then nodded. "And if they can't?"

"I wonder."

"I don't." She almost whispered, "It'll be like the Romans."

"The who?"

"The B.C. Romans who conquered and sacked Syracuse. The first person, the very first, they killed was Archimedes. He happened to be the greatest scientist of the age. But they didn't want any of his inventions to be used against them. That's military thinking for you. It's what I was remembering when I decided Adam would be better off with Ted Bristol's committee. Scientists aren't absolutely convinced that the rest of the world is wrong and they are right. They leave a little space for mistakes. They don't play Russian roulette with a bullet in every chamber of the revolver."

They walked slowly along Fifth Avenue and turned right after a few blocks toward the self-parking garage where they had left the car. They started up the ramp into the garage.

"Did you feel anything?" Margaret asked.

"What?"

"Something passed by us."

The ramp led up to the second floor. They walked toward the Volvo, parked slantwise among other similarly parked cars.

Margaret clutched Don's arm. "Look!"

The rear door of the Volvo opened and closed.

Don said, "Get in the car."

He unlocked the front doors and Margaret got in. He went around and got in from the driver's side. He started the ignition and released the emergency brake. As the car backed out Margaret looked in the rearview mirror and saw Adam in the rear seat.

"They're following us," she warned.

Don said: "Keep down. I'll try to shake them."

He drove slowly down the ramp, presented his ticket to the cashier at the booth. As the barrier rose he swung out quickly into the street, turning left in the wrong direction on a one-way street. A taxi honked angrily at them. At the corner of Sixth Avenue he moved out with the uptown flow of traffic, and at the next block turned quickly right again, heading for the East Side.

Before they reached Madison Avenue, three more cars were in line behind them. The taxi was third in the line. Don turned left on Madison Avenue, drove three blocks, turned right, and on Park Avenue turned right again, heading downtown toward Grand Central and the Pan Am Building. Of the cars that had been behind them only the taxi and a black Cadillac remained.

Don said, "Once more for luck."

He turned left in front of the Pan Am Building. The black Cadillac kept going straight ahead up the ramp around Grand Central. The taxi turned left also. Don turned downtown again on Lexington, then crosstown. He ran a red light on Park Avenue and turned uptown. The taxi was no longer behind him. He kept going uptown on Park Avenue, catching the staggered lights.

At Fiftieth Street the black Cadillac cut in again on his trail.

When he was almost past the turn onto Fifty-first Street, he swung about and entered the street. The black Cadillac continued uptown. Don turned right, heading downtown again on Lexington Avenue.

"There's the taxi," Margaret said.

"The same one?"

"The driver has a visored hat. The car has a dent in the front grille. And there's another man in back."

"They've got us locked in a pattern. They must be checking each other by radio."

He wheeled quickly into a side street where a large sanitation truck was blocking passage. He drove through a small space between parked cars at a fire hydrant and bumped onto the sidewalk. Pedestrians scurried for cover. There was a good deal of shouting and yelling. Once past the sanitation truck, he returned to the street. At the corner he turned on a red light, sped in and out of traffic at fifty miles an hour. At Fifty-eighth Street the black Cadillac moved into place directly behind him.

"I can't break out of it," Don said. "All I can do is keep leading them around in circles."

"Adam," Margaret said, "we need a little help."

From a side street a small truck waiting for the light to change suddenly shot forward and struck the black Cadillac on the side, sending it into a spin that ended with it pointing downtown. As the light changed, cars from the side streets began to cross. The Cadillac was caught in the middle of the flow of cars that parted and packed it in a solid phalanx of metal.

"Nice," Don muttered.

They reached Seventy-fourth Street before Don saw the taxi again. He sped up, but the taxi stayed close. He ran a yellow light turning red, but the taxi came through the light with him.

"They don't care about being spotted anymore," Don said.

On the access to the FDR Drive at Seventy-ninth Street the taxi was only half a car's length behind. Don maneuvered into the tight narrow turn onto the downtown access. He expected the taxi to turn with him, but instead it went straight ahead into the dividing barrier. There was a rending crash as the front crumpled. Two men stumbled out.

Under her breath Margaret said to Don, "Where to now?"

"We can't risk going to the Committee. Their offices will probably be watched. I've another idea."

He drove down to Battery Park and left the car in a parking lot. Again she saw no sign of Adam. Don hailed a taxi. Just before the taxi started off, the door opened and Adam got in.

Don told the taxi driver where to take them. "A friend of mine is staying there," he told Margaret.

Don and Margaret went up in the hotel elevator. Adam took the stairs and was waiting when they arrived on the tenth floor.

"Wait here," Don told him. "And keep out of sight."

A young woman answered the door to Room 1009. She was dark-haired, cameo-faced, and wore large square rimless eyeglasses.

"I'm Dr. Swenson. I'd like to speak to Mrs. Juana Campo, please."

"I am Mrs. Campo's secretary. May I be of assistance?"

"I have to speak to her personally."

The secretary led them into a tastefully furnished living room. "Mrs. Campo is on the long-distance telephone. It's an important call."

"This is urgent. Will you please tell her I'm here?"

A few minutes later Juana Campo came in from another room. She wore a heavy brocaded robe and her hair was done up in a severe bun. She looked pale and less attractive than when Margaret first met her at the farmhouse.

"My secretary said you came on urgent business."

"Yes." Don glanced at the secretary.

"Would you mind stepping outside, dear?" Juana Campo asked her secretary.

270

As soon as the door closed behind the woman, Don said, "It's about Adam." In a few minutes he explained the situation.

Color returned to Juana Campo's cheeks, and she showed some of her usual vivacity as she promised whatever assistance they needed.

"I can make arrangements with people who will help Adam to get out of the country. But where is he? I thought you said he came with you."

"He's outside."

"I'm very anxious to see this young man." She turned to Margaret. "Ask him to come in. Meanwhile I will contact my friends. There's little time to waste."

Margaret stepped out into the hotel corridor. Through an inset rectangle of glass in the fire exit door, Adam was looking at her. She gestured to him to come out.

"Mrs. Campo is willing to help us," she told him. "And she'd like to meet you."

Adam followed her back into the suite. Don was alone in the living room. A few moments later Juana Campo returned, her face flushed with excitement.

"I've talked to my friends and they will take care of everything." She went toward Adam, holding out her hand. "You're safe now."

Adam looked at her with a quizzical expression. He took a step back, and she let her hand fall to her side.

She laughed nervously. "Apparently he doesn't like me."

Adam turned to Margaret. The words came so rapidly that they joined into a blurred indecipherable sound.

"Speak more slowly," she told him.

His face contorted as though he had an incapacitating stammer and was trying to force words to come. Finally he uttered another stream of indistinguishable sound.

"Is he having some sort of fit?" Juana Campo asked anxiously.

Margaret answered, "I've never seen him like this before." She felt a sudden unreasonable twinge of apprehension. "Try again, Adam. Please."

Don said, "It's no use. Don't you understand what's happened? The control of speech has been transferred from his neocortex to his new brain. He's gone beyond ordinary verbal communication. For him it's become redundant."

Adam's eyes filled with the anguish of someone who has suddenly acquired an insuperable disability. He strode across the room, reset the controls on the dictating machine on the secretary's desk, and uttered the same indecipherable stream of sound into the microphone. He put the machine on playback, slowed down to a fraction of its normal speed. "Ssssshhhhhh-eeeeeissssssnooottttttmyyyyyfriiiieennnddddd."

Margaret got it first. "He means her," she told Don. "He says she's not a friend."

Don said, "Adam, you're wrong. She's taking a risk for you, a very big risk."

Margaret's apprehension changed into a searing certainty. She had been going along with Don's appraisal: This woman will try to help us. Now she realized she had been listening to what Juana was saying but not to the echoes. The echoes of voices carry a different, often contradictory message.

"We're leaving," she told Don.

His stare reflected his disbelief. "Why?"

Juana Campo took a tentative step forward. "Forgive me. I am sorry. I really do believe this is best for everyone."

"Juana! What is this all about?" Don asked.

"No matter what Adam thinks, I am not his enemy. I am fighting for something very important to me. My husband's life."

"Your husband?"

"He would have been executed. No one could have helped him. I just called the minister in charge of security. In return for Adam, he promised to set my husband free. A valuable human life will be saved. And no harm will come to Adam." She had the air of a woman trying to convince herself.

272

Margaret opened the door and gestured to Adam to follow her.

Juana Campo said, "Stop her. Please! If you go now, it will be bad for everyone."

"Juana, this is crazy," Don said. He followed Margaret into the hall. An indicator light showed an elevator rising toward their floor.

"It may be them," Margaret warned.

"Take the stairs. Hurry!"

They were halfway down the first flight when she heard the heavy tread of rushing feet coming up. The staircase descended in two flights, turning sharply to the right. A stocky swarthy man appeared on the floor landing below. He shouted in Spanish, waving his gun.

"Adam!" Margaret cried. "Help!"

The man's body was whipped around with tremendous force. Then it whipped around again. And again. And again. When the force released him he fell and lay spread-eagled on the floor. His gun lay near him.

Margaret and Adam ran past him.

On the floor above, the elevator stopped. She heard excited voices in Spanish and then the clatter of pursuit coming down. Don picked up the gun from the floor and waited behind the stairs in the shelter of the wall. A swarthy head appeared at the turn above. Don fired.

The man flung his body across to the opposite wall, where he had a better view of the floor landing. As Don turned to go, the man fired.

An inch-long projectile traveling at sufficient speed can penetrate the hard bony surface of the skull and go through, making a splintered opening into the brain, fissuring the soft internal substance, puncturing the membrane of dura mater which encloses the spinal fluid and draining cerebrospinal fluid. The brain does not feel pain because it lacks the necessary sensors; it can sense pain anywhere in the body except within itself.

Don did not feel pain as the bullet passed in a millionth of a second through his cerebral hemisphere and the cerebellum. He saw only a sharp startling change

273

from bright to dark as his occipital lobe was destroyed along with the verbal and nonverbal regions.

He was for every practical purpose dead before his body began to tumble grotesquely down the stairs.

In the hotel lobby, clerks were working discreetly at the reception desk. Adam and Margaret crossed the lobby under the subdued amber glow of chandeliers. Their footsteps were cushioned by deep pile carpeting. The Argentines were careless—they had thought it a sufficient precaution to close off the elevator and stairways as methods of escape and had not stationed anyone in the lobby.

Before they reached the exit door, a thought turned Margaret back.

"Don! We have to wait for him."

Adam's grip on her arm held her and she felt herself, unable to resist, propelled out through the door to the street.

She said faintly, "We can't leave him. It isn't fair."

A car raced to the curb outside the hotel and came to a tire-screaming halt. She caught a glimpse of men in the front seat who looked like Orientals. Their car seemed to buckle in the middle, the front and rear ends rising higher as a chasm opened in the street beneath it. One man leapt out into the midst of traffic. Several cars snaked around him but another coming through the opening buzzed its horn like a huge angry wasp and struck him. Still standing, he slid awkwardly like someone skating backward across ice before toppling over. The other two men in the car reached the safety of the street before their car vanished into the chasm that had opened.

They ran toward Adam and Margaret. An invisible projectile appeared to explode between them—an explosion visible only in its effects. Both men were flung outward. One came to rest on the roof of a passing bus where he lay sprawled like a boneless floppy man-sized doll. The other was flung upward against the facade of the hotel at the third-floor level. His thin body was pinned there, drooping as if suspended from a coat hanger. One shoe dangled precariously from his foot before it dropped silently to the sidewalk.

Everyone began to shout at once. Scores of people were running toward the hotel. Others were pouring out from the hotel lobby.

At the height of the excitement, Adam guided Margaret in the opposite direction. They reentered the hotel.

They took the elevator to the top floor, and climbed a short flight of stairs to the roof. From the parapet they looked down at the confusion in the street. A large crowd was gathered and several police cars with whirling lights were parked in front of the hotel. A police emergency vehicle had been driven up onto the sidewalk, and an extension ladder was in place to reach the thin Oriental man pinned to the hotel facade.

Margaret turned from watching the scene. "What's happened to Don?" She had the uncomfortable sensation that Adam could actually see the syllables falling from her lips as she spoke.

He is dead.

He had not uttered a word but simply put the thought into her mind.

She felt faint and sick and at the same time incredulous. She did not question how he knew; she accepted it, just as she accepted that his mental processes had become so swift he could no longer communicate in a spoken language.

He was watching the sky. Not a wrinkle disturbed his serene expression. She thought: He is removed from the corrosive effects of emotions such as grief or anxiety. He is as isolated emotionally from ordinary humans as he was in his primitive state.

A moment later she saw a helicopter in the distance. Crouching, she and Adam took shelter behind an air shaft.

The helicopter skimmed over the rooftops as it approached. Its ungainly body hovered fifty feet above

275

them, like a bird of prey about to pounce. She heard a metallic rasping as if the machine were clearing its throat.

"WE'RE GOING TO LAND SO THAT ONE OF OUR MEN CAN TALK WITH YOU. HE WILL NOT BE ARMED. YOU HAVE NOTHING TO FE—"

The thundering noise of the helicopter engines accelerated. The craft tilted sharply down to the right. At the same time it was thrust away from the building roof. She caught a momentary view of the pilot fighting the controls. Then the helicopter began to move rapidly away at a steadily increasing speed until it dwindled to a large black speck in the sky.

Others will come, she thought. They won't give up.

I know, he answered. They are coming now.

She looked around. The rooftop was empty, but the door to the roof seemed to bulge slightly. Black-clad men erupted through it. She was not afraid, not with Adam beside her.

Then to her surprise the black-clad men were all around her. One pinioned her arms. His hold was tight, painfully stretching her shoulders.

Moments later another man called from the parapet enclosing the roof: "He can't have jumped. There's no body down there."

A quick stirring in the air beside her—Margaret was unsure if it was real or imagined—but she heard clearly the message in her mind: Goodbye, Margaret.

She struggled to free herself.

"Adam!" she cried.

There was no answer.

Her eyes slowly filled with tears. She still heard Adam's last words clearly, as she would hear them for the rest of her life. But she would never see him again.

Goodbye, Adam.

Goodbye.

chapter 22

The muddy brown waters of the tributary began
swirling in wide slow circles of surrender as they met
the mighty current of the Sepik River. On the riverbank the wild boy emerged from heavy glistening jungle growth. An eddy washed over a submerged sandbar,
frothing yellowish foam.

He was hungry and tired and afraid. If only he could
cross the water to the other shore, he would be safe.

Behind him a jabbering arose. A lizard on a low
branch glittered sunlight on green scales. The boy was
drained of strength, nearly dead of weariness. He wished
he could slide under the river and lie there as still and
wide-eyed as a fish.

He heard jabbering as his pursuers pressed closer.
Then the foliage parted and his pursuers arrived. They
wore plumed headdresses and war paint; their faces
were masked in white clay. More came through the
shadows of the jungle.

He stared at the semicircle of his captors closing in.
He recognized them: Swenson and Miles and Margaret,
the men from the Security Bureau, the quarreling couple who picked him up in a car, Juana Campo, Elfie
the call girl. Their faces were blurred by war paint as,
grinning, they put deadly blowguns to their lips. The
first dart struck and turned his blood to ice. He was
pierced by their poison. More darts thudded into his
body as consciousness faded...

Adam woke.

Somewhere in his new brain a connection had been
made to old memory, and the result was the confusing
coherence of his dream. He did not wish to dream that
again and he so informed the marvelously intricate
machinery of his brain.

He stood up and stretched. His silhouette was dark

and upright against the moon and the dark tree branches. There were many stirrings in the still jungle forest, and he could hear the patient indefatigable gnawing of tiny insects. From her sleeping place, Mada hopped toward him, answering his silent summons.

Adam paused to get his orientation. With Mada hopping beside him, he moved on with direct sureness. Vaporous mist rising from the ground seemed to absorb the sound of his footsteps. Occasionally a pair of yellow eyes stared from the bush.

In a short time Adam found the place he was looking for.

Years ago a clearing had been made here by a fire's burning. Now the clearing had returned to the jungle. From the clasp of interlocked vines, he pulled a large fragment of metal. Part of a plane's wing.

He rubbed his hand over the scorched metal and saw a man's grim face at the controls of a plunging plane, felt a woman's arms clutching him tightly, so tightly he could hear the repressed scream in her chest and the powerful beat of her heart. Then the image broke, dissolved, became a flowering red light in darkness. He could smell the fire leaping, devouring the trees and undergrowth.

Mada hopped near him. You have found it?

He nodded.

Over one of Mada's ears she wore an electrode that was like a hearing aid. This provided her with the ability to receive and express thought patterns. Adam knew she was puzzled. She could not provide an explanation for human motivations. There was only so much one could expect from a tree kangaroo.

We will go home now, he informed her.

They followed their own path back through the jungle, clambering over fallen tree trunks, pushing aside obstructing foliage that had been pushed aside on their journey here. At times the grass was shoulder-high.

Adam strode on swiftly with a dim awareness that he was obeying a summons. He had learned to trust these signals that appeared to come out of nowhere.

The air in the jungle seemed trapped in the oppressive heat. Mada hopped along, her mouth opened to breathe, giving her lean features an odd aspect.

As they reached the savannah, the morning sun was rising and their long shadows preceded them. A pulse of danger beat strongly. Adam stopped to search the sky. Then he saw it—a long sleek cylinder soaring through the upper atmosphere, trailing apocalyptic light.

It has begun, he thought.

He hurried on until he came to a low, peculiarly shaped hump of ground amid the coarse grass and stunted trees of the savannah. A square patch of light appeared in this elevated ground as a door opened. The figure of a woman was silhouetted against the light.

Amelia wore a simple flowing white gown. She was tall and slender, and her dark hair was tied in a braid on the right side of her head. She was beautiful. She moved toward Adam, smiling, and gave him her hands. That was the only communication they needed. Her smile faded and she turned her face upward.

The distant sky was now ribboned with sleek silver-swift messengers on unspeakable errands. Amelia's eyes suddenly glistened with tears and she hid her face against Adam's shoulder.

He continued to watch with wonder and an overwhelming sadness until sunlight glittered on empty vapor trails crossing the cloudless sky. He knew he had witnessed the loss of something irrecoverably precious.

Why? he asked, seeking a purpose beyond his understanding.

World without end.

Upswelling from a secret place hidden to his reason, the message came to him.

Adam put his arms about Amelia. She raised her head as she shared his brief thrilling vision of the destiny they were meant to fulfill. A glow began in her pale cheeks that went up to brighten her eyes with awe.

They entered the mound of earth and descended into their home.

> *And God said unto them,*
> *Be fruitful, and multiply,*
> *and replenish the earth ...*
> *(Genesis 1:28)*

About the Author

WILLIAM WOOLFOLK is the author of eighteen books of fiction and nonfiction, many of which were chosen by major book clubs. His books have sold a total of over six million copies in all editions. Some years ago he was chief writer and story editor for the television series *The Defenders*, which is still on everyone's list of the best dramatic series ever to appear on TV. Mr. Woolfolk has also been a successful magazine publisher and is the founder of *Space World*, the first popular magazine of astronautics.

Mr. Woolfolk's novels include MY NAME IS MORGAN, OPINION OF THE COURT, THE OVERLORDS, THE PRESIDENT'S DOCTOR, THE SENDAI, and others. Among his nonfiction best sellers are THE GREAT AMERICAN BIRTH RITE and DADDY'S LITTLE GIRL, which he coauthored with his daughter Donna Woolfolk Cross.

Mr. Woolfolk currently resides in New Canaan, Connecticut, with his wife, Joanna, who is also an author.